NO MORE 1

To Gemma

Best Wishes

Neil Mo...

NO MORE TEARS

NOEL MORAN

JANUS PUBLISHING COMPANY
London, England

First published in Great Britain 1998
by Janus Publishing Company Limited,
Edinburgh House, 19 Nassau Street,
London W1N 7RE

www.januspublishing.co.uk

Copyright © 1998 by Noel Moran
The author has asserted his moral rights

ISBN 1 85756 314 X

The characters and situations in this book are fictitious, any
resemblance to actual people or events being unintentional.

Phototypeset in 11 on 12.5 Trump Medieval
by Keyboard Services, Luton, Beds

Cover design John Anastasio – Creative Line

Printed and bound in Great Britain by
Antony Rowe Ltd, Chippenham, Wiltshire

CHAPTER ONE

Joe Quinn glanced at his Rolex as his car eased between the twelve-feet-high solid stone pillars. It was three minutes to midday. He switched off the ignition, slid out of his seat and made his way through the solid oak doors. He waited for a few minutes until the receptionist finished her telephone conversation. Finally she looked up at him.

'Mr Quinn to see Mr Conroy,' he told her.

She spoke into a microphone on her desk. 'Matron to the front desk. Matron to the front desk please.'

A burly nurse approached the desk and conversed with the receptionist for a minute. Joe, who stood a few feet away, watched as the matron approached him.

'You're early,' she growled, in a voice which would have turned the meanest Rottweiler into a Poodle in seconds.

'I'm sorry,' Joe began.

'It'll be at least an hour,' she broke in, 'before Mr Conroy is prepared to receive visitors. You may wait in the lounge if you wish,' she barked.

'I'll take a stroll around the grounds, if you don't mind.'

'Suit yourself.'

Seconds later Joe was outside the building, delighted to be putting distance between himself and that awful matron. Looking up at the sky, 'Good,' he said, as he watched the few scattered clouds slowly drift eastwards. The sky will be cloudless in a few minutes, he told himself. Ten minutes later Joe stood before a pond. It was about eighty feet in length and twenty feet wide. He sat on the wooden bench, his back to the building. After a few minutes some ducks emerged from the reeds on the far side of the pond and Joe began to watch their antics as they searched for food. He laughed out loud as he watched three of the ducks squabble over what must have been a morsel of food. The squabble ended as fast as it had begun. Each of the ducks paddled away in a different direction, continuing their quest for food. Joe took his handkerchief from his trouser pocket and blew his nose. The squabble between the ducks had revived a memory deep in the mind of Joe Quinn.

*　　*　　*

Peter Quinn had been pacing up and down the corridor of the maternity hospital for an hour and a half. His nervousness was beginning to agitate the nurses who were fluttering past him from one ward to another, but they held their patience. Peter's wife had been at the hospital on three other occasions, and each time she had lost the baby. Secretly they prayed that this time it would be different. Their prayers were answered.

'Mr Quinn,' a voice called. He turned in its direction and, throwing her arms around him, a smiling nurse told him, 'You have a beautiful, perfectly healthy, seven pound baby boy.'

'And the wife?' he inquired, his eyes misty.

'Fine, just fine,' the nurse told him. So at five p.m. on July the fifth, 1950, Joseph Quinn's life began.

*　　*　　*

For the next nine years Peter and his wife, Betty, and their son lived in a two-roomed tenement flat in the centre of the city. Two weeks after Joe's ninth birthday they moved to their new home on a corporation estate some three miles from the city, and for the first time in his life Joe had a bedroom all to himself. Up until then

2

Joe had led a rather sheltered life. His mother understandably watched his every move like a hawk. She would stand by her bedroom window, which took in the entire street, and if Joe got into an argument with other children he would be immediately whisked away by her. It was a mild mannered Joseph Quinn who was thrust into the rough and tumble that was the O'Dwyer Estate.

From the first day at his new school, the Bullies began to show their authority. When Joe arrived home from school one afternoon. his nose bloodied and one of his front teeth loose, his poor mother almost had a seizure. Taking Joe by the hand to see the Principal next morning only added fuel to the Bullies' fire.

'Mother's pet, mother's pet.' Punch, kick, the torment never ceased. To and from school the taunting continued – 'Squealer, mother's pet, squealer.' When Joe went out to play after finishing his homework, the accidental pushes and tripping would begin. From the first day Joe moved into the estate, his attitude and behaviour were being observed by one Seamus Conroy.

It was Joe's fourth week in the estate, during a football match on the local green. Joe and five friends were playing a six-a-side. The Bullies had decided on picking the teams. It was 'sheer coincidence' that the Bullies all ended up on the same team. The Bullies told the Refined that the match should be played for two hours. Whoever scored the more goals at the end of two hours would be declared the winners. Yvonne O'Meara, the local tomboy, was given the honour of timing the match, due to the fact that she was the only person on the entire estate who had a wrist watch.

The game, as might be expected, was rough, very rough indeed, but the Refined's better skill was keeping the score even. Ten minutes from time, Charlie 'Chubby' O'Holloran went off crying. His legs, like all the Refined's team, were black and blue. Joe's team now numbered only five. But Joe felt very proud. His team had taken everything the Bullies dished out and now, with only two

3

minutes to go, only one goal separated them. The Bullies had twenty-one, and the Refined twenty. A large crowd of children had gathered by now and they all seemed to be cheering on the Refined. The Bullies gave away a touch one yard from their own wide ball line. Joe asked Lanky Foran to take it. Lanky's long throw landed perfectly on Joe's head. Joe headed the ball between the Bullies keeper's hands. The children on the side lines went wild. Twenty-one all. The ball was at Joe's feet. He dribbled past two Bullies. Now he had only the keeper to beat. As he was about to score a certain goal, the Bullies' leader elbowed Joe, sending him crashing to the ground.

'Penalty, penalty!' Yvonne O'Meara screamed.

Five minutes later, after much heated discussion, the Bullies gave in to Yvonne and the crowd. The Bullies' leader took up position in the goal mouth. In an instant he had gone from full forward to goalkeeper. The tactic was, of course, that his menacing presence would put off the penalty taker. The Refined decided that Joe should take the penalty. Running towards the ball, Joe pointed his right hand towards the right-hand corner of the goal. As the keeper dived right, Joe sent the ball along the ground into the left-hand corner of the imaginary net.

'Full time, full time,' screamed Yvonne O'Meara. The Bullies disputed for some minutes with Yvonne, but she stood firm. The match was over. Bullies twenty-one, Refined twenty-two.

'Better luck next time,' Joe shouted in the direction of the Bullies.

'You trying to be funny?' the Bullies' leader enquired.

'No ... no,' stuttered Joe.

By now the Bullies had circled him. One of them got down on all fours. The leader pushed Joe who staggered back, tripping over the Bully on the ground. The back of Joe's head smashed hard into the ground. Joe Quinn had had enough. He got to his feet, fists clenched, and led with a right, sending it into the face of the leader. His head jerked back and immediately his nose began to bleed. Instantly the other Bullies began to punch and kick Joe, who was taking a pounding from the gang.

'Leave him alone,' came an authoritative voice. The punishment subsided.

'What's it to you, Seamus?' the leader asked.

'Six against one. Let's say six against two,' Seamus said, sticking a finger deep into the Bully's shoulder. 'Come on, what do you say, tough man?'

There was silence for a minute. Then the Bullies began drifting away, declining his offer. They knew full well that Seamus was the toughest boy in the estate. He also had three even tougher older brothers. Joe got to his feet, wiping his blooded nose.

'Thanks,' he said.

'You're the new kid, aren't you?'

'Yes, my name is Joe Quinn. What's yours?'

Seamus Conroy then said, 'For a soft kid, you've got guts.' As they walked from the green, Seamus said. 'Never lead with your right, OK?' Joe nodded.

This was the first time Joe Quinn had laid eyes on Seamus Conroy.

From that day Seamus had put an end to Joe's torment. From then on they became inseparable. Seamus was a god, as far as Joe was concerned.

CHAPTER TWO

Seamus was three years older than Joe, and on his fourteenth birthday he took a job in a butcher's shop as a messenger boy. From his first week's pay Seamus opened a savings account at the Post Office. He saved hard for the next two years, then took all his savings to the pawn shop in town where he purchased a secondhand electric guitar. Joe would sit for hours listening to Seamus sing and master the guitar. He took to both like a duck to water.

By 1970 Seamus Conroy was well established as one of the finest rhythm guitarists in the country. His skill with the guitar, and his husky voice, made him a household name in his native city. He had formed a group back in '67, consisting of lead and bass guitar, plus drummer and himself. They called themselves 'Ground Control'. After a year, playing mostly in pubs, sometimes they were asked to support more popular bands. Slowly they were gaining the admiration and respect of the younger generation.

Joe Quinn made his parents proud no end by staying on at school until he was eighteen, then went to college for two more years. Now he worked in one of the most prestigious banks in the city. Once a week, every Tuesday, Joe and Seamus would meet in a quiet pub. Joe would listen with great interest as Seamus talked about how popular his group had become in their native city.

'Do you know, Joe, we are booked up until the end of

this year for weddings. We even have two weddings some Saturday afternoons and evenings.'

'I've always told you, you're very good Seamus, you deserve all the success in the world.'

Christmas approached and, like all Christmases, brought with it great sorrow as well as great joy. Thus it was great sadness which brought Brian Ford back to his native city that Christmas. Brian walked through the gates of the graveyard, where he had just buried his father. Together with his younger twin brothers, he made his way to the pub where his late father had spent many years sampling his favourite beverage and a game of forty-five with his friends. Brian and his brothers each in turn bought a round for the house, as was the tradition. After a couple of hours, Brian excused himself. He wasn't a drinking man himself, so he returned to his mother's home to comfort her.

Three days later, on Saturday evening, Brian sat in an armchair reading a newspaper.

'Ma, these jeans are dirty. Where's my other ones?' Brian looked at his mother, who was ironing. She threw her eyes heavenwards.

'Did you look in your wardrobe?' she replied.

'Grand, Ma, I have 'em,' he shouted back.

'Ma,' the other twin was shouting, 'where's my green shirt?'

'Hot press.'

'Thanks, Ma.'

Half an hour later, the twins were admiring themselves in the mirror over the fireplace in the sitting room.

'God, the stench of Brylcream mixed with Old Spice is overwhelming,' Brian said, laughing. His brothers ignored the remark. 'Where you off to, anyway?' he enquired.

'Never you mind, auld man,' one of the twins said as he adjusted his tie. 'Anyway, you're too old to be hanging round with us.' Brian Ford was thirty years old. His brothers were ten years younger.

'I didn't say I wanted to join you, just asked where you were off to.'

'If you must know,' the other twin said, laying a hand on Brian's shoulder, 'Seamus Conroy's band *Ground Control* are performing at the opening of the new lounge bar, Naughton's Bar. You know the one, 'bout four miles outside the city.' Brian nodded. 'Well, it's been completely refurbished. We're headed off early, there'll be a massive crowd there. Seamus Conroy is the most popular singer in these parts, as you might say in your line of business.'

'We're off then, Mam; see you later. You too, auld man,' they taunted. 'Brian, then again, you'll probably be fast asleep by the time we get home.'

Naughton was given an extension until one a.m. They were gone in a flash. Brian returned to his newspaper.

'You know, Brian,' his mother said, without taking her eyes from her ironing, 'you should go out to Naughton's. That young man, Conroy, is pretty good. He played at several weddings I attended. I think he's got a lovely catchy voice.' If Brian admired anything, and there were many qualities to admire about his mother, it was her ear for music. She might belong to the Mario Lanza era, but when she heard a rock singer with a good voice she praised it.

An hour later Brian folded his newspaper. 'You know something, mother, I think I'll take your advice. I'll see you later,' he said, kissing her on the cheek.

Brian sat with his back to the wall at the bar in Naughton's lounge. There was a group of three musicians playing and screaming something. Brian couldn't make head nor tail of it. He toyed with the orange juice before him as he waited patiently for the main attraction to appear. An hour and a half later, at eleven thirty, the master of ceremonies removed the microphone from its stand.

'Ladies and Gentlemen' – at that the crowd went wild

with great expectation – 'Naughton's proudly presents *Ground Control!*'

Brian thought he'd go deaf from the screaming and clapping. It was minutes before the noise subsided. The group opened with the Beatles number, *Help*, and the crowd went wild again. Two hours later, as the group left the stage, Brian was totally convinced of one thing; the group's leader, Seamus Conroy, had talent – and plenty of it. His mother was right; his husky voice, to say the least, was unusual and should be heard by millions, not just the four or five hundred he estimated were here tonight. Brian introduced himself to the proprietor, who went in search of Seamus Conroy.

The proprietor returned and asked Brian to follow him. 'In here,' he said to Brian, opening a door to his tiny office at the back of the building.

'Please have a seat,' Seamus said, indicating a chair. Offering Brian his hand he said, 'I'm Seamus Conroy and this is my friend, Joe Quinn.' Brian shook hands with both of them. Brian took a small card from his wallet and handed it to Seamus. Seamus whistled and handed the card to Joe saying 'Very impressive.' On the card was printed 'Brian Ford, Official Talent Spotter for Mecca Records, London, England'.

Brian began, 'I'm here partly because of my mother and partly out of curiosity. She said I should come and hear you. She was right,' he added; 'you're good, Seamus, very good. 'I know it's late now, but could you meet me some place today, say around five? That's if you're interested.'

'Of course I'm interested. Say the lounge in Phillips Hotel, you know it?'

'Yes,' Brian replied, 'five then. OK.' They all shook hands again. As Brian closed the door behind him, Seamus made a comical face at Joe. Shaking his hand, Joe said, 'Best of luck later today.'

At five that afternoon, Brian and Seamus sat in a quiet corner of the hotel's lounge. When they had finished their conversation more than an hour later, Brian had convinced Seamus to fly to London in a week's time to meet and sing for his bosses at Mecca.

*   *   *

Joe sat with Seamus in the airport bar, both sipping orange juice. A voice broke over the intercom system, 'Aer Lingus Flight 129 for London now boarding.'

'That's you,' Joe said, getting off his stool.

'Wish me luck,' Seamus said, offering his hand. Joe grabbed Seamus by the shoulders and pulled him towards him. Into Seamus's ear he said in a low voice, 'Remember two things. You're the best, and don't be nervous.'

'I promise you one thing, old friend,' Seamus said, 'I'm going to give it my best shot. After all, I may never get another.' Joe watched as his best friend disappeared down the corridor towards his flight and his destiny.

*   *   *

Instead of staying two days in London as originally plan-ned, so taken were the directors of Mecca Records with Seamus's voice that they asked him to stay on and make a record. Apart from an extra pair of jeans and under-pants, the only other piece of luggage Seamus had brought was an old briefcase. Inside it were more than twenty of Seamus's own compositions which he had written since he was seventeen years old. Mecca's producer went through the songs very carefully until finally he chose one. It was called *No one tells me*, a fast rock-'n'-roll number.

Three weeks later Seamus recorded it, but before Mecca would release it they asked Seamus very tactfully if he wouldn't mind choosing a first name other than Seamus. He had to agree with them: Seamus Conroy didn't sound very attractive. He gave it some thought, then after a while he said, 'How does Brad Conroy grab ye?'

'Great, couldn't have chosen a better one,' they told him.

'My mother's maiden name is Bradford, so what could be more appropriate?'

One week later Mecca released the first record sung by their newly discovered talent, Brad Conroy. Five days after its release it was number four in the top ten charts. Eight days later it reached number one. Brad Conroy was a huge hit on *Top Of The Pops*. Over the next four weeks it seemed every radio presenter wanted an interview with Brad. He obliged them all. Mecca arranged a tour of England, Scotland and Wales as well as a tour of his own country, Ireland. By the end of his first tour Brad Conroy was an established star. The blond, blue-eyed, six-footer from the corporation estate was ready to take on the whole world.

Before Brad started his first tour, the directors of Mecca gave him a few days off to return to his native city to attend to some business. Joe Quinn was taken totally by surprise when he raised his head from some paperwork at the bank to see his best friend standing before him.

'How much do these people pay you a year?' he asked Joe after they had greeted each other.

'Two thousand,' Joe replied.

'Like to earn ten?' The amazement showed on Joe's face. Brad leaned on the hatch counter, putting his fingers under Joe's chin. He pressed it upwards.

'There,' he said, 'now the flies will have to go some place else.' Brad looked at his watch.

'It's now two thirty,' he told his friend. 'The day is Monday. I leave for London at eleven o'clock Saturday morning. I'm in dire straits for a manager. Tell these people you can't work for the pittance they pay you any more.' As he walked to the bank's door, he turned and said, 'I'll call for you at eight this evening.' Joe's mouth dropped open again.

CHAPTER THREE

It was now February, 1972. In one year Brad Conroy had achieved more fame and fortune than any other single singer/songwriter in Europe. Already he had had four number one hits in the charts and the three albums he had made were all in the Top Five Best Selling Albums Chart at the same time. He had also had sell-out concerts in France, Germany and Spain. Now Brad Conroy was ready to conquer America, and all before his twenty-fifth birthday.

By the time Brad had finished his American tour, he was a well and truly crowned superstar. The American newspapers gave him rave reviews. Brad's concert attendances were equal to Presley and Beatles concerts. When Brad read the reviews, he told Joe he had reached the peak of his career.

*　　*　　*

Joe Quinn sat reading a magazine in his suite at the Dorchester Hotel. The date caught his eye, 25th January, 1984. God, he thought, where did the years go? It seemed like only yesterday that Brad had asked him to be his manager. That was thirteen years ago. The first ten years had gone by trouble-free. Then Joe had noticed that Brad began popping pills into his mouth. When Joe asked Brad what they were for, Brad would just shrug his shoulders and say, 'Nothing to worry your head about, old friend. They help me stay awake.'

But Joe did worry. He had seen many a career destroyed by pop stars who started on the road to destruction by popping such pills into their mouths, and then going on to cocaine and finally heroin. There had been fatalities, far too many fatalities. Brad would have to be watched closely, very closely.

But in spite of Joe's observations, Brad had indeed graduated to cocaine and finally to heroin. Every time Joe challenged Brad he had walked away from the argument the loser. He picked up the framed photograph from the coffee table and smiled down at the four faces smiling back at him.

Joe had met Sally Brennan during one of Brad's concerts in Dublin. For both of them it was love at first sight. Twelve months later they married, with Brad as best man. That was six years ago. Brad and Sally were sitting on a couch. Brad held Ann, Joe's eldest daughter, on his knee. She was four years old. Sally held Kerry in her arms. Kerry was just ten months old. Joe flicked a tear from the corner of his eye and placed the photograph back on the table. He had made up his mind. He would have one more confrontation with Brad about his habit. If Brad refused to meet him halfway, he would resign.

Joe knocked on the door to Brad's suite.

'Good evening,' the huge minder said to Joe.

'Where is he?' Joe asked.

'Bedroom, sir.'

As Joe made his way towards it, the minder said, 'He's not alone, Mr Quinn.'

Joe looked back at him. 'When is he ever?'

Joe walked right in. Brad was sitting at the side of the bed. On the bedside locker were four tiny, four-inch-long mountains of white powder. Brad took a gold sniffer from his pyjama top pocket. He placed the tip of the sniffer at the back of the first mountain and in a second it disappeared up his nostril. The remaining three disappeared likewise.

'Would you excuse us, Joe?' asked the blonde young

lady who knelt behind Brad, pressing her fingers into his shoulders.

'Would you mind, young lady, leaving us for a few minutes?'

She gave Brad that lost look, eyelids fluttering. He nodded at her. She put Brad's robe around her shoulders and left the bedroom. Brad stood up, hands on hips.

'We're not going to have one of those father-to-son talks you're getting so fond of, are we?' he said, in a tone which had become all too familiar to Joe.

'Look, Brad, I've watched your health deteriorate bit by bit over the last two or three years because of that rubbish you're shovelling into your system, and no matter what I do to cut off your suppliers you always somehow manage to find someone to get it to you. I must have sacked two dozen minders who I suspected were getting it for you since you started, but I have to admit it, Brad, you're more cunning than me.'

'You're making a mountain...' Brad began, but Joe cut him short.

'Look, Brad, let's call a spade a spade. You've lost nearly two stone in weight, your voice isn't as near as good as it should be and your performance on stage leaves a lot, an awful lot, to be desired.'

'That's your opinion,' Brad screamed. 'I don't hear any complaints from Mecca or the video makers. Who the hell gives you the right to degrade me like that? Nobody has the right to talk to me like that, least of all you,' Brad continued. 'Only for me you'd be back home bowing to some pencil pushing banker, yes sir, no sir, of course sir, right away sir, pull down your pants and I'll kiss your arse sir. Remember something, pal,' Brad said, pointing an authoritative finger and with a cutting edge to his tone, 'I made you a rich man, a very rich man.'

At that moment Joe wanted to walk out of Brad's life forever, but something inside made him go the extra yard. The two men faced each other, inches separating their faces.

'I ask you for friendship's sake,' Joe said, 'please quit the drugs.' Brad ignored the request and remained staring at Joe in silence. 'If you don't at least promise to try to quit, I'm out of here tonight.'

For a few moments the shock of his statement showed on Brad's face, then he turned his back on Joe.

'You found your way in all by yourself, I'm sure you can find the way out even easier.'

'Goodbye, Brad,' Joe said in a low tone.

As Joe closed the door behind him, Brad threw the glass of Scotch he had just poured hard against the bedroom wall. 'The hell with him,' he screamed.

*   *   *

Three months later, Joe was at home having dinner with his wife when their maid came into the dining room.

'There's a telephone call for you, Mr Quinn, it's a Mr Ford.'

Joe thanked the maid and went to take the call. Returning to the dining room, Joe told his wife that Brian Ford wanted to meet him tomorrow evening at eight o'clock in Freddies Restaurant.

Joe was shown to a private booth when he arrived at Freddies Restaurant in the east end of London. He was glancing through his diary.

'Do you think you could find it in your heart to forgive a loud-mouthed eejit?'

He looked up. Brad was standing before him. In an instant Joe was on his feet, throwing his arms round Brad. He said 'You're a sight for sore eyes, old friend.'

Over the next hour Brad apologised more than a dozen times for his behaviour towards Joe. Joe brushed his apologies aside.

'No, Joe, I was totally out of line, especially about making you a rich man. Managing myself for the last three months proves that. You earned every penny. Funny how one takes another's job for granted.'

Brad enquired of Joe's wife and two daughters. 'I asked Brian Ford to ring you. I wasn't sure you'd even talk to me over the phone.'

'Idiot,' Joe said, smiling.

'Look, Joe, I haven't had anything for the last week, and as you can plainly see I'm in a bad way. I've decided to take a year off. Do you think you could find a discreet clinic where I could book in for a few months, say six months?'

Joe smiled. 'A year ago I made enquiries about such a clinic and found one with a ninety five per cent success rate.'

'Smashing,' Brad said, rubbing his hands together. 'Where is it?'

'Colorado, in the States. Yes, Brad, it's about forty miles south of Pueblo. One phone call and you're in.'

'Make it,' said Brad.

In the first week of May 1984, Brad walked through the doors of the clinic. The staff were courteous, kind and sympathetic. His treatment began immediately. Brad was booked in for six months, but extended it to ten months. He was determined to be totally cured by the time he walked back out through those same doors. Also he told Joe he wanted absolutely no visitors, absolutely none. The press were told that Brad was taking a year off, mostly to find inspiration for a new album. This was accepted.

CHAPTER FOUR

On the last day of February 1985 Brad left the clinic a new man, and decided to see some of America by car. He was sporting a six-month black beard. He had also dyed his hair black. Before he left the clinic he checked his appearance in a mirror. 'Not even Joe would recognise me,' he laughed.

'Where to, Mac?' the taxi driver said as Brad climbed into the back seat.

'The first garage you know that sells cars,' Brad said. Brad thanked the taxi driver and tipped him generously. He inspected the new cars in Hank's showroom. The salesman didn't break any records rushing over to serve him, and who could blame him? Wearing jeans and fur lined jacket to match, with a scruffy beard and his hair in a ponytail, Brad looked a perfect hippy.

'Was there something yah wanted in particular?'

'Can't seem to make up my mind,' Brad replied. The salesman, thinking Brad was English, decided to have some fun.

'Would yah like for me to order a Rolls-Royce for yah?'

'Now there's a thought,' Brad said. 'Perfect!' he suddenly shouted.

'Which one, sir?'

Brad brushed past him. Outside the showroom was a seventy-eight Ford pickup.

'This belong to you?' he asked the salesman.

'You're kiddin'; that belongs to the kid who pumps the gas here.'

'Think he'd sell it?'

'He's in the office over there.'

The young man was drinking coffee as he listened through his earphones to a tape in his Walkman.

'You interested in sellin' your truck?'

'Sure, what'll you give me for it?'

'What's it worth?'

'At least five.'

'That's fair enough,' Brad said, removing a five dollar bill from his wallet.

'What are you, mister, a comedian or something?' The young man replaced his earphones.

'Country and western?' Brad said to the young man, indicating the Walkman.

The young man unplugged the earphones. 'Nope. Ever hear him before?' he asked.

'Think so,' Brad said.

'He's beyond all doubt the best.'

'How about Springsteen?'

'Naw. Boulton. Naw, this guy's the best, the very best.'

'Tell you what, I'll make a deal with you.'

'Oh yeah?'

'Yes, you choose any car in the showroom, I'll buy it and swap it for your pickup. Deal?'

'You crazy or sometin', Mister? You look like you couldn't rub two cents together.'

'Pick one,' Brad said.

'OK, Mister. You bring that new jeep over here and you got a deal. Lunatic,' the young man muttered under his breath. He put the earphones on.

As Brad drove away, the young man tried to clear the cobwebs from his brain. The salesman came running towards him.

'Spick, hey Spick, what's the name of that lunatic rock star you're always deafening us with?'

'Conroy, Brad Conroy.'

18

'Well, I'll be! You've just traded trucks with him.'

'What you talkin' about?'

'Look, look!' The salesman shoved a slip of paper into his face. 'He paid me for the truck with his gold card. Brad Conroy, Ireland. It checked out, too. Does Brad Conroy come from Ireland?' he asked.

But the young man couldn't answer. He lay on the ground, passed out.

Brad drove through Albuquerque, New Mexico, El Paso, San Angelo. He booked in at the Stakeout Hotel in Santa Fe. He was cruising some ten miles outside Santa Fe when a sign caught his eye. It read, 'See Colorado, The Old Fashioned Way'.

'Why not,' he said.

'Here you go,' said a man who looked every inch a cowboy. 'Betsy here will take good care of you. I put some tinned food, a blanket, there's ammo for the Winchester in the saddle bags. Take this too,' he said, handing Brad a Bowie knife complete with scabbard and belt. 'You got a lighter?'

'Yes,' said Brad.

'Smokes?'

'Haven't touched one in eight months.'

'Good for you. Now, remember what I told you in the office.'

'I know,' Brad said, 'particular eye out for rattlers.'

'Good luck, don't drift off the marked path and don't drift east, mighty rough country east of here. Keep an eye to the west for bad weather.'

Brad touched the rim of the black Stetson he had purchased in the owner's office. 'See you in a couple of days. Giddee up, Betsy,' he said to the horse and they headed north towards the mountains.

Man and animal were about three miles from the Rockies terrain when Brad tugged on the reins. The animal responded immediately and turned east. What the hell, Brad thought, if everyone stayed on the straight and narrow we'd be still living in caves.

Brad stopped halfway up the mountain. He took a swig of water from his canteen. Never thought water could taste so sweet. He raised the field glasses to his eyes and gazed at the plains down below. They seemed to go on forever. Who could blame the Indians for putting up such a fight to hold on to country such as this? He turned the glasses to his right. He gazed in awe at the snow-capped mountains. He said only one word. 'Magnificent.'

A few hours later deep in the woods, as he sat by his camp fire eating from a tin of salmon, he laughed out loud. 'God, I feel just like John Wayne,' he told whoever wanted to listen. Using his saddle for a pillow, he drew his blanket round his shoulders. 'Goodnight, world,' he said and fell into a deep sleep.

It was approaching midday when Brad rode into what could only be described as a meadow. He stopped and stared down at the furthest corner of the field. 'I see him, boy,' he said, running his gloved hand down the horse's neck. Brad came to within a few feet of the riderless horse. It was grazing under the branches of a huge oak tree, as if sheltering from the sun's tremendous heat. He checked the horse for injuries. There was none. 'Where's your owner, fella, eh?' The horse kept on grazing. Brad walked parallel with the trees. There was a gap in the opposite corner. This must be where he came in. He climbed a huge mound of rock. If he were going to spot anyone it would be from this vantage point. Brad scanned the entire area three times. There wasn't the remotest sign of another human being. He sat down and rested. He was about to climb down when something caught his eye. Peering through the glasses he could make out that it was a white piece of cloth. Something else he had missed before also caught his eye. To get to where that piece of cloth lay hanging from the lowest branch of a tree was a deep ravine. A horse could get down all right, but it would be too steep to get back up again. Brad tied large rocks to the reins of each horse to prevent them from straying but allowing them to feed. He loaded the Winchester, threw his lasso round one shoulder, the canteen over the other, and set off in the direction of the cloth.

It took Brad an hour to reach the ravine. He was about to descend into it. 'Hold your horses,' he said to himself. 'If I find that guy and he's injured, how the hell am I going to get him up?' He started walking along the edge of the ravine. Ten minutes later Brad was throwing ice cold water onto his face. He drank his fill from the stream, emptied his canteen and refilled it with fresh water, then continued on his journey. It was another hour before the cloth came into view.

'Thank God,' he said as soon as he spotted it. He was about two hundred feet from the cloth when he spotted a body lying face down on a dried mud patch. Fifty feet further on he was stopped dead in his tracks by a distinct sound. He had heard that sound in so many movies and on television. It was the sound of a rattle snake. He kept his eyes on the immediate vicinity of the body. A yard in front of the body the snake lay poised.

Brad knelt down on one knee. He had been regarded as a pretty good shot with an air rifle in his teenage years. He silently prayed to God that he could be as good just one more time. The snake was only a foot from its victim. Brad pressed the butt of the rifle tight into his shoulder. As he looked down the long barrel, its sight was perfectly levelled on the back of the snake's head. Very gently he squeezed the trigger. The snake's head exploded into tiny fragments. Brad wiped the perspiration from his face and forehead. 'Thank You, Lord,' he whispered. 'Thank you.'

'What the hell was all the racket about, mister?' The voice like thunder brought Brad to his feet. There was no mistaking her origin; she had a distinct southern accent. As he walked towards her, once again her voice almost deafened him. 'You normally go around the countryside scarin' people half to death with that cannon of yours?'

21

He stopped a few feet from her. He sized her up from head to toe. 'God,' he said to himself, 'what a mess.'

She could see he was controlling himself from laughing. 'I fell off the stupid nag o' mine twice.'

Brad's laughter echoed round the mountain. He decided to have a little fun with her. In the best southern accent he could remember from *Gone With The Wind*, he said, 'Why, Ma'am, you fell off your horse twice and you call *him* stupid?' Again his laughter echoed round the mountain. When he stopped laughing and looked at her, he could not remember another human being even looking so angry.

'Why, I'm mighty pleased you find my discomfort so funny,' she said.

'You just returning from the Battle of Gettysburg?' he joked.

'First fall I had was on hard ground, second was at the edge of a creek.' She was covered in hard mud. 'I've been following my horse all night. 'Bout an hour ago I laid down for a few minutes to get some shuteye, don't know how long I've been sleepin.'

Keep up the accent, he thought. 'Well let's go, the horses are a few hours that way.' He pointed. He had taken a few steps when she let out a loud scream. 'What is it now?'

'There,' she said, pointing at the grass and looking at the spot where the headless snake's body was twisting and turning on the ground.

'He can't hurt you. C'mon,' he said, 'we have a ways to go.'

'Did you shoot it?' Her voice was low and mellow.

'Nope, he shot himself in the back of the head.'

She looked at him, grinding her teeth. 'What kind of snake is it?' she enquired, looking at the snake, its nerves still twitching in its body.

'You could say he is a shake rattle and roll snake.'

'Funny, funny. Gaad, I must be the luckiest girl in the world. In the middle of the wilderness, I have to come across Grizzly Adams with a cannon and tryin' to be funny like Bob Hope.'

'Will you look at you,' he drawled. 'Why, Miss Scarlett, you're filthy. We've wasted enough time, let's be goin'.'

'My scarf, would you get it for me?'

He walked past her and snatched the white scarf from the branch. Handing it to her he said, 'Women!'

A few yards on, she staggered and fell. He bent down and grabbed her by the elbow. She pulled it from his grip. 'Don't try to get too familiar, Mister,' venom in her voice. After ten minutes it became clear to him that she was walking with great difficulty.

'Sit there,' he told her, pointing at a large rock. She obeyed. 'Which foot?' he asked.

'This one,' she said, tapping her right knee. He removed her boot and thick sock.

'Just like I figured, its sprained.' She put the sock and boot back on. He bent down. 'C'mon, lady, get on my back.' She hesitated. 'Look, lady, you want to spend a month on this mountain?' She climbed on.

Half an hour later, teeming in sweat, he asked, 'You ever thought 'bout losin' weight, lady?'

'One hundred and forty pounds is perfect for a lady five ten and a half,' she told him.

Brad took many intervals on the journey. By the time they reached the stream where he had filled the canteen previously, he felt like lying down and sleeping for a month. He laid her down gently onto a rock. She had carried the Winchester, holding it with both hands against his chest. Taking the rifle from her, he laid it against the rock.

'Me first,' he said, and staggered towards the stream. He dropped down onto the hard stones and began drinking deeply. He pushed his face into the water several times. It was freezing, but oh it felt good.

She thought she was seeing things as she watched the puma edge closer to Brad. Her call to him didn't scare the cat off, nor did he hear her, because of the water in his ears and the noise of the rippling stream. Grabbing the rifle, she took aim and pulled on the trigger. The bullet grazed the puma's right hind leg, ricocheted off a stone and passed within a half inch of Brad's right ear.

He was filling the canteen when an explosion almost shattered his hearing. Clutching at his right ear he turned round, temper showing on his face. He only got a glance of the cat as it disappeared into the thicket of the woods. She held the Winchester in her right hand, the butt resting on her thigh. He regained his composure.

Handing her the canteen, he said, 'How did you miss me from this distance?' She wasn't sure if he had seen the puma or not. After taking two swigs from the canteen, she said, 'Mountain lion almost had your butt,'

'What mountain lion?' he asked in a surprised voice.

'Never mind,' she said.

'Anyway, if there was a cat he probably only wanted a drink.'

'Yeah, your blood,' she said, making a face at him.

When they arrived at the ravine, Brad climbed down. She threw him the canteen and rifle.

'Ease yourself down on your back,' he told her. 'Do you think you could manage to pull yourself up by that rope? I'll help you from the top. You know, pull from above.'

'This ravine is about fifteen feet deep, agreed?' He nodded. 'Why don't I stand on your shoulders? Then I'll only have to pull myself up three feet.'

'I thought you'd never think of it,' he said.

By the time they got back to where the horses were it was almost dark. Brad gathered as much wood as he could find. After lighting a fire, he tied the horses to trees at either side of them. If any unwelcome visitors showed, the horses would sound the alarm. Opening a tin of salmon and a tin of peaches, he handed them to her.

'Use this,' he said, handing her the knife. They lay side

by side chatting, their heads resting on the saddles. The night's silence was broken by a terrible shriek. She threw her arms around him, holding on to him like a terrified child clinging to her father.

'It's OK,' he said. 'It's only an owl.' She fought off the sleep till she could fight it no more. Slowly her head tilted until it rested firmly on his chest.

When she woke next morning, Brad had both horses saddled. Casting aside the blanket he had given her, underneath her was his fur-lined denim jacket. Handing it to him, she said, 'Thanks.'

'Think nothin' of it, Miss Scarlett.'

'I don't,' she snapped.

Helping her on to her horse, he said, 'Moy oh moy, but your Ashley's sure got his work cut out. I sure don't envy him.'

They rode together in total silence for the next half hour. He decided to break it.

'Where you from, anyway?'

'Richmond,' was all she offered.

'That's in Virginia, ain't it?'

'Give the genius a prize,' she said in a mocking voice.

'I'm from Charlestown myself, if anyone's interested.'

'No one is,' she snapped.

'Why are you always in such a damn bad mood?'

She ignored the question. An hour and a half later they were walking while they gave the horses a break. She was looking down at a bald eagle as it skimmed the surface of the river. Brad stepped on some loose rocks and stumbled against her. Pushing him off she said, 'You trying to hit on me, mister?'

'I only...' She cut him short, 'Cause if you are, forget it. You have as much chance of making it with me...' As she hesitated, her eyes caught sight of the eagle once more as it soared high over the tall pine trees. She continued, '...as you have flyin' on the tail of an eagle.'

'I give up,' he said, slapping the reins on his right leg. 'Mount up.'

25

This time an hour went by with neither of them breaking the silence. Brad was leading the way along a narrow path which divided two quarries. A rabbit darted across the path of his horse. The horse reared, sending Brad crashing hard onto the ground. He slid from the path, head over heels down into the rock quarry.

She was off her horse in seconds, screaming and shouting, 'Are you all right?' He lay at the bottom of the quarry for a minute, then noticing how distressed she was he waved to her. He felt sore as he climbed back up. He felt more embarrassed than hurt. He was about to mount his horse when he noticed she had her face pressed against the side of her saddle. Standing a couple of feet from her he said laughingly, 'Why, Miss Scarlett. I do declare, you're crying.'

Wiping the tears from her eyes with the back of her hand, she yelled, 'Damn you! All that worried me was that you were dead and I wouldn't be able to find the way back on my own.'

He wiped a trickle of blood from beneath his hairline. 'Figures,' he said, and mounted his horse. They started down the mountain towards the ranch.

As they rode up to the ranch the owner came running towards them. 'God almighty, thank the Lord you're all right. You sure had us worried, Miss Gordon. When your three friends returned without you and you didn't show up that night,' he whistled, 'you sure had us worried.' He helped her down off her horse. Noticing the pain on her face as her feet hit the ground, he ordered two of the hands to carry her to his office then he went out of the office in search of Brad. But all he saw was the back of Brad's pickup as its wheels sent clouds of dust high into the sky.

'That guy have a name?' she enquired.

'Don't remember him givin' his name,' the owner said as he scratched his cheek. 'Came in here, asked to hire a horse for a couple of days, paid cash up front, seemed like a real nice feller. Doctor will be here in a jiffy to look at your leg, Miss Gordon. In the meantime, I suppose you wouldn't say no to a hot cuppa coffee?'

'Thank you,' she said.

CHAPTER FIVE

Brad stood before a mirror in his suite. 'You sure do look like Grizzly Adams,' he said, smiling. He stepped into the shower and stayed there until the black dye was washed from his hair. Drying himself with a towel, he picked up the phone.

'Would you send the barber to suite 739, please?'

'Immediately sir.'

'Thank you.' He hung up. The next two days Brad spent swimming and relaxing by the hotel's pool. The following two days he spent playing golf.

Brad sat in a quiet corner of the hotel's dining room. He had given the waiter his order and was reading a newspaper. Four young ladies came in and sat at a table at the other end of the room. One of them used a walking stick for support. It looked like her, but he couldn't say for certain. He couldn't take his eyes from her. She looked different. Then who wouldn't? Out there in the wilderness you are as you are. But this lady looked absolutely stunning. She wore a long blue silk dress and around her neck was a gold chain, with gold earrings to match.

Thirty minutes later her three friends got up from the table and left. Brad called the waiter, stuck a fifty dollar note into his jacket pocket and whispered into the waiter's ear. Five minutes later the waiter walked into the dining room and went from table to table saying, 'Telephone call for Miss Gordon.' Finally he arrived at the lady in the blue dress. She nodded. Brad's heart skipped several beats as he watched the waiter plug the phone extension into the socket on the wall. By now Brad had moved to the dining room door. He pretended to read something in his newspaper.

'Hello? Amanda Gordon. Hello, hello?'

'They must have been disconnected,' he heard her say to the waiter.

Brad returned to his table. He watched as she rose from the table minutes later and limped out of the room. He followed at a safe distance. She sat in the Residents' Lounge and began reading her magazine. Brad went down the hall. Stopping outside a shop, he walked in.

He returned and sat in the lounge. He had the advantage, as her back was to him. Over the next two hours she ordered only two coffees. After two hours her friends returned and joined her. They chatted excitedly as only women can. Over the next forty-five minutes Brad caught the girl directly in front of Amanda look his way a dozen times or more. She got up from her table and headed in his direction. Watching her walk in his direction he told himself, 'Oh, oh, I've been sussed.'

Brad's gaze returned to his newspaper.

'Excuse me for disturbing you, but aren't you Chuck Bradley?' Brad felt the tension leave his body.

'Beg your pardon Chuck, Chuck Bradley.' Offering her hand, 'I'm Lori Denis. We worked the catwalk upstate New York, oh, two years ago ... oh, I'm terribly, terribly sorry.' Seeing her genuinely embarrassed, he offered to elevate the situation.

'Now that you've walked over here, could I get you something to drink?' Realising there were dozens of eyes fixed on her, she nodded her head and sat down beside him.

'I haven't been so embarrassed since I tripped over my dress my very first night on the catwalk, back in Seattle eight years ago,' she told him.

'I know the feeling well,' he told her.

'Are you in the modelling business?' she asked.

'Not exactly, but I've been in one or two embarrassing situations in my time. Forgive my manners, what would you like to drink?'

'Vodka and coke, please.'

He told the waiter to make it a large one.

'It's absolutely amazing how alike Chuck and you are,' she told him.

'Well you know what they say, everyone's got a double somewhere.'

They both laughed. 'Tell you the truth, I only worked with Chuck for three days.' She squeezed his arm. 'Had a terrible crush on him. Unfortunately, he didn't feel the same way.'

'The guy must have been blind,' Brad told her.

'You're very kind,' she said, smiling. The waiter placed their drinks before them.

'Orange juice?'

'Afraid so.' Leaning towards her he whispered, 'Liquor and me ain't on swallowing terms just now.' They both laughed.

'So,' he said, 'you and your friends are here in Sante Fe for the fashion exhibition?'

'Yes, Cheryl, Chris and me are doing the evening's last session in about an hour.'

'I saw ye as ye came into the dining room. One of your friends seemed to be limping,' he said, enquiringly.

'Oh, that's Amanda. You know, she was lost the best part of two days up there in the mountains.'

'You don't say,' he said, amazement showing on his face. 'That must have been real scary. I sure wouldn't like to be up there all alone, no siree,' he added.

'She somehow got separated from us. We searched round for hours, but there wasn't a sign of her.'

Brad's face was resting on the palm of his right hand. 'How did she get back down?' he enquired.

'This fella found her. All she ever said was the guy was big, had dark hair and a beard which covered almost all his face.'

'What happened to her foot?'

'Oh that, she fell from her horse and sprained it. Doctor told her to keep off it for a few days. She hasn't modelled since. She should be fine in a couple of more days though.'

'Tell you something else,' she said in a low voice. 'She hasn't been the same since her return from those mountains.'

'What do you mean?'

'Well, something happened up there.'

'You mean the guy took liberties?'

'No, no nothing like that.'

'That's a relief,' Brad sighed.

'She's been ever so quiet, doesn't seem to be herself, there's a sadness about her which wasn't there before. Tell you the truth, I think she fell in love up there in the mountains, that's my opinion.' She glanced at her watch. 'God, I'll have to be going. Work, you know.'

He stood up. 'You're a very nice man. Would you do me a huge favour?'

'Name it,' he said.

'She's going to sit there alone for the next couple of hours waiting for us to finish. Would it be asking too much to sit with her; you know, cheer her up, keep her company for a spell?'

There is nothing on God's earth would please me more, Brad was thinking. 'It'd be my pleasure,' he replied.

'God, I don't even know your name. How will I introduce you?'

Brad thought for a second. 'Why not as your old school friend, Chuck Bradley?' he said, smiling.

'You're a genius,' she said. 'Girls, this is an old school

friend of mine.' The girls in turn shook hands with Brad. Turning to Amanda, she said, 'Would you mind keeping Chuck company until I finish work?'

'I was going to retire early, Lori.'

'Oh for God's sake, don't be a old woman,' the other two girls said, annoyed with her.

'I'm sorry,' she said, looking at Brad. 'I'd be delighted.'

When the three girls had left, Brad, who was sitting directly opposite Amanda, asked, 'Would you like something to drink?'

'Coffee's fine, thank you.' A few minutes had passed in silence. Her thoughts seemed elsewhere.

'Unusual,' he said.

'What's that,' she said, totally unconcerned.

'A woman with nothing to say.' This remark brought a smile to her face. 'God,' Brad was thinking, 'she's so beautiful.'

'Please forgive me, I'm not very good company these days.'

'Foot hurtin'?' he asked.

'Not really.'

He decided to gamble. 'Lori was telling me about your adventure up there in the mountains.' Immediately he sensed her body tense up. She toyed with the gold chain hanging round her neck. 'You must have been terribly scared.' Her mind was drifting again. 'My apologies, I didn't mean to pry.'

Shaking her head, 'There's nothing for you to apologise for,' she told him. She bit on her lower lip. 'It's, it's just that he was so kind, and I acted like a real bitch. He carried me for miles on his back. His back must have been breaking while he carried me and all I did was complain. He fed me and gave me his blanket and jacket to keep me warm at night. I complained. He saved me from a rattlesnake,' she smiled.

'Nothin' to smile about, rattlers,' he said.

'You don't understand. When I asked him what kind of snake it was – you see, it was wriggling round on the grass headless – he told me it was a shake rattle and roll snake.'

'Sounds more like a wise guy than anything to me,' Brad replied.

'He wasn't a wise guy, it's just he had a sense of humour, that's all. On the way down he stumbled and fell, he must have hurt himself real bad and all. I told him that if he died I might never get down from the mountain. He did everything for me and all he got for his trouble was grief.'

'Oh, think nothing of it, my dear. Those mountain men are thick skinned, it probably ran off him like water off a duck. Anyway, you were understandably very scared.'

'Never so scared in my life. But he was so kind and considerate, I should have realised it long before.' She stopped.

'Before?' he enquired.

'Before we got back to the ranch. Would you believe I didn't even ask him his name?' They both remained silent for a time. Brad rubbed his chin.

'Amanda, do you mind if I ask you a question?' She shook her head. 'At what point up there in those mountains did you realise you were in love with that fella?'

Without stopping to think she said, 'When he fell off his horse onto the rough gravel.' Shooting him a glance she said, 'But I never said that I loved him to anyone.' Brad prised the palms of his hands apart, making a frowned face at the same time. 'Is it that obvious?' she enquired.

''Fraid so,' he told her. Brad removed a handkerchief from an inside pocket and offered it to her. Thanking him, she accepted it.

'I'll return it to you later,' she told him.

'How about at dinner this evening?'

'I, I, I don't think so. Forgive me if I seem ungrateful.'

'Look,' he continued, 'your friends could be held up after the fashion show – you know, meeting with possible buyers, the press, etc, etc. I'm here alone. Just one meal, then maybe a drink. I'll make a solemn promise here and now that it will be a night to remember.' He knelt down on one knee and pressed his right hand against his heart. 'Please don't say no.'

The other guests, smiling and applauding, encouraged her to say yes. Amanda felt every drop of blood in her body had rushed to her head.

'OK, OK, yes. The answer's yes. Please get up off your knee.'

Brad watched her walk to the elevator. When the door closed behind her Brad stood up, looking at the guests. He said, 'I thank you, I thank you, I thank you,' then bowed his head like an actor receiving the accolades of the crowd.

At precisely eight o'clock Brad knocked on the door to Amanda's suite. When she opened the door the shock on her face startled Brad.

'Were you expecting somebody else?' he asked nervously.

'Forgive me. Please come in,' she indicated towards a chair. 'It's just that I expected you to be wearing jeans and a chequered shirt. I thought we were going casual.'

'I can return to my room and change in no time,' he offered.

'What must you think of me, going out to dinner in jeans and a sweater?' She removed a plastic covered garment from her closet. 'I'll be just a tick,' she said, and closed the bathroom door. Brad had felt like an idiot after she had agreed to have dinner with him. He had hired a tuxedo, white shirt, wine bow tie, and black and white spats. When Amanda emerged some minutes later, she took Brad's breath away. She had replaced her jeans and sweater with a purple pleated off-the-shoulders, just-below-the-knee stand-out frock. She rummaged through the floor of her closet. 'Here we are.' She placed the stilettos on her feet and they matched her frock perfectly.

She wrapped a white silk scarf around her shoulders. 'Now,' she said, 'at last we're off.'

Brad closed the door behind them and they made for the elevator. Amanda had discarded her walking cane for the evening. As they approached the hotel steps, Brad offered Amanda his arm. He helped her into the waiting cab.

'You choose the restaurant,' he suggested.

'OK,' she said, smiling, 'but I hope you won't be disappointed.'

'I won't,' he said, smiling back at her. Amanda gave the driver directions and the cab sped away.

Some twenty minutes later, after taking a side road, the cab pulled up outside a long log-cabin type building. Brad paid the driver, tipping him generously. Once inside, Amanda realised she had make a mistake. There was a queue of some thirty couples waiting for a table to become available. Turning to Brad she said 'I'm sorry, I should have known we'd need a reservation.'

'Let's try the bar,' he suggested.

'But we'll lose our place in the queue.'

'I'll make sure we don't, I promise.' Brad placed a Scotch before Amanda and sat down beside her. He took a sip from his orange juice.

'Vodka and orange?' she enquired.

'Just orange juice. Been on nothing stronger for almost a year.' Brad was grateful that she hadn't pried.

They had been chatting for ten minutes when a uniformed youth came over to their table.

'Miss Amanda?' Glancing at the youth she said, 'Yes.'

'Your table is ready now, Ma'am.' She looked at Brad.

'Seems like you've got friends in high places,' he said.

When the waiter came to take their order, Amanda ordered fresh salmon salad. 'Make it two,' Brad told him. Half way through the meal, Amanda whispered to Brad, 'I wonder who pulled strings and got us such a well placed table?'

'Tell you the truth, I slipped a hundred dollar bill to the maitre de,' Brad said sheepishly.

Fifteen minutes later the master of ceremonies took the microphone from its stand. 'Good evening, ladies and gentlemen. I hope you are all having a good time.' The crowd applauded. 'Well let me tell you, it's going to get better. Tonight, direct from their triumphant appearance at *Ye Auld Opera*, The Pine Cabin presents *The Hilly Billy Hogs*. The crowd went wild. Ten minutes into their show Brad asked Amanda, 'This your favourite kind of music?'

Shaking her head she said, ''Fraid not. I'm old fashioned, I love classical music. But,' she added, 'there's no music I don't like.' Brad and Amanda had several dances until Brad protested about her sore foot.

'If you can suffer my dancing,' she told him, 'so can I.' Half way through their last dance she told Brad, 'Enough is enough.' They retired to their table and watched the huge crowd enjoying themselves.

As they sat enjoying the music and dancing, a tall cowboy said to Amanda, 'You like to dance, Ma'am?' Looking up at him, she smiled, 'No thank you.' Brad was about to explain that she had a sore foot. The cowboy cut him short.

'Nobody's talkin' to you, butt head, so why don't you butt out?' Brad stood up. Though Brad was six feet tall, the cowboy was almost a head taller than him.

'The lady said no, Roy,' Brad said through clenched teeth. By now a crowd had gathered round them. Looking round the crowd, the cowboy said, 'Seems like this here dude in the monkey suit is hankerin' for a hidin'.' The cowboy removed his huge stetson and threw it on the table. He sent his massive left fist crashing into Brad's already sore ribs. As Brad's head tilted forward, the cowboy brought an uppercut under Brad's chin, sending him flying across the room. As Brad got to his feet, the cowboy was sneering, a matchstick clenched firmly between this teeth. The two men faced each other.

'I'll say one thing for you, dude. You're game.' The cowboy led with his left, aiming for Brad's face. Brad grabbed his wrist and sent a powerful blow into the cowboy's stomach. Still holding the cowboy's wrist, Brad punched him repeatedly on the jaw. The cowboy crumbled to the floor, raising his left hand as in submission. Another cowboy ran to Brad, holding his right hand in the air.

'Ladies and gentlemen, I declare the dude's the winner!'

The cab came to a halt outside their hotel. As they climbed the steps, Amanda supported by Brad's left arm, he stumbled and fell against the corner of one of the steps.

'I'll get some help,' Amanda said.

'No, no, I'm all right, just a little bit sore is all. Would you get me a glass of water from the kitchen?' he asked, as they went through the hotel doors. While Amanda went in search of water, Brad asked for the key to his suite. Amanda handed him a glass of water. He swallowed it in one gulp.

'I'll get your key from reception,' she said.

'I've already got it,' he said, showing it to her. As they walked from the elevator, Amanda put her arm around Brad's wrist.

'I'm not complaining, but I'm not that bad,' he said, smiling.

Amanda opened the door to Brad's suite. 'The medicine cabinet is in the bathroom, through there,' he pointed. She returned with some bandages.

'Off with your shirt.' He obeyed. 'That sure looks awful bruised. Must be awful sore.' Amanda brought the bandage round his shoulder.

'You seem to have experience at this,' he said.

'Well, being an only girl with six brothers it became compulsory in our house.' As they lay on the couch, Brad said, 'You look like you could do with a Scotch.' Pointing, he said, 'The liquor cabinet's over there.'

'And you?'

'Just iced water, thank you.'

Amanda handed Brad a tall glass of iced water. Standing before him, she swallowed the Scotch in one gulp.

'May I?' she asked.

'Help yourself.' Amanda poured herself a generous measure, then sat beside Brad on the sofa.

'I was so frightened,' she told him. 'He, he, he was so big I thought he'd kill you.'

'Big, but out of shape. There's an awful difference.' She took another sip from her glass.

'Excuse me, I have to use the bathroom,' Brad told her.

As Brad came out of the bathroom, Amanda's sobbing stopped him in his tracks. He watched her for a minute. Inwardly he was laughing hard. He returned to her side. Above him lay his jacket. He rolled it down and removed his handkerchief from the inside pocket. Handing it to her, he said, 'This could get expensive.' She laughed out loud. 'That's better, no more tears ... please,' he asked.

'I'll never forget those two punches you took, and all because of me.'

'That's the least I could do. Your honour was at stake.' She began to sob again.

'Why, Miss Scarlett, I do declare you're crying.' Very slowly she prised her face from his handkerchief.

'Yes, my love, it's me. Grizzly Adams himself. You saved me from the puma. Yes, I saw it dart away, my love, and you're crying 'cause I took a couple of punches.' Her mouth hung open. He covered her mouth with his, kissing her for a full minute.

'Before you removed the mud from that beautiful face up in that mountain, I was captivated by you.'

'But I was so cruel.'

He pressed a finger to her lips. 'I love you with every fibre of my being.' He stuck his hand into his jacket pocket and placed a white velvet box on the table before her.

'I bought that before I spoke one word to you in this hotel, cross my heart,' he told her. Before she opened it, she gave her answer. 'Yes.'

They kissed passionately for several minutes. After opening the box she remained silent for some time.

'Cat got your tongue?'

Looking at him, she said, 'This must have cost a hundred thousand dollars. Where on earth would you, Chuck, get that kind of money?'

'Sweetheart, it isn't Chuck Bradley, it's Brad Conroy.' It didn't register with her.

'Are you a jeweller, Brad?'

'No,' he laughed. 'Nothing so distinguished, I'm afraid. I'm a so-called rock singer.'

She clasped her fingers round her mouth. 'Of course, Brad Conroy! All the girls on the catwalk would do anything, anything, to be where I am right now.'

'But, honey, none of those girls saved me from a mountain lion.'

'We'll arrange for our parents to meet as soon as possible.'

'I want us to be married about ten minutes after they meet.' They began kissing passionately once again.

When Brad had set eyes on Amanda in the dining room and realised it was the girl from the mountain, he had gone to the jeweller's shop in the hotel. As the assistant placed the tray before her, he very quickly chose a ring.

'The one with the tag for one hundred thousand dollars, Sir?'

'No, Miss,' he replied. 'The one with the tag for one million dollars.'

CHAPTER SIX

Amanda and Brad stood on the steps of St Peter's Church, sixty miles south of Charleston, South Carolina. Amanda was in a splendid white wedding gown, her veil trailing six feet behind her. Brad wore grey striped trousers with matching waistcoat, white shirt, black bow tie and black jacket.

'How does it feel to be Mrs Brad Conroy?' he whispered, a broad beam across his lips. Squeezing his hand she replied, 'Positively beautiful.'

Amanda was twenty-two, Brad was thirty-nine. There had been two hundred guests invited to the wedding, with an open invitation to anyone who felt like it just to drop in at the hotel, if only to say hello. Amanda had been born in Charleston and her family, being Catholic, travelled the sixty miles every Sunday to attend Mass. Two of Amanda's brothers had gone to work in Sydney, Australia, two more to Los Angeles, and the other two worked, as Amanda put it, 'just down the road' in Memphis. Brad had insisted on paying their expenses in order to attend the wedding. Brad also paid for his parents, three brothers, and two of his mother's brothers. Joe Quinn wouldn't hear of Brad paying for Joe or his wife to travel from London to attend.

Brad and Amanda thought the handshaking would never come to an end outside the tiny church, but they were very courteous to everyone. Many of Brad's fans had turned up to wish them both well. Brad's mother was crying as she threw her arms around Amanda, telling her, 'Brad couldn't have chosen a nicer or more beautiful girl.' She whispered in Amanda's ear, as she squeezed her arms, 'Please make my boy happy.'

'That, Mrs Conroy, I promise you,' Amanda assured her.

After the breakfast and all the speeches, everyone retired to the bar to allow the hotel staff to clear the tables so that the dancing could commence.

As Brad and Amanda took the floor for their bridal dance, there was thunderous applause from the now increased five hundred crowd.

'Stunning, absolutely stunning, is the only word for you, Mrs Conroy.'

'Don't make me blush, Brad, you know I blush easily.'

He pulled her close. 'Before God, I promise you you'll be the only woman in my life as long as I live,' he told her. After their dance they went about shaking hands and speaking to as many of the invited and the uninvited guests as possible.

About an hour later the leader of the eight-piece orchestra spoke into the microphone.

'Ladies and gentlemen, I'm sure that you will agree with me if I extend an invitation to Mr Conroy to join us here on stage and treat us to some songs from those wonderful pipes of his.'

The applause was deafening. Brad held the mike in his hand and the orchestra began to play. The first song Brad chose was the *Hawaiian Wedding Song*. Amanda was sitting at a distance directly in front of him. As he sang the words, 'Here and now, dear, all my love I vow, dear', Amanda brought her handkerchief to her eyes. Spotting this, Brad stopped singing and spoke into the mike.

'Why, Miss Scarlett, I do declare you're crying.' With that, Amanda's face became a radiant smile. The next song Brad chose was Barry Manilow's *Amanda*. Handing the mike to the band leader, he said, 'Thank you.' He bowed and said, 'It's all yours, gentlemen.'

Brad's and Amanda's family sat in the VIP lounge at Atlanta Airport. Amanda's six brothers had gathered round Brad. They were very keen to hear Brad speak about his native land. Their father's father, they told him, had emigrated to the States from a place called Elphin, County Roscommon, around the year 1880.

'You six organise your holidays, that's "vacation" to you,' he joked, 'at the same time, say next September, and together with Amanda we'll all make a trip over there. How's that?'

They agreed to try. The flight was called. Brad and Amanda kissed and shook hands with everyone and made their way to board their flight.

About half an hour out from Atlanta Airport, the stewardess handed Amanda a telegram. It read, 'Congratulations to you both. Would be grateful if you would give me a call if you wish to continue modelling after honeymoon.' It was signed by Antonio Stratti. Amanda squeezed Brad's arm.

'You know the only reason he sent me this is because now I'm Mrs Brad Conroy.'

Brad made a face. 'You know,' he said, 'you could get a part in Cinderella – as one of the ugly sisters, of course.' They both laughed heartily. They had chosen Hawaii for their month's honeymoon.

Thirty days later Brad and Amanda stepped off their flight from Hawaii and made their way to the limousine waiting for them, courtesy of Mecca Records. The limousine pulled up outside the plush office of Antonio Stratti's Model Agency. Brad escorted Amanda to the reception area. He had offered to sit through the negotiations, as she had decided to work freelance and in her own words had told Brad "There is no time like the present to start fighting my own corner". While Brad waited, a couple of dozen models had sought his autograph. He obliged and chatted with them. They had all handed him their card, their phone numbers handwritten on them. As soon as

Amanda came through Stratti's office door, Brad threw the cards into a waste basket.

As they sat in the back seat of the limo, Amanda threw her arms around Brad. She was as excited as a child at Christmas after receiving its favourite toy.

'What would you think I'm worth, darling?' she asked.

Brad thought for a minute. 'Somewhere between forty-five and fifty million,' he said.

'No, no, don't tease me, please, Brad. As a model I mean.'

'Sorry, love. You tell me.' He was kissing her hands.

'I negotiated ten thousand dollars a day, plus expenses, How about that?'

'How much were you getting when we met?' he asked.

'Fifteen hundred a week and no expenses.'

'You sold yourself short.'

'What do you mean?' she frowned.

'The most beautiful girl in the world just doesn't have a price tag.'

She cupped his face in her hands. 'You know the exact words to say to a girl, you old romantic.' They kissed passionately.

Over the next twelve months Amanda's modelling assignments took her to the four corners of the world. Brad stayed resident in London, working on four new singles and two albums. When their schedules allowed, they would fly to meet each other. Sometimes they would be together for as little as four hours. They phoned each other twice a day, regardless of time variations.

When Mecca released Brad's new composition, *Forever Yours*, a romantic ballad, it went to number one in four days. Two weeks later it reached the number one spot in every country in Europe. America and Japan took a week longer. Four weeks later Mecca released his new album, all fourteen songs written by Brad. It went to number one worldwide in three weeks. Brad Conroy was back on top once more.

CHAPTER SEVEN

Brad picked up the phone and dialled.

'Joe Quinn.'

'Howa, Joe?'

'Fine, Brad. Yourself?'

'Well, except for a little loneliness, just fine. Look, Joe, I'm just dying for a home cooked meal. Would Rose mind?'

Joe cut in. 'Our home is yours. You don't need a bloody invitation to join us for dinner. Anything in particular you'd like Rose to cook?'

'Hows about plain old fashioned Irish stew?'

'You got it. Eight o'clock all right?'

'Fine, see you then.'

Brad arrived at Joe's home at five minutes to eight with flowers and wine, which he handed to Rose as he kissed her cheek. Joe's two daughters came running at him shouting, 'Uncle Brad, Uncle Brad.'

Picking them up, one in each arm, he kissed them, then spent fifteen minutes listening to their school adventures. As their mother was about to send them to bed Brad said, 'Barbara, left pocket.' She stuck her tiny hand in, removing a tiny gift-wrapped square box. He called to Kerry, 'Right pocket.' Excitedly they removed the wrapping.

'Look, Mammy!' They showed the contents of the velvet boxes. Inside were Rolex watches. They had cost Brad just under one thousand pounds each.

'Damn it, Brad, you have those kids spoiled,' Joe said angrily.

Brad only smiled. 'Isn't that what kids are for? Anyway, Barbara is my godchild; I'm entitled.'

Joe shook his head. 'There's just no talking to you, Brad.'

When Joe and Rose had married, during the reception Brad had handed Rose an envelope, saying, 'A little something from the Conroy family.' The little something was the four-storeyed house in Chelsea which they had now lived in for the last ten years.

Joe and Brad were sitting in Joe's den.

'Joe,' Brad began, 'I want you to organise a European tour. We'll start in Ireland. Where we finish is entirely up to you. How long will it take you to organise?'

'No longer than two weeks.'

'Great, I can't wait to get back doing live shows.'

That out of the way, Joe said, 'How's everything with Amanda?'

'Well she loves what she's doing, though it keeps us apart a lot. Knowing how much I love what *I* do, I understand.'

Joe and Brad chatted about old times for another two hours. Brad kissed Rose goodnight.

'By the way, Joe, I'd like to visit Limerick for a couple of days before we start the tour. Make sure you allow for that, please.'

They wished each other goodnight. Brad climbed into his Porsche and drove away.

Brad was back on Irish soil again. He hired a car at Shannon and drove straight to his parents' home. After a couple of hours Brad's mother told him to phone his brothers.

'The four of ye go out tonight and meet as many of the musicians you played with as possible. Talk over old times.'

Brad and his brothers visited half a dozen old haunts.

Brad was sporting dark glasses. All the groups playing were very young and he didn't get to meet any of his old friends at all. He was disappointed, but didn't let it show.

*   *   *

At eight that same evening, Brad's mother got into her car and drove to Newcastle West to visit an old friend who was feeling poorly. On her way home, five miles from Limerick, her car came to a sudden stop in the middle of nowhere on a dark country road. She removed the torch from the glove compartment. She signalled several cars but they just whizzed by her. She checked her watch. Ten-thirty. She had been seeking help now forty-five minutes. She decided to sit in the car, as it was getting rather chilly. A light shone into her face and a voice woke her from her slumber.

'Are you all right, Mam?' the torch holder enquired.

'It just broke down.'

'Let me try,' the young lady offered. 'Dead as a doornail I'm afraid. Where are you going? Can I drop you off?'

'I'm living a short distance from the city on the other side.'

'Hop in, I'll drive you home.'

'You're very sweet and kind,' Brad's mother said as they drove along. 'Where are you off to this late at night? A disco?'

The young lady laughed. 'I wish. I'm actually going to work.'

'It's a mortal sin, young ladies working in factories throughout the night, a mortal sin so it is.'

'Actually I'm working at a local radio station in the city. I play the records.' No point in telling this old lady that she played CDs. She'd be an hour trying to explain what a CD was.

'What's your name, dear?' Brad's mother enquired.

'Sue, Susan Brown. And yours?'

'Nora Conroy, love,' Brad's mother replied.

The young girl had to give Brad's mother her address,

she insisted so much. The reason given was so that she could send her a Christmas card for her act of kindness.

At breakfast next morning, Brad listened as his mother relayed the story of the night before.

'God Almighty, mother, anything could have happened to you out there. A car, a horse, a cow, any of them could have run you down, not to mention...' He didn't continue. 'Get the girl's name?' he enquired.

Smiling, she said, 'I got more than her name, son. I got her address.' She produced a slip of paper from her handbag and handed it to him.

'How did you manage this?'

'I told her that I wanted to send her a Christmas card for her kindness, but I'd like to treat her to something special.'

'I'm going into town now,' Brad said, 'I'll take care of it.' Kissing her on the forehead, 'You're still as crafty as ever, Ma,' he told her. 'See you later.'

Nora Conroy knocked on the door. It was four-thirty in the afternoon. A girl in school uniform answered.

'Hello, love, is Susan in?'

'She's, she's in bed.'

'Just then a voice called from inside, 'Who's at the door, Angela?'

'A lady, Mam.'

'May I help you?' she asked.

'I'm so sorry. I didn't realise that Susan would be in bed.'

'Is it important? She gets up at five.'

'Well, it really is.'

'Reluctantly, the woman of the house invited her in.

'I've got my son with me. He's in the car. May he come in also?'

'I suppose so.'

Brad came at his mother's beckoning.

'Angela, tell your sister that there are some people waiting downstairs to see her, would you, please?'

Before Brad reached the front door, Angela was up the

stairs. Mrs Brown directed them into the sitting room, leaving the door ajar. Brad and his mother smiled as they heard the words, 'Who the hell is looking for me at this time of the day?'

She pushed the sitting room door open. Before her sat Nora Conroy. The door almost obscured Brad, who was leaning against the wall behind it. Surprise and annoyance showed on Sue's face.

'Mrs . . .' She couldn't think of her second name.

'Conroy, love,' Nora said. 'It's just that my son wanted to thank you personally for the trouble you took to get me home safely last night.'

'Your son,' Susan mumbled.

'Brad,' Nora said.

Brad came round from behind the door. Susan's face went crimson red in seconds. Offering his hand, he said, 'So very pleased to meet you, Susan.' Her hand was shaking out of control as she accepted his. She stood there motionless, both hands clasped round her lips. Brad had seen it all before.

'Wouldn't we be more comfortable sitting?' he suggested. Nodding, she sat next to Nora on the couch. Brad sat on the armchair opposite.

'I can't tell you how much I appreciate what you did for my mother last night, Susan. May I call you Susan?' She hadn't taken her hands from her mouth. She nodded.

'The fact that you stopped alone shows you're a person who cares, and the thought of my mother fast asleep in that car . . . I shudder to think. I'm terribly, terribly grateful.'

'I can't believe that you're here in my own home,' she sighed.

'Ah, ye young girls are all the same. He's only flesh and blood, same as you and me,' Brad's mother said. Susan gave her a half smile, and jumped at the ringing of Brad's mobile phone.

'Will you excuse me, please?' Sue nodded.

48

'Hello? 'How are you, darling?' He covered the mouth-piece. 'It's Amanda.' He conveyed Susan's kindness to her. Handing Susan the phone, he said, 'My wife would like to thank you also.' Susan surprised herself by chatting as if to an old friend for five minutes with Amanda. Brad chatted for another five minutes and promised to ring right back.

Mrs Brown came into the room and laid a tray on the coffee table.

'Please help yourself,' she said. Brad stood up.

'We haven't met,' he said to her, extending his hand. Susan got to her feet.

'Mam, this is Brad Conroy, and his mother Mrs Nora Conroy.'

'Forgive me for being a little distant at first, but I didn't have a clue who you were.' She shook hands with both of them.

'Won't you join us, please, Mrs Brown?'

'Dora, please.' Mrs Brown called to Angela, who came into the room very coy.

'Do you mind if I ask you a question, Mrs Conroy'

'Please call me Nora,' then added, 'ask any question you like.'

'How does it feel to have such a famous son?'

'That's easy,' Nora said securely.

Brad decided to get them to talk about anything but himself. 'Mam tells me you're a disc jockey;' his words were directed at Susan.

'Yes. Yes, Brad, I'm with a local station here in town.'

'Do you enjoy it?'

'Well, yes.'

'You sound a little apprehensive.'

'I do midnight to seven a.m. It's hard to keep cheerful for seven straight hours.'

'I can imagine. You must be drained at the end of each shift.' Susan nodded.

'And you Angela?' He wanted to include the girl in the

conversation. 'Are you enjoying school?' She shook her head.

'Speak up, girl,' her mother said.

'She's just a little girl being a little girl,' Nora said. She finished her cup of tea. 'We've taken up enough of your time as it is, Dora. We'd better be going.' She turned to Susan. Thanks again, love.'

Placing his saucer on the tray, 'Very refreshing, Dora, thank you,' Brad added.

As they stood up to leave, the doorbell rang.

'I'll get it,' Angela said. Angela came back into the room. 'Mam, there's a man at the door and I think he's got the wrong address.'

Nora looked at Brad and nodded her head in the direction of the hall.

'No, no, you must have the wrong address,' Dora Brown was saying to the delivery man. Brad put his hand on her shoulder.

'I think I can straighten this out, Dora.' Brad checked the invoice. 'It's OK, you've got the right address.'

'Back in the sitting room, Brad explained that he'd like to show more than his face as appreciation to Susan.

'The delivery man will drop a few things in and he will connect them for you.' They all shook hands. 'I'll surprise you some night on the radio, Susan, that's a promise,' Brad said. Susan looked very sad as Brad drove away.

Over an hour later, the delivery man left the Brown home. Susan, her mother and sister sat flabbergasted, admiring the goods he had delivered. A thirty-six inch stereo television set, state of the art video, a viewfinder camcorder, a Sony midi system, a Sony CD Walkman, and a CD player with some forty games and films. The envelope which Brad had discreetly placed on the tea tray contained a voucher for tapes and/or CDs to the value of one thousand pounds.

'Nobody, but nobody, is going to believe that Brad and Mrs Conroy sat in our sitting room drinking tea with us, not to mention presenting us with these wonderful gifts, mother. They must have cost a fortune,' Susan said in a whispering voice.

The following evening Brad embraced his mother, father and brothers at the airport. He threw them kisses as he made his way to board the aircraft.

'See you all after the tour.'

'You're not goin to cry again, mother,' Brad's father said, smiling at Nora.

Joe Quinn came into Brad's suite. He sat directly opposite Brad. 'OK,' he said, 'here's the tour roster.' Brad rubbed his eyes.

'Read it to me please, Joe.'

'We start the tour as you requested, in Ireland, first gig at the Limerick University, then Dublin's Point, Belfast, back to London, then Birmingham, up to Liverpool then to Glasgow. Next stop Paris, then Lyons. On to Barcelona, Madrid, over to Lisbon, then up to Brussels, then Amsterdam. In Germany we play in Hamburg, Berlin, Dusseldorf. Then on to Prague, then Warsaw, down then to Budapest. From there we slip down to Athens, on then to Rome, then back home to London.'

'How long?' Brad asked.

''Bout four months.' Joe replied.

Brad looked at his watch; eight p.m. 'It's three p.m. New York time.' He picked up the phone and gave the operator Amanda's number.

'Brad, Brad, is that you Brad?'

'Yes, darling.'

'Why so long to speak?' she enquired.

'I was savouring the sound of your voice, my love. How are things in New York?'

'Hectic. Tomorrow we fly to Boston, then back to Philadelphia, then on to Washington. And you, my love?'

'All over Europe for the next four months.' They chatted for an hour.

When Brad hung up he wiped the mist from his eyes.

'Joe, will you make sure that the Brown family in Limerick get tickets for the show at the University? Make sure a limo picks them up and returns them home. Ask them if they would like to have dinner with me after the show. They're a wonderful family.'

'Done, Boss,' Joe said.

'I wish Mam and Dad would attend, but the noise is too much for them, so Mam says.'

'Maybe if you sang like Mario Lanza they would attend,' Joe joked.

Even before his tour began it was sold out throughout Europe. Brad was halfway through his tour when Joe realised how much he loved and missed Amanda, but he was a real professional and would let his guard down only in Joe's presence.

It was three o'clock in the morning and Brad was fast asleep. He had finished the first of two concerts in Barcelona. The light switched on in his room and woke him immediately. Sitting up, he rubbed his eyes.

'Amanda! Amanda, is that really you?'

'In the flesh, darling.'

'I thought I was dreaming.'

As she began undressing, she said in a sexy voice, 'Well, darling, it's going to be the most realistic dream you've ever experienced.'

Brad and Amanda sat eating breakfast on the balcony of Brad's suite.

'The view is breathtaking,' she gasped.

Holding her hand, Brad said, 'Just like you, my love. How did you know where I'd be?' Brad enquired.

'Are you going soft or something? Didn't you post me your itinerary times, dates, venues before you started this tour.'

'Oh, yes,' he said. 'But how did you come to have a couple of days off? Your itinerary is as hectic as mine.'

'Dress consignments plus dates got mixed up,' she lied. Joe Quinn had phoned the day before, telling her that Brad's heart was breaking from being separated so much from her. Amanda was in Paris when she received Joe's call. She simply told Stratti that she was taking a couple of days off to be with her husband. He protested angrily but had to give in to her. He knew what a strong-willed lady she was.

Amanda was studying Brad as he sat gazing out of the window at the airport.

'Penny for them,' she asked.

He turned to her. 'Sorry, my love.'

'You were in deep thought just then.'

'Oh, my mind drifted back to the days when Joe and I were kids on the estate. There was this fish 'n' chip shop. We would stand on the corner and now and again someone would offer us a chip from their bag. That time, by the way, I didn't have an arse to my trousers.' Brad didn't continue.

'Darling, darling, I don't get the point of what you've just told me,'

He took her hands in his. 'Well, my queen, when someone would offer you a chip it tasted so good you would have loved to have had the whole bag.'

'I'm still lost, darling.'

Brad looked at the floor and laughed. 'Do I have to write a book, sweetheart?'

Amanda could feel her face heating up. She shifted restlessly in her seat. Brad kept staring at her like a puppy dog. Finally she said, 'I understand. I'm the chip.'

'What a clever girl I married,' he mocked.

An hour later Amanda stood up. 'That's my flight they're paging.'

'I hate these goodbyes,' Brad said, an angry tone in his voice. 'If you didn't love what you do so much I'd never have agreed to let you do it,' he told her.

'Don't you think I know that, darling? And I love you

53

all the more for it.' Now Amanda was fighting back the tears. He held her as if he was never going to see her again.

'You know something, sweetheart?'

'What's that?' she asked.

'There are very few people on this planet who are blessed with the privilege of doing what they really love and getting paid for it to boot. We are two of those people.' They kissed until they heard the final announcement for her flight. He handed Amanda her cosmetic basket.

'Please God, may the next two months fly,' he whispered as she walked away through the boarding area.

The aircraft climbed higher and the terminal grew smaller.

'When my contract expires next February, I'm not going to renew it. I'm not being a bit fair to Brad.' She blew her nose and turned her face from the window. February was five months away.

CHAPTER EIGHT

The next two months really did fly. Brad gave interviews to women's magazines, the press, did radio and TV talk shows. All these helped stop him counting the hours until his tour ended and he could be with Amanda. He took his final bow in Rome. When he walked off stage he climbed into his limo and went back to his hotel. Joe and Brad's five-piece rock group sat round Brad's suite.

'Best tour ever,' Joe said. All heads were nodding. The critics in each of the countries had once again given Brad rave reviews. They had crowned him the king of rock and roll.

There was a knock on the door. Joe answered it. Walking to where Brad was laid out on a couch, a white towel wrapped around his neck, he said, 'It's for you, Brad.' After reading the note, Brad tossed it on the magazine table. Everybody looked at each other.

'Not bad news I hope, Brad?' Joe asked.

'No.'

After a few minutes, Brad stood up. 'Lads, you'll have to forgive my bad manners of late.'

'We understand, Boss. No need to apologise, Boss.'

'Read the telegram to the boys, Joe, it concerns them.' Joe read out loud.

The Academy of Motion Pictures, Arts and Science takes great pleasure in announcing that the composition written and sung by you has been nominated for an Academy Award. The date for this venue is March 21st, 1988. Congratulations, best of luck.

Signed......

When the group had finished congratulating Brad and one another, Brad said, 'Don't you lot have young ladies to attend to?' They immediately knew Brad wanted to be alone. He bade them goodnight and they left. Joe handed Brad a tall glass of iced water. He poured a Scotch for himself. They had been chatting for an hour when Joe stood up and turned on the radio. The radio station had played three of Brad's records in a row without interruption from the DJ. After the third song the DJ said, 'That was the one and only Brad Conroy.'

Brad sat up, smiled at Joe and said, 'Pass me the phone please, Joe.'

'Hello, good morning, Radio Limerick. Lovely to hear your voice again.' The DJ laughed. Another drunk, she said to herself.

'Your voice comes really lovely over the air.'

She laughed into the phone. 'Have I spoken to you face to face?' she enquired.

'Once.'

'Oh, when was that?'

'Little over four months ago.'

'I don't recognise your voice I'm afraid.'

Brad decided to string her along for another while. 'To hear you say that hurts me.'

'Well, you do have the advantage.'

'When we met, I was sure you fell head over heels in love with me.'

She was becoming impatient with him. 'Did we meet in bar, or at a function, or where?'

'You really don't recognise my voice?'

'Definitely not.'

'Are we on the air?' Brad asked.

'Why?'

56

'Because if we were, I'd sing a song just for you. Then you'd remember my voice.'

'OK,' she said, throwing her eyes to the ceiling. She spoke into the mike.

'Well, I have someone on the line who refuses to tell me his name. He wants to sing, so here goes. Remember this is his idea, not mine. In your own time, caller.'

Brad was on his feet, walking around his suite. He chose to sing one of his singles which had kept him at the number one spot for ten weeks.

Susan sat back. She had unwrapped her sandwich and taken a bite. Less than one minute into his song she almost choked on her sandwich. Her face was roaring red. 'Br, Bra, Brad,' she blurted out.

When Brad had finished singing, he added that that was especially for his good friend, Susan Brown.

'Hello, hello, are you still there?'

'Susan,' Brad said into the phone.

'Brad, Brad, I'm so sorry.'

'For what, my love? You'd never have recognised my voice. I love to mimic and try impersonations as a distraction from the pressures of touring.'

They continued to chat for forty-five minutes off air. Before they finished talking, Susan told Brad that the switchboard was jammed with callers, most of them wanting to know how she came to be a personal friend of Brad Conroy.

'I promised to surprise you when I visited your home.'

'That you did, Brad. And Brad, my family and I really appreciate those wonderful gifts. On behalf of my family and me, thank you very much.'

'My pleasure, love. Next time in Limerick, I'll drop in for some tea. OK?'

'My heart is pounding at the thought,' she said.

'So's mine,' he said generously. They said goodnight and hung up.

'Won't feel it now,' Joe said to Brad. Brad, who was reading a newspaper, turned to Joe and said, 'What was that?'

57

'Christmas. Two weeks away.' I said we won't feel it now.'

'Oh yes,' Brad replied.

Joe was shaking his head and laughing to himself. Brad put down the paper.

'Like to let me in on it?' he said to Joe.

Joe took a hankie from a pocket and wiped his eyes.

'I was thinking back to another Christmas. What were we, fourteen, fifteen years old? We were in your father's work-shed. You were trying to work a miracle with an old beat-up Spanish guitar. 'I'm sure Caruso must have owned it at one time.'

Brad was laughing heartily. 'I remember it well. You,' he said, pointing at Joe, 'had hammered the top off a biscuit tin onto a chunk of wood and tried to play the drums on it.'

They both burst out laughing. When the laughter had subsided, Joe said, 'Life is funny, all the same.'

'How do you mean?' Brad asked.

'That Christmas we were happy, very happy, with our rubbish instruments in a draughty shed with only a candle as a means of light.'

'Yes,' Brad said, 'but back then everyone, in our estate anyway, was in the same boat.'

'Yes,' Joe said, 'but just look around this suite. That chandelier alone must have cost at least ten grand. Look at the furniture. Dudley Moore would be at eye level standing on that carpet. A jacuzzi, your bath is large enough to wash ten people at the same time, and what are you paying for this suite?'

'You tell me. You're my manager,' Brad said.

'Too right, I know. I sign the cheques. Fifteen hundred quid a night. Still,' Joe continued, 'you deserve it all, Brad. God knows you've worked hard enough for it.'

'That's a relief,' Brad sighed, 'for a minute there I thought you wanted me to give it all away.'

'Sorry, Brad, I just got a bit melancholy for a spell,

that's all. What time is it,' Joe asked. 'I left my watch in my suite.'

'Almost three p.m.,' Brad said. He slapped his left palm on his forehead. 'That reminds me. Fancy a little fresh air?' I have one gift in particular to buy for someone very special.'

'Let's go then,' Joe said.

*　　*　　*

'Flight 128 from Cape Town now arriving at gate 15.' Amanda spotted Brad first. In her anxiety she almost knocked him over. They had a long lingering kiss. He held her at arm's length.

'Let me look at you. I'm convinced you are getting more beautiful with each passing day.'

She moved into his arms, kissing him hard on the mouth. Cameras were flashing all around them, Press and public alike, but they seemed oblivious to them.

As their limo drove away from Heathrow, Brad asked, 'How was the flight?'

'Long,' she replied, 'all 5,634 miles of it.'

'You actually counted them,' Brad said, laughing.

'That tell you anything?' she said, giving him that look. They embraced until they reached the Dorchester Hotel.

One week later Brad, Amanda and Nora Conroy stepped off their flight at Shannon Airport. Brad had insisted that his mother flew over to London four days earlier to shop at Harrods. Amanda, who had taken her to all the best shops and stores, told Brad that at Harrods Nora had asked one of the assistants the price of a pair of earrings to which she had taken a fancy. Nora had almost fainted when the assistant told her the price. Brad laughed so loudly that Amanda had to give him a glass of water, his throat had become so dry. Placing the glass on the table he asked, 'How much were they, anyway?'

'Five thousand quid, as you say over here,' she replied.

'I can guarantee you one thing,' he said, still smiling, 'she didn't buy them.'

'That's right, darling, but I did. I'll surprise her Christmas morning.'

Still laughing, Brad said, 'If she had her way, I'd still be eating breast bones.'

'Breast bones?' Amanda asked.

Waving his hand, 'I'll explain later' he told her.

The night before Christmas Eve, the driver climbed out of the limo, walked up the pathway and knocked on the door. Mr Brown answered and invited the driver to come in. Paddy Brown was fidgeting with his bow tie.

'Let me do that for you, or we'll be here all night,' Dora said. 'There. Now put your jacket on.' She handed the chauffeur a large whisky.

'I shouldn't, Mam,' he said.

'For God's sake,' she said, 'it's Christmas.' He thanked her and downed it in two gulps.

Angela stood before her mother. 'How do I look?'

'Beautiful, my love. Susan,' she shouted up the stairs, 'the driver's waiting.'

As the limo pulled away, 'Will you look at that?' Mr Brown said.

What?' his wife asked.

'Who'd believe it? A car with a TV and a bar.'

'Where have you been, Daddy?' Susan asked.

Pointing towards the sky, Dora Brown said, 'Armstrong must have left him up there.' The driver joined in the laughter.

As they walked through the hotel lobby, the driver went straight over to the Reception desk. The hotel manager seemed to appear from nowhere.

'Good evening,' he said, bowing. 'Mr Conroy's party? This way, please.'

They followed him as he led them to the Residents' Only Bar. Brad, Amanda, Brad's parents, his three brothers and their wives were gathered round a huge open log fire. Brad walked over and welcomed them as they approached. Mr Conroy and his three sons stood up. Young Angela was very impressed and felt very important. Brad introduced everybody to each of the Brown family. He himself was meeting Paddy Brown for the first time.

'Come,' Amanda said, indicating to Angela, 'sit by me.'

'Thank you,' Angela said in a whisper.

'What age are you, dear?' Amanda asked.

'Fourteen.'

'Your frock is beautiful,' Amanda told her.

'Thank you. I've seen your photograph in lots of magazines, but you're more beautiful in real life,' Angela got up the courage to say.

Throwing her arms around her, Amanda said to the group, 'I've just made a friend for life.'

A waiter came over and they each in turn ordered their favourite drink. Brad sat beside Susan.

'How's the radio business?' he asked, putting his arm around her.

'Fine, Brad, just fine.'

'You look absolutely gorgeous.'

'Don't make me blush, please,' she said, the colour already creeping up her face.

'For God's sake,' he said, 'we're old friends. No more of the blushing nonsense. Ah, if only I wasn't already married, Susan.'

'There you go again,' she said. Brad gave her a hug and kissed her on the cheek.

'God, Brad,' she said, 'you're so lucky in life. You have a great voice and millions of adoring fans all over the world.'

'Don't forget the money,' he mocked, 'and the apartments.'

'How many have you, if I'm not too impertinent?'

'Not at all. Let me see.' He scratched under his chin. 'New York, Los Angeles, Nassau, Paris, Athens and a kinda hut in the Seychelles – and, of course, London.'

'Mr Conroy, your table's ready when you are,' the head waiter informed him.

After they had eaten, they returned to the Residents' Bar, where they had more privacy. When they were in the dining room, Susan had noticed every female's eyes were fixed on Brad, who seemed totally unconcerned. An hour later the waiter, beckoned by Brad, came over to take their order once again.

'I think I've had enough,' Paddy Brown told Brad. 'After drink, travelling by car plays havoc with my stomach.'

'But you're not travelling tonight, Paddy,' Brad told him.

With a bemused look, Paddy asked,' And how am I going to get home?' Squeezing his arm Nora said, 'Everybody here is booked in for the night, so enjoy yourself. Drink up, man.'

At midnight Brad winked at Amanda, who asked the barman for the packages she had left with him earlier. She handed each of the Brown family a package, starting with the mother.

'May I open mine?' Angela asked.

'Of course, darling,' Amanda said.

Dora Brown's contained a string of pearls, Paddy Brown's a solid gold watch. Angela's contained a solid gold bracelet and matching earrings. When Susan opened hers, her eyes lit up.

Her package contained a solid gold, diamond-encrusted Rolex wristwatch. When they all thanked Brad, he simply said, 'My pleasure.'

After breakfast next morning, everybody embraced each other, wished each other a Happy Christmas and drove, or were driven, to their own homes.

* * *

The last two months had been hectic for both Brad and Amanda, she modelling in every corner of the globe, Brad working on a new album as well as preparing for his toughest tour ever. Brad and Joe left the recording studio. It was seven p.m.

'Suppose there's no chance of a home-cooked meal?' Brad said to Joe.

'I'm sorry, Brad. Rose and I have something planned for this evening.'

Disappointment showed on Brad's face. 'Another time,' Joe told him.

As Brad drove out of the car park he thought, 'He never mentioned having anything planned for this evening.' It wasn't like Joe. He'd always mentioned such things before. As he drove he was thinking to himself, it's probably my fault. I haven't been exactly Gandhi these last weeks. The Porsche eased to a halt outside the Dorchester. Tossing the porter the keys, 'Park it for me, please' he asked. As soon as the elevator doors closed he thought, 'I'm whacked. Probably would have fallen asleep if I'd eaten at Joe's anyway.

Brad didn't bother to switch on the lights in the lounge as he made his way straight to the shower. After fifteen minutes in the shower, Brad towelled himself dry. He walked towards the bed in darkness. He lay on his left side as usual, his eyes were laden with sleep. In less than five minutes he was in a slumber.

A hand began gently caressing his chest. Brad seemed unaware. Slowly the hand travelled down his stomach. As it went inside his underpants, Brad tossed the duvet across the bed, leaping from it at the same time. He fumbled with the table lamp on the bedside locker. Finding the button, he switched it on. 'Amanda!' There was total surprise on his face.

'Were you expecting someone else?'

'No, but you weren't due till tomorrow.'

'That's what I led you to believe. That's why I phoned Joe this morning, telling him to make sure that you wouldn't be anywhere else except at your hotel.'

'Figures,' he said, smiling.

'I don't understand.'

'Tell you tomorrow,' he said. Brad stood transfixed. 'Darling, darling.' He couldn't take his eyes from her half naked bronzed body.

With outstretched arms she said, 'Come to Mammy.'

They lay in each other's arms next morning. 'Darling,' she said, running her fingers through his magnificent shock of blond hair, 'I have something to tell you, which I hope won't upset you.' A look of terror masked his face. She was fidgeting with his hairline.

'For God's sake, Amanda, spit it out!'

For the first time in their marriage she witnessed ice in his voice. Her mind shot a glance back to the night she had helped him to his hotel after he had fought the cowboy. Inwardly smiling, she thought to herself he sure took his time that night before he revealed his true identity.

'Well? Are you going to tell me or do I have to wait until the morning papers arrive?'

She remained silent. Brad went into the bathroom. Amanda's head was shaking with laughter. He thinks there's another man. Brad came out of the bathroom with a towel around his waist. He tore it off in a temper and threw it blindly at the ceiling.

'Is it someone I know?' he asked, his eyes fixed on the floor.

'Well ... yes.'

Without taking his eyes from the floor he asked, 'Where did you meet him?'

'America,' she said.

'Well, that narrows it down,' he barked. 'Is he an actor?'

'No.'

'Producer?'

'No.'

'Director?'

'No.'

He looked up at her. 'Some billionaire.'

'Well, he's got quite a fortune, but he hasn't reached that status yet.'

'Yet!' he yelled. He walked back into the bathroom. It was ten minutes before he emerged. He pressed a towel to his face.

'Why, grizzly! I do declare you're crying.' Patting the bed, she said, 'Come over here, you slob.'

He sat on the side of the bed She knelt behind him and massaged his shoulders.

'What I had to tell you is – I'm not a model any more. I quit yesterday.'

'Turning towards her, he said, 'Amanda, darling, can you forgive me?'

'It's I who need forgiveness for making you think what you thought.' She lay back on the bed.

Kneeling over her, Brad said, 'You probably heard it in the movies a thousand times, my love, but if you left me, I'd die.' He lowered his lips to hers.

CHAPTER NINE

'How are things in the old country?' Brad asked into the phone.

'Dull and damp as usual,' Joe Quinn answered.

'How are your parents?'

'Fine Brad, they're both in great health. I called to see your parents yesterday.'

'Everything all right with them?' Brad enquired.

'Couldn't be better. They both have their fingers crossed for you for Sunday night. Your mother has never said so many rosaries.'

Brad laughed hard into the phone.

'I can well imagine the old fella sitting by the fire, the mother sitting across from him praying. Are you and the family enjoying your well-deserved holiday?'

'Yes, Brad. Most of the time we visit relations – you know the drill.'

'Don't remind me,' Brad replied with a laugh.

'How are you physically and mentally?'

'Couldn't be better. Having Amanda round all the time is just magic, you know what I mean.'

'Of course. You sure love that woman.'

'You said a mouthful there, my friend.'

'I'd better let you get back to whatever you were doing.'

'You flying to L.A. Sunday week?' Brad asked.

'Yes. I want to make sure there are no hiccups before the tour begins on Tuesday.'

'You're a worrier. See you Sunday week.' Brad hung up.

'How's Joe?' Amanda called from the bedroom. Brad walked in. Amanda was sitting before her dressing table, applying the last of her makeup.

'Everything's fine, darling, just fine.' He bent down and began kissing the back of her neck. His hands travelled slowly down her naked arms, around her waist. Then he encircled her breasts. She turned to face him, kissing him lightly on the lips.

'One more minute of that and I'll have to do my makeup all over again,' she purred in his ear. Just then the phone rang. She picked up the extension on her dresser.

'Hello, Mrs Conroy speaking.'

'The limousine is ready when you are, Ma'am.'

'Thanks, I'll be right there. There,' she said smiling, 'saved by the bell.'

'No one cares,' he said.

'Poor baby.' She cupped his face in her hands. 'You know I have to buy something special for the Academy Awards. You don't want people to think I married a pauper. I do so much want to make you proud, darling.'

'You did that last May fifth.'

'You always say the right words. I'll only be a few hours, darling.' She kissed him and left. May the fifth was the day they had married.

Brad switched on the TV and stretched out on the couch. He glanced at his watch. A couple of minutes to go. He picked up the remote control and pressed the button. The forty-six inch screen came to life. There was a Clint Eastwood, a *Dirty Harry* film about to start, one which Brad had not seen before. He filled a large glass with ice from the fridge, took a large bottle of mineral water, and filled the glass to the brim. As he lay back on the couch, the film's credits came up on the screen.

67

After the film ended the TV announcer said, 'We'll be back with the news right after these commercials.' The anchor man had been reading the news for about five minutes, mostly about the conflict in Nicaragua.

'It is with great sadness, ladies and gentlemen, that I have to report to you the death of one of America's heroes of World War Two. Louis 'Lucky' Brady was set on by three youths after leaving a bar in downtown L.A. last night. Here now with a report from the scene is Curtis Ford.

'Thanks, John. Louis Brady came out of this bar behind me last night at around ten-thirty. I was informed by the bar owner that Louis and some dozen army buddies have met at this bar on the same day once a year since 1946. That group had thinned through the years to just four. Louis' three pals left the bar around ten. He had gone only half a block when the three muggers sprang their attack. They demanded money from him at knife point. An elderly lady looking out of her window across the street said that Louis punched the guy with the knife, knocking him to the ground. She said the other two then began punching and kicking him. She said that Louis fought back well for a man of his age. The two youths had Louis pinned against a wall, punching him. The third youth gathered himself from the ground. Pulling one of the youths out of his way, he proceeded to plunge the knife into Louis' chest. Louis crumbled to the ground. The elderly lady dialled 919. An ambulance pulled up minutes behind a police car. Louis was placed in the ambulance, but was pronounced dead on admission to hospital. When the doctor went through Louis' pockets for identification, the only money he had on him was four dollars, thirty-five cents.'

'Thank you for your report, Curtis. Louis "Lucky" Brady,' the anchor man continued, 'joined the Marines the day Pearl Harbor was attacked. He earned his first silver star in the Philippines while his unit was retreating from overwhelming odds. Louis and three other marines volunteered to make a stand so as to give their buddies time to escape. The unit escaped, but three of the volunteers were cut to pieces. Louis made back to his unit unscathed, thus the nickname "Lucky". Louis volunteered once again to join a special unit who were trained to use explosives. Their mission was the fuel dumps at Tobruk, practically under Rommel's nose. The unit succeeded in blowing the fuel dump sky high. Three quarters of the unit were killed or captured, but once again Louis was lucky. For this action, General Montgomery awarded Louis the Distinguished Service Cross.

'Louis earned his second silver star on the beaches of Iwo Jima. Louis had gone in at night one week before the main task force and discovered several of the Japanese heavy gun positions before the marines stormed the beaches. Louis gave the gun co-ordinates to the battleships lying off shore, thus saving many lives.

'Louis' finest hour came when his unit were with the flotilla which was sailing towards the French coast – his unit's destination Omaha Beach. Half his unit were cut down before they made it to the beach. The other half had made it as far as the iron anti-tank emplacements, but they were caught between murderous crossfire coming from two pill boxes. Out of sheer frustration, Louis made a dash up the sand dunes. Somehow he made it. The two bags of grenades he had brought with him he tossed through the mouth of each of the pill boxes. In less than a minute they lay silent. As Louis lay wiping the sweat from his face, one of his unit said, "Louis, you're hit." Without knowing it, Louis had taken a piece of grenade shrapnel in the right shoulder and a bullet in the left thigh.

'This picture shows Louis Brady in the Rose Garden of the White House, being presented with the Congressional Medal of Honor by General Dwight D. Eisenhower. The President himself insisted on placing the blue and white ribbon around Louis' neck for his bravery at Omaha Beach.'

Brad had watched the black-and-white film of Louis through misty eyes. The anchor man was back on.

'There you have it, ladies and gentlemen. What two powerful armies failed to do three youths found no trouble at all, taking the life of Louis 'Lucky' Brady.'

Brad switched off the set. Blowing his nose, he said, 'Bastards, cowardly bastards, four dollars and thirty-five cents! A shame is what it is.'

How many other veterans are out there, probably broke, hungry and homeless, how many forgotten heroes are in that situation? Brad felt he had to do something to help such brave men, and the place to start was at the Academy Awards. He had made many friends in Hollywood and he felt sure they would be delighted to support such a worthwhile cause.

*   *   *

Brad came out of the shower. He put on his black and gold striped robe.

'I'm home, darling,' Amanda's voice called from the drawing room. 'Walk straight through to the bedroom, guys.'

Brad nodded to half a dozen porters as they passed him on their way to the bedroom, each one laden with boxes and large paper bags. Brad took a roll of bills from a drawer and peeled off several, handing them to one of the porters.

'Split that amongst ye.'

'Thank you very much, Mr Conroy.'

'Same to you,' Brad said. Brad sat on the couch, Amanda came over and sat next to him. 'Looks like you bought Macy's.'

'There was one dress that I fell in love with, but I couldn't make up my mind about which colour, so I bought all six.' Kissing him, she said, 'You, darling, can decide on which colour.'

Brad began kissing her passionately. Amanda stood up, offering him her hand. He took it as she walked him to the bedroom. Brad sat at the foot of the bed. He watched as Amanda began to undress to her slip. She walked over to him. He pressed his face to her stomach, she ran her fingers through his hair. 'Miss me, darling?' she asked.

'Every second you're out of my sight is torture.'

She pushed him back on to the bed. Looking down at him, she said, 'We must be the two luckiest people in the world.'

The white stretch limousine crawled to a halt. Amanda got out first, behind her Brad. A tremendous roar went up from the huge crowd, who had waited for hours hoping to catch a glimpse of their favourite movie stars.

'We love you, Brad! You're the best,' a section of the crowd chanted. Brad, holding Amanda's hand, bowed to the crowd and with his free hand threw them kisses.

'Thank you, thank you,' he called to them.

*　　*　　*

Two hours later Chuck Brack, the newest Hollywood heart-throb, together with the newest bombshell, Linda Begg, walked to the podium.

'Now we come to the category *Best Original Song*.' Amanda squeezed Brad's hand.

Linda said, 'Paul Rex for *Never Again*.'

Chuck said, 'Lief Canerh for *Just For You*.'

Linda said. 'And last but not least, Brad Conroy for *Nobody's Lucky Twice, But Me*.' When the applause subsided, Chuck said, 'And the lucky winner is...' Linda seemed to take forever to open the envelope, and when she did she hesitated for what seemed a lifetime.

'Brad Conroy.'

Thunderous applause, as Brad was a genuinely popular winner. After kissing Amanda he walked to the stage. Linda Begg handed Brad the statuette, then she kissed Brad full on the lips for almost a minute. Brad, embarrassed, had to pull himself away from her.

'Tart,' Amanda muttered under her breath.

Brad stood before the microphone, the statue held high in his left fist. He waited for the applause to die down.

'Tonight, ladies and gentlemen, I'm a hero.' Laughter from the audience.

He brought his hand down, placing the statue in front of him. 'It took me two hours to write that song, so now I'm a hero, a hero because this Oscar will add five, maybe ten, million dollars at the box office. But what about the real heroes? I'd like to take this opportunity tonight to mention just one. I don't know if any of you were watching the news on Friday night. Three thugs attacked a sixty-eight-year-old man and subsequently ended his life. In his pocket was four dollars, thirty-five cents. In the richest nation on earth, that's a shame – no, it's a *disgrace*. My friends, I'd like to organise a benefit for the other forgotten heroes, not just for the allied soldiers but for the soldiers of all the nations. I'll be amongst you later if any of you would like to contribute in any way at all. I'd be ever so grateful. I thank you all for the award and for being patient with me. Goodnight, God bless you all.'

The entire auditorium rose to their feet and stayed that way, applauding for fifteen minutes. Brad Conroy had struck a chord. Amanda Conroy was the proudest woman in the world at that moment.

At the reception after the ceremony ended, it seemed that everyone wanted to speak to and shake hands with Brad. Brad was flabbergasted with the response to his appeal. Every actor, actress, director, producer or studio head, all wanted to be part of Brad's benefit.

Amanda got separated towards the end of the reception. She was surrounded by several top actors including Chuck Brack, who whispered that he had wanted to make love to her since he first caught a glimpse of her on a catwalk presentation some three years previously. Politely but firmly she told him, 'I'm strictly a one man woman.'

'What a waste,' he replied.

'Not if you knew my man,' she said, with a huge smile on her face. He got the message. As she continued to chat to the other actors she caught a glimpse of Linda Begg approaching Brad. Amanda's eyes were transfixed on Linda. Linda was chatting and beaming into Brad's face. She's obviously begging him for it, Amanda thought to herself. Linda laid her hand on Brad's chest. Brad looked uncomfortable. Linda's hand slid slowly down to Brad's genitals.

Rage rose up inside Amanda. 'Excuse me,' she said to the actors, who watched her storm away. She caught Linda's left shoulder, ripping her dress as she spun her around. Before Brad could react, Amanda sent her tightly clenched fist into Linda's face, sending her crashing into a table which seated six of the biggest studio heads and their wives. Bottles and glasses were strewn everywhere. The Press were having a field day. As Linda was helped up from the table, her nose was bloody and her left breast was in full view.

'Next time you lay a hand on my man, I'll pull your head off and stick it up your ass. You receiving me loud and clear, tramp?'

Linda wiped her bloodied nose with the back of her hand and stormed out of the room, with Chuck Brack hot on her tail. Amanda got as much applause as Brad had after his speech. The studio bosses' wives congratulated Amanda.

'That's been coming to Miss Big Tits for a long time,' they told her. Chris Brown, a long-time friend since her catwalk days with Amanda, said,

'She's laid everything in Hollywood except a paving stone.' The two burst out laughing.

'Phew, am I glad I was not on the receiving end of that,' Brad said to Amanda as the limousine pulled away.

'God, she made me so angry! The thought of bringing myself down to her level ... and the Press, there were cameras flashing all over the place. That bitch, kissing you like that on stage before a billion viewers world-wide. People like her have no conscience, and as every-one knows those kind of people are extremely danger-ous.' Brad put his arm around her.

'Well, honey, you told the world one thing tonight.

'What's that?'

'That you love me.' He kissed her and whispered, 'Can't wait to get home.'

'Me too,' she told him.

'Mornin', hon', Brad said as he came out of the bedroom, yawning and scratching his head. Amanda was half way through breakfast.

'Morning, darling. Don't bother to read the newspapers.

'Why?' he said, smiling.

'I made a complete ass of myself, that's why.

He picked up the *Los Angeles Tribune*. On the front page in full colour was a photo of Linda being helped from the table, with a bloodied nose and her huge left breast exposed for the whole world to admire. Brad read out loud, 'It seems Linda Begg made a play for Rock Superstar Brad Conroy after the Awards Cere-mony last night, but Brad's wife, ex-model Amanda Gordon, wasn't having any of it. She punched Linda square on the schnozzle, causing it to bleed. Linda's dress was torn in the fracas. You could say it was tit for tat.'

'That's enough,' Amanda said. 'I'm glad you find it so funny.'

Tears were streaming down Brad's face. He picked up another paper. 'Linda begged for it and Amanda obliged.' Brad was holding his side, laughing. He sat down and swallowed his glass of orange juice.

'Anything planned for today, hon?'

'You're joking! After last night I'd be afraid to step outside of the hotel.'

'Well, that's going to be very awkward.'

'Whatever do you mean?' she enquired.

'How are we going to get to the airport without leaving the hotel?'

'Would you mind explaining, or did I miss something?'

Brad reached into his jacket pocket at the back of his chair. He placed an envelope at the side of Amanda's coffee cup.

'What's this?'

'Why don't you open it and find out?'

'*Acapulco!*' she yelled.

'Yes, my love. I'm going to be on tour during our anniversary, so I'm trying to make up for the inconvenience.'

'You're so thoughtful.' She came round and sat on his lap. 'You're the most considerate,' she said, running her fingers through his hair.

'Well, to be honest, I was really thinking of me a lot.'

She kissed him. Six days and, more important, six nights.

'What time does our flight leave?'

'Midday.'

She checked her watch. Ten after nine. 'There's time,' she said, walking into the bedroom.

'Time for what?' he said innocently.

She turned, facing him. She undid the knot in her robe, letting it slide to the floor. 'Get the picture?'

CHAPTER TEN

The head porter walked Brad and Amanda to the elevator. He inserted a key into the gold-plated keyhole of the Presidential Suite. Handing the key to Brad, 'Nobody else can gain access to your suite, senor,' he told him.

Brad nodded, and tipped him.

'Brad, I've been in some exquisite suites worldwide, but this,' she said, spinning around, 'takes my breath away.' The dining area had a table which seated twelve. The rich brown leather-backed chairs were gold studded. The lounge measured eighty feet square, the white settee with matching armchairs measured twenty five feet long, the TV screen was twenty feet long and ten feet high. The paintings which adorned the walls were balanced between still life and the latest modern art. As Amanda walked through the teak French doors towards her balcony, 'Brad,' she yelled. He rushed to her, more out of concern than curiosity.

'Look! Our own swimming pool, Jacuzzi and sauna.' She was as excited as a child opening her presents at Christmas. She walked out onto the balcony. 'Brad, come look at this view.' He came up behind her, placing his arms round her waist. 'Isn't that beautiful?' she said, staring out at the ocean.

Kissing the nape of her neck, he said, 'That's the good old South Pacific.'

'I touch your hands and my arms grow strong
Like a pair of bird's that burst with song'...

He hummed the next couple of lines because he couldn't remember the words, then continued

'Younger than springtime are you,
Softer than starlight are you.'

She turned round. 'You are an old romantic at heart, and I love you for it.'

'Let's try the Jacuzzi, then explore Acapulco.'

They were strolling hand in hand, like any other couple on vacation, both wearing jeans and short-sleeved shirts.

'God, I've never known a week to fly so fast.'

He squeezed her hand. 'As they say, hon, when you're enjoying yourself...'

It was Saturday evening, their last night in Acapulco. Their flight was leaving at eight next morning. That week they had water skied and wind surfed. Brad had hired a high-speed motor boat, but Amanda wouldn't allow him to do more than fifty miles an hour. They jet skied, and Brad had tried parachute flying, towed by a speed boat. He loved it.

Brad had also hired a boat to try deep sea fishing. They had been out for almost four hours, neither of them getting as much as a nibble on their baits. As they made back to shore, Amanda's line seemed to go berserk. Brad unstrapped himself from his chair and came behind her.

'Start reeling in, darling,' he said excitedly.

'God, it's a terrible strain,' she shouted.

The boat owner was more excited than both of them. 'Give him more slack, Senora, more slack.' Amanda obeyed.

A minute later, 'Pull hard,' the boat owner advised. Brad helped her.

The rod was almost vertical. About a hundred yards to their right, a huge marlin leapt six feet out of the water.

'Senor, he is a big one, maybe eight feet long, yes?'
'If he's an inch, Pedro,' Brad agreed.

The fish fought valiantly for forty minutes. Amanda had reeled him to within ten feet of the craft. Removing her knife from its scabbard, she cut the line. The marlin disappeared.

'Mama mia, Mama mia. Why you do that, pretty lady?' Pedro asked.

'Because if I had killed it, I would have lost,' she said.

Removing his white cap, Pedro scratched his thick black hair. 'Mama mia, women I never understand.'

What Amanda really fell in love with was pony trekking. They had driven south late in the afternoon, just cruising, taking in the countryside. Amanda spotted the sign 'Pony Trekking Ranch two miles ahead.' They had been riding for two hours with not another human being in sight.

'Let's make for that cluster of trees,' Brad suggested. They sat under the trees. Her head was resting on his chest.

'Penny for them,' Amanda said.

Brad removed his stetson. 'Don't this remind you of something?'

She decided to tease him. 'No, darling, can't say that it does.'

He looked dejected. He fanned his face with the stetson.

'Why do you think I suggested we came pony trekking?' she said, smiling.

He held her in his arms. 'The two nights I spent up on that mountain, I wanted so much to make love to you,' he told her.

'I brought you out here to the wilderness so I could make it up to you,' she beamed.

'You mean...?'

'Yes,' she interrupted, 'right here. I don't think the birds or the bees have any objections,' she giggled.

After making love twice, they headed back to the ranch house.

They had strolled off the main thoroughfare and were in a section of the city where each building looked at least a hundred years old.

'Look,' Amanda said, pointing to the exterior of a small restaurant, 'it looks exactly like one of those Western movies.'

Smiling, Brad said, 'I must agree with you.'

'Let's have something to eat in there,' she suggested.

'Honey, it wasn't exactly what I had planned,' he told her.

Grabbing his hand, she pulled him through the doors. Instantly Brad was taken with the place. Its immediate impression gave him the feeling he was home from home. There were only four couples seated, eating and chatting, taking no notice as Brad and Amanda walked in.

A fat man aged about sixty, wearing a white apron, came to their table.

'Welcome, senor, senora,' he said, bowing slightly. Handing each a menu, 'Something to drink, yes?' Amanda looked at Brad.

'Pineapple juice,' he nodded.

'Two pineapple juice please, lots of ice.'

'Si, senora.' He disappeared behind the counter. They had decided on plain salads. A beautiful young girl brought their salads to the table.

'Would the senora, senor, wish for anything else?'

'No thank you,' they told her.

Brad and Amanda were half way through their meal when the sound of a mandolin made them put down their knives and forks. A Mexican in his mid-thirties sat on a high stool on a tiny bandstand. The sound from the strings of his mandolin was enchanting.

'Everything all right?' a fat lady asked Brad and Amanda.

'Perfect,' Amanda said.

'But you not finish you food.'

'Oh, we were enjoying the young man.' She nodded at the musician.

'Oh, Chico, he my son. You met husband, he took order. My daughter Maria, she serve you, that all my family.'

'You have a lovely family Mrs...'

'Gonzales.'

'Mrs Gonzales.' Amanda told her, 'Amanda and Brad Conroy.'

Mrs Gonzales wiped her hands on her apron and shook hands with both of them.

'You call me you need anything.'

'Thank you, Mrs Gonzales.'

They continued with their meal.

'He's very good,' Amanda said.

'Very good? He's excellent,' Brad replied, 'a natural.'

They had been listening to the young man for half an hour. 'Do you notice something, dear?'

'Yes, love, I do, Brad said, without taking his eyes from the musician.

'So now you're able to read my mind?' Amanda said angrily.

Brad was smiling as he turned and faced her. Holding her hand, he said,

'Darling, what you noticed is every tune the young man's playing is an Elvis number.' He squeezed her hand. 'I am in the business, or had you forgotten, my good woman?' he said in a suave English accent.

'Sorry,' she said. Amanda ordered two more pineapple juices. Mrs Gonzales brought them to her.

'Mrs Gonzales, why doesn't Chico sing to his music?'

'Oh, he English terrible. He useless to learn.'

'He seems to be a big fan of Elvis Presley.'

'He Elvis on the brain,' she said, pointing to her forehead.

'B-R-A-D,' Amanda said, in her asking voice.

Looking at her, 'Of course I will, darling.'

'But I haven't asked you anything yet.'

'I know, sweetheart, but I know you so well. You'd like me to sing a few numbers. You reckon that young Chico wouldn't mind.'

'He'd love it, dear.'

Brad stood up. 'I can refuse you nothing. By the way, I've been horsin' this around with me since we left L.A.' He placed a small package on the table in front of her.

Chico had stopped for a break. Brad stuck out his hand. 'Hi, Chico. I'm Brad.'

'Hi, Brad.' Chico said.

'You mind you play, I sing? I love Elvis too.'

Chico beamed. 'Si, si Senor Brad.'

'You play any tune you like, I try sing.' The first tune Chico chose was *It's Now or Never*.

Amanda removed the pink ribbon from the package. Inside the green satin box was a diamond and emerald bracelet. Beside it lay a matching ring. Brad was enjoying himself immensely on the tiny stage. The restaurant was beginning to fill. Mr and Mrs Gonzales and their daughter watched Brad in amazement. He was doing a great impersonation of Elvis. The customers didn't seem to mind the fact that they weren't being served with the normal efficiency of the Gonzales household. An hour later Brad was still on stage. Amanda watched him with glowing admiration.

'That's what he was born to do,' she told herself, 'entertain people.'

By eleven o'clock the restaurant was jam-packed. Brad announced he would sing one more song. He told Chico the song's title. As Brad sang the song he walked through the crowd and towards Amanda's table, Chico in tow behind him. He sat before her, taking her hand in his. The song was *Can't Help Falling In Love With You*.

Brad stuck a bunch of dollar bills into the top pocket of Chico's jacket. 'For the food and the drinks, and especially the music,' he shouted into Chico's ear.

Chico shook hands with them both. 'Vaya con Dios' he bade them both.

At eight o'clock next morning their flight taxied down the runway.

'I feel awful not having bought you something for our anniversary, even if it is five weeks away.'

'Don't be silly,' he told her. 'Come to think of it, you gave me the most satisfying anniversary gift last evening.'

'I'm lost.'

'Well, when you asked me to join Chico on stage. To be up there as an ordinary Joe Soap, singing those old Elvis numbers, I got the greatest pleasure.'

Amanda squeezed his arm. Looking at her, he laughed out loud and said, 'Well, the second greatest.'

'Don't get your priorities mixed up again,' she told him.

*   *   *

Brad had been trying to calm the massive crowd for ten minutes. It took another five minutes before they gave him the silence he asked for.

'Ladies and gentlemen,' he began 'you may have seen the news a couple of weeks ago concerning the attack and slaying of one of America's finest heroes. I refer, of course, to Louis "Lucky" Brady.' Now Brad had their undivided attention and you could hear a pin drop.

'Three brave hoodlums attacked a sixty-eight-year-old man after he left a bar, after meeting a few other brave veterans of World War Two. Even at sixty-eight he didn't go down without a fight, God bless his soul. I've got a message for such thugs and hoodlums, Brad screamed into the mike. 'Your Country Don't Need You.' He repeated this several times. The crowd joined in. When the crowd became quiet again, he said, 'Friends of mine in both the music world and Hollywood are pleased to organise a benefit, with the entire proceeds going to the Red Cross, who will distribute the proceeds to Veterans In Need on all sides of the World War Two conflict.' Brad received tremendous applause.

'I have written a song I'd like to share with you. I wrote mostly because of what happened to Louis Brady. If an odd line from a Clint Eastwood movie pops up now and then, I beg your forgiveness. By the way, we will be recording this number, and everybody concerned with the making of the record will gladly forfeit all their royalties. They will be given to the Red Cross.' The bass guitar and the saxophone were the only instruments required for the sad tune.

MAKE MY DAY
Here you stand in a corner
Shakin' like a leaf
A force to be reckoned with
The main man on your street

But if they could see you now
Sweatin', feet like clay
To a cowardly punk like you I say
Go ahead, make my day

Chorus

Brave men each of you are
Prowling around in the dark
Take away your knives and guns
And you'd be crying for yer mas

Punks like you are vermin
Crawlin' from cracks in the wall
Preyin' on the old and the vulnerable
Who give no resistance at all

But sooner or later you stumble
Into the park where I play
That's what makes my job worthwhile
So go ahead, punk, make my day

Chorus repeated

When Brad finished the song, the crowd went wild. Backstage he said to Joe Quinn, 'Think they agreed with it at least.'

'Anything concerning law and order can't fail,' Joe predicted.

That was Brad's first of three concerts to be given in Los Angeles and the beginning of a gruelling tour that would take him to forty States.

Amanda stood in the VIP Lounge of the San Francisco International Airport. She watched as Brad and his band's chartered flight eased from the ground and rose like an eagle effortlessly into the clouded sky. Taking a hankie from her sleeve she wiped her eyes. The chauffeur, spotting her as she came through the terminal doors, was out of the car and holding the door open as she approached. As she got in, he closed the door. Turning from his seat he asked, 'Anywhere special, Mrs Conroy?' He could see she was in deep thought.

After a minute she replied, 'Sorry, Peter, back to the apartment please.'

Secretly she was saying, 'Wish you would drive to Oregon so I could be with Brad.'

Brad had convinced her that she should not join him on tour. Tour life, he told her, was too hectic. One night here, two nights there. Dashing from hotel to airport, airport to hotel to venue. He had seen many marriages break up due to short fuses, fatigue, illness, rigging problems, unions, security. The problems were endless, he told her. That's not for us, no way.

Amanda had spent the last hour sitting without saying a word, like a teenager not being allowed to go to the prom. Brad tried with all his charm and patience to justify his reasons, telling her that he never wanted them to quarrel, at least during his touring. Amanda just sat staring mindlessly at the television set. Finally he stood up, as if out of patience, and blocked her view of the movie.

'Honey, are we having our first fight?' She remained silent. Brad stayed standing, blocking her view. After five minutes she averted her eyes to a painting on the wall. Ten minutes later neither of them had spoken a word. Amanda stood up in a temper, and threw the cushion she had been clasping to her stomach hard against the wall. She brushed past him angrily and walked into the bedroom, slamming the door behind her.

Brad had been packing for almost an hour. He clicked his fingers while he searched around until he found what he was looking for. Finding it, he scribbled down the number. Brad went through the guest bedroom and into the bathroom. He sat on the third marbled step leading into the bath and dialled. That was Sunday night. Brad's tour was beginning on Tuesday.

The telephone had rung just once. Brad had been awake for the last five minutes. The voice said, 'Eight a.m., Mr Conroy.'

'Thank you,' Gently he placed it back on its cradle. When he had joined Amanda in bed later that night, she was asleep. He had a recording session at ten next morning. Mecca had decided he should record *Make My Day* as a single before he began his tour. By the time he left California it would be in the shops, they told him. Sliding quietly from the bed, he tiptoed to the bathroom. Amanda smiled as she watched his naked buttocks disappear into the shower.

CHAPTER ELEVEN

Two hours later, Amanda sat on her bed drying her hair. The doorbell rang. She switched off the hairdryer and went to answer it.

'Your breakfast, Miss Gordon.'

'Thank you; just there will be fine.'

As he closed the door she held a hand to her mouth as she laughed. The waiter was about her own age and must have been an admirer of hers.

'Miss Gordon,' he said out loud. Half a minute into the room she sensed he had removed the large towel which clung to her body. 'Men!' she said, shaking her head.

She was only half way through her cereal when her mobile phone rang.

'Hello, how are you, cowboy?' Amanda's face broke into a huge grin.

'Cindy! Oh, it's so good to hear your voice.' She had met Cindy Clune during a catwalk session six years previously and they had become instant friends. After Amanda had relayed how she and Brad had met, any time they met or Cindy phoned the first words out of Cindy's mouth were, 'How are you, cowboy?' At their wedding, Cindy had been Amanda's bridesmaid.

'I'm fine, Cindy, just fine.'

'How's that hunk o' yours?'

'As the Irish say, there's fear of the men. He starts his tour after his concert tonight here in Los Angeles.'

'You don't sound very happy, hon. Anything the matter?'

Amanda explained everything to Cindy, telling her she thought Brad was doing everything in his power not to have her with him on the tour.

'Listen, cowboy, nobody knows me more than you.'

'Right, right, OK.'

'Well, you know I'm no angel, right?'

'Right.'

'You don't have to agree with every word that comes out of my mouth,' Cindy barked down the phone. They both laughed.

'As you know, in my younger years I toured with several top rock groups. Well,' she added, 'as a groupie, you might say, I witnessed close up what can and does happen when wives accompany their husbands. Total chaos. Guaranteed, within three weeks they're ready to shred each other to pieces. The pressure's too much.'

Cindy, without having to think, reeled off a dozen names. 'All of them ended up where?' Answering her own question, 'In the divorce court, all within months after their wives had accompanied them on tour.'

'But, Cindy,' Amanda began.

Cindy interrupted her. 'Amanda, darling, I know what you're thinking. I've known Brad what, eighteen, nineteen months? And I can honestly tell you he's got two rare qualities, for a man that is. His devotion to you and he will never be unfaithful to you.'

'How can you be so sure?' Amanda asked, 'You an expert, or what?'

Cindy sensed the ice in Amanda's voice. 'Forgive me, darling, for sounding like the Almighty, but if I know anything I know the love he has for you. I've watched you both at parties, in restaurants. I've been with you out on the town. He hardly leaves your side. I may be neurotic, but a blind man can sense the love he's got for you. Like the song says, sometimes you can be standing up too close. Darling, it must be torture for him not to have you with him on the tour. Believe you me, darling, you've got something very special. Never let it go.'

Cindy waited for Amanda to reply, knowing full well that she had caused her best friend to cry, but for the best reason in the world – love.

When Amanda came back on the phone her voice was more relaxed. 'If I can't listen and take the advice of my best friend, who is there to believe? Forgive me, Cindy, I haven't even asked you where you're ringing from.'

'Fort Worth, Texas. Fashion show here all this week, then next week on to Cincinnati, then a week in Cleveland, on then for a week in Washington.'

'What happens after Washington?' Amanda enquired.

'New York for a month. Fashion show for a week, photo session for a week, fashion show again for a week, then another photo session the last week of May.'

'Cindy, may I make a suggestion?'

Cindy was already smiling. Amanda's voice for the first time sounded cheerful.

'Of course, darling.'

Amanda continued, 'I've had a thought. I could visit with my parents for the coming month, then we could meet at some restaurant. It goes without saying you'd stay at our apartment for the duration of your stay in New York.'

'Best offer I've had in almost a year,' Cindy replied. They chatted for another hour.

*   *   *

At one o'clock Amanda walked through the doors of Romero's Restaurant on Fifth Avenue. Romero seemed to appear out of nowhere.

'Good afternoon, Mrs Conroy.'

'Good afternoon, Romero.'

'May I say how beautiful you look,' Romero said, touching his designer beard.

'Thank you, you old charmer,' she replied, smiling.

'Your table is right over here, if you'll follow me.'

Amanda wore a grey two-piece suit. The jacket was double breasted, the skirt a couple of inches above the knee. Under the jacket her blouse was a pale blue. Her chestnut brown hair was combed back quiff style, tied with a blue silk scarf. The restaurant was almost full. Male and female eyes watched her as she followed Romero to her booth.

'Would Madam like a drink while she's waiting?' Romero asked.

'A tall glass of iced spring water, please, Romero.' Snapping his fingers, he passed the order to a waiter, dismissing himself gracefully. Amanda sipped the water. She had the distinct feeling she was being watched. She picked up the menu, pretending to read it. She glanced round the room from her vantage point. Her eyes settled on Chuck Brack. He smiled and bowed slightly. Amanda pretended not to have noticed him in the least.

Amanda glanced at her watch. One-twenty. God, what's keeping Cindy? Amanda had made the reservations the previous week. Romero's, Fifth Avenue, one o'clock, Saturday the first of May. Amanda caught a glimpse of Chuck Brack rising from his seat. 'Oh, no,' she said to herself as she watched him make straight for her booth.

'It *is* you,' he said. Amanda closed the menu and looked up.

'Amanda, how are you? You look absolutely gorgeous, if you don't mind my saying.'

'Thank you, Chuck, nice to see you. How are things with you?' She didn't ask him to sit down.

'May I?' he asked.

'Please do.'

He sat opposite her. 'Oh, I can't complain,' he said. 'That's my lawyer's private secretary I'm having lunch with. She's up from L.A. with some papers for me to sign. It concerns a four week mini-series I'm doing here in New York.'

As Chuck spoke, Amanda was looking at the woman

Chuck was having lunch with. She was about thirty-eight, looked very business-like, black framed glasses, her silk black hair tied back in a bun. Amanda studied the face, no makeup except for lipstick. She had fine bone structure, and a figure any model would die for, but Amanda sensed there was a terrible sadness behind that business-like face. Amanda's thoughts were interrupted as she saw the secretary almost stand to attention as she was joined by another woman. They shook hands. The secretary nodded in the direction of Amanda's table. The other woman turned round. Her pleasant face turned to stone as soon as she set eyes on Amanda. Chuck, who had hardly stopped talking, didn't realise she had arrived.

'Chuck.' He kept talking. 'Chuck, please.'

'I'm sorry, Amanda, I talk too much.'

Amanda leaned forward. 'I think your presence is required at your table.'

Without looking round he said, 'No problem, Frances. That's her name, by the way, Frances Kelly. She's used to my leaving her to talk to friends.'

'Were you expecting someone else to join you?' Amanda asked calmly.

Turning round, he quickly got to his feet. 'Guess there's no point in asking you to join us?'

'I don't think so.'

Offering his hand, he said, 'It was lovely seeing you again.'

'And you,' she replied.

Chuck was seated at his table for only thirty seconds when Linda Begg stood up and stormed out of the restaurant, Chuck hot on her tail.

Amanda watched as Frances Kelly paid the bill, her face strewn with embarrassment. Picking up her briefcase as she stood up, her eyes met Amanda's. She nodded politely. Amanda acknowledged with a smile. Frances Kelly walked out of the restaurant alone, into the beautiful sunshine. You poor, poor woman, Amanda was thinking. Amanda had realised the reason for the sadness behind that business-like face. Frances Kelly was in love with Chuck Brack.

'Darling, darling, please forgive me,' Cindy said as she came almost running towards Amanda. Amanda stood up. They embraced warmly and kissed each other's cheeks.

'On the way in from the airport there was an accident.'

'No one hurt, I hope,' Amanda asked.

'No, but the two drivers were at each other's throats. They held the traffic up for ever.'

It was one-fifty by the time Cindy joined Amanda.

'You've been sitting here since one,' Cindy tapped the back of Amanda's hand. 'You poor thing.'

'Actually, I was entertained for a while.'

'You were? Now you have aroused my curiosity. Give, let's have the details,' Cindy begged.

'Later, it's not in the least important,' Amanda assured her. 'What would you like to drink?'

'The usual please,' Cindy said.

Handing Cindy the glass, Amanda sat on the couch beside her.

'You still on mineral water?'

Amanda nodded.

'I wish I had your willpower.'

On returning from the restaurant, Cindy and Amanda had relaxed in the Jacuzzi for forty-five minutes. Cindy sighed, 'God, that Jacuzzi really felt good, really helps relax the body.'

'So much flying is so tiring.'

'Would you listen to me,' Cindy said, grabbing Amanda's wrist. 'You're missing him terribly, darling.'

Amanda nodded.

'He's going through the same, darling.' Cindy dried the tears running down Amanda's cheeks. 'It won't last for ever, darling. There's one month gone already, you have me for the next four weeks.' 'Why don't you visit Brad's parents for the month of June?' she suggested. 'I'll be with you across the Atlantic, I'll fly to London on the thirty-first of May.'

'OK, agreed then,' Amanda nodded.

Cindy stood up. 'You're not the only one feeling lonely tonight, madam.'

Slowly, Amanda got to her feet. As they stood eye to eye Cindy nodded, at the same time biting on her lower lip.

Amanda threw her arms around Cindy. 'I'm so happy for you, darling.' Amanda held Cindy's wrists. 'How long?'

'Six months.'

'Six months! Six months you waited to tell your best friend.' They sat back on the couch.

'Well to be truthful, hon, there's nothing concrete.'

'I don't understand,' Amanda said, frowning.

'I met him in Chicago, he's in real estate there. His name's Bob Santos, tall, dark, handsome and he's never been married. We see each other most weekends, sometimes only for a few hours. We fly from different parts of the country to meet each other.'

'So,' Amanda asked, 'what's the problem?'

'Well, nothing's been said. You know, it's purely physical.' Cindy smiled. 'Fabulously physical.'

'It was Amanda's turn to dry Cindy's tears.

'God, Amanda, I love him so much. He's so different from all the other men I've known – gentle, kind, considerate, you know, the holding the door for you type. But he's never told me he loves me.'

'Have you told him how you feel?' Amanda asked.

'Are you kidding? Give him the edge? Come on!' Cindy jeered. 'From my experience, the minute you tell a fella you love him he's out the door like a blue-assed fly.'

'When are you seeing him again?'

'Next weekend, he's flying to New York Friday night.'

'Then I'll have to make myself scarce.'

'What do you mean?'

'Well I'm not going to play gooseberry, am I?' Amanda said, shrugging her shoulders.

'I'm really grateful to you, darling, but this is your home: yours and Brad's. We'll book in to some hotel. Can't be turning a friend out of her own home.'

'There's an awful lot of lovin' gone on in this apartment. Maybe it'll bounce off the walls and hit Bob right on the heart.' Amanda picked up the telephone book. 'Let's see – hotels.'

Cindy protested, but was hushed up immediately.

'Now that's done. I'm booked in at the Royal indefinitely. The rest is up to you.'

'I think you can be a little devious,' Cindy said, smiling.

'Look at the comfort you have: Jacuzzi, bath, shower, a bed that does everything but.' Amanda stretched her arms. 'When I think how I looked when Brad and I first set eyes on each other.'

Cindy offered her open arms to Amanda. As they embraced, Cindy said, 'Didn't I tell you he was someone special?'

'What would you like to do this evening, if you're not too tired?'

Cindy thought for a minute. 'How about a show?'

'That's my girl! Which one would you like to see?'

'How about *Phantom*?'

'No, that's booked out for the next two years.'

'Who said?'

Picking up the phone, Amanda dialled.

'Thank you so much, Andrew. I am ever so grateful, bye, bye.' Turning to Cindy,

'We have our own box. Now, let's prepare. The curtain goes up at eight.'

Cindy sat brushing her hair. 'Wasn't Michael Crawford terrific last night?'

'Can't disagree with you on that.'

She turned on the stool to face Amanda, who was lying on the bed. 'Oh, the filthy rich. I've got to be at rehearsals by ten and you could lie there for years, waited on hand and foot.'

Amanda rolled onto her stomach. 'Brad could have been a plumber or a rubbish collector and it wouldn't have mattered. But,' she said, raising a finger, 'being famous and rich *is* a bonus.'

Cindy smiled as she listened to Amanda laughing into the pillow. 'Listen, lazy bones, why don't you throw on a pair of jeans and accompany me to the hotel – you know, a little moral support?'

'Amanda threw a pillow at her. 'Why didn't I think of that?'

Amanda sat completely relaxed and at ease as she watched the girls go through their paces. After ten minutes she was already missing the hustle and tussle, the pressures and excitement at the top of the modelling world.

When one of the models walked down the catwalk wearing a gold strapless silk gown, its bodice strewn with diamonds, emeralds and pearls, it took her breath away. During the lunch break Amanda never stopped talking about the gown.

'Have you seen the price tag on that particular gown?' Amanda said, 'A girl can dream, can't she?'

Fifteen minutes into the second rehearsal, David Morris walked down the aisle. 'Sorry, children. Sorry I missed the first session.' Calling to his director, 'Shall we begin again please?'

Spotting Amanda's outline, he said as he approached her, 'Didn't know we were going to have an audience.'

Amanda stood up. Turning towards him she said, 'I'm sorry if my presence disturbs you.' Throwing her jacket over her arm, she started for the exit. She had gone several paces past him.

'Amanda, Amanda Gordon.'

She turned to face him. 'Amanda Conroy, actually.'

'Forgive me, forgive me, please. I didn't recognise you. You modelled one of my first designs back in Minneapolis six years ago.'

'That's right Mr Morris.'

'Never mind the Mister stuff.' Taking her by the hand, 'Please, please, let us watch the show together. You are more beautiful than ever, my dear. Marriage becomes you. Oh, and by the way, how is Brad?'

'You're very sweet, David. Brad is fine, he's touring for the next three months. Afraid I won't see him till the end of July, but thank you for asking.'

'We're ready now, Mr Morris,' the director called.

About an hour into the show, Cindy walked onto the stage. Shielding her eyes from the stage lights, she called, 'Amanda, telephone call for you.'

'Excuse me, David.'

'Certainly,' Morris said, standing up to let her through.

'Who is it?' she whispered to Cindy.

'No idea.'

When Amanda came out of the tiny office backstage, Cindy was waiting for her, arms folded, a huge smile on her face.

'You sneak,' Amanda shouted in the loudest whisper. They embraced for a minute. 'I'll return the compliment some time.'

The phone call was from Brad. Amanda had left the hotel's number on her answering machine in case Brad or other family members rang.

Amanda had been sitting chatting and enjoying the show with Morris. More than an hour had passed. The director walked down the catwalk.

'Mr Morris, sorry to interrupt sir. There's a call for you.'

'Yes sir, yes sir, yes sir, I understand completely. It will be attended to exactly as you require. My pleasure sir, you have my undying gratitude. Have a nice day sir, bye-bye sir.'

He hung up. Morris discreetly called his director on

95

one side. After some minutes of consultation, Morris returned to his seat.

'Sorry to leave you alone for so long.'

'You have to attend to your business, David,' Amanda told him.

Thirty minutes later the director walked down from the stage, knelt down and whispered into Morris' ear. Morris' angry outburst took Amanda by total surprise.

'Problems, problems, nothing but problems,' he shouted, not caring who heard him. The director made a hasty exit back to the stage. Morris sat down and wiped the perspiration from his face.

Amanda gave him a few minutes to compose himself, then said, 'Mind if I ask what the problem is, David?'

Morris, his face in his hands, looked at her as if for the first time.

'Oh, Amanda, I'm so sorry for that awful outburst. Will you forgive me?'

'Of course. In this business problems wait in the wings.'

'You're so right,' he said, tapping her hand.

'So?' she said, frowning.

'One of my models had to go home.'

'Go home? I don't understand.'

Morris looked awkward. 'Women's problems,' he whispered into her ear.

'So, you've got plenty of others,' Amanda offered.

'Yes, but not exactly five feet ten and a half inches tall. You see, Amanda, I have this magnificent blue silk dress especially made for a very famous rich client, who will be here tonight and who's that height exactly. She's married to some sheikh, blue is her favourite colour and I just know she'll go for it. The price is mind-boggling, but to a sheikh it's so much gold dust brushed off his sandals.'

'This sale means a lot to you.'

He clasped his hands. 'Amanda, that dress alone would pay for my next collection.'

'Maybe I can help.'

96

He looked at her with the eyes of an urchin begging in the streets. 'My dear Amanda, if only you could.'

'Well, I'm five ten and a half exactly, but have I got the figure?'

His face lit up like a Christmas tree. 'Amanda!' he shouted, making a loud clap with his hands. 'Would you try, please?'

'No trouble.'

He held her hand as she rose from her seat.

As they reached the stage, she sensed his discomfort. Laughing, she said, 'David, I haven't been away from the business a hundred years. I know you have to measure me.'

'Oh, you are so kind and considerate. Let's go in here.' He opened the door to the same office where she had taken the call.

Amanda was standing in briefs and bra; Morris began his measuring. 'I know they have to be meticulous at measuring' Amanda thought, 'but for a man who does this every day of the week, Morris sure seems nervous.'

They were almost through when a young man about eighteen years old came through the door, sandwich in hand. He had already taken a bite before he entered, but when he gazed upon Amanda's perfectly shaped and tanned body, his mouth dropped open, its contents falling as if in slow motion to the floor.

'Out, out, out!' Morris shouted, walking over to the young man. He pressed the boy's chin upwards, closing his mouth. 'Go eat somewhere else,' he told him. Turning to Amanda, 'A thousand apologies, Amanda.'

Amanda was laughing so heartily Morris joined in with her.

The show that night was such a success that Morris invited everyone connected with it to a Greek restaurant on Broadway as a reward. As the night wore on, he cornered Amanda. Tonight you saved my life. How can I thank you?'

Amanda, who stood a good four inches taller than

Morris, ran her fingers through his hair. 'Six years ago, at your first showing, it was my first assignment too. I was a scrawny thing back then. You could have hired better, but you didn't. You gave a nobody a chance, so tonight makes us even – agreed?'

'You are letting me off lightly. Very lightly,' he told her.

'By the way, did the dress I wore sell?'

'Oh yes. The sheikh was crazy about it, but to tell you the truth,' he put his hand to her ear, 'he seemed more crazy about the model who was wearing it.'

'Well,' she said,' matter of fact, I haven't lost my touch.'

'You, Amanda? Never, never,' Morris retorted with a cross face.

CHAPTER TWELVE

Amanda was sitting having breakfast. 'Are you ever going to get out of that tub?' she called to Cindy.

'All right, all right. You're getting worse than my mother,' Cindy called back.

Amanda began reading the morning paper. She smiled as she read the entertainments page. 'Brad Conroy can't put a foot wrong. Every venue has been sold out months in advance since he released *Make My Day*, which is still number one all over Europe, America, Canada, Australia, New Zealand and, believe it or not, it's at number one since last week in Japan. Yes, folks, Japan. If anyone there has got tickets for the remainder of Brad's concerts, you can now get up to thirty times their face value.'

'*Ouch!* The scream from the bathroom made Amanda drop the paper and run for the bathroom. Cindy was sitting on the floor, nursing her right ankle.

'What happened, darling?' Amanda asked.

'Ah, I only slipped. Think I sprained my ankle. Let's see. Don't be a fuddy duddy; help me up, please.'

Amanda helped her to the couch. 'Shall I call the doctor?'

'For this? You kidding? Fetch me a basin of ice from the ice box. An hour in that should do the trick.'

'You sure?'

'Yes, ma,' Cindy mocked.

Amanda laid the basin of ice at Cindy's feet. Then she

rolled the breakfast tray over beside her. As Cindy began eating, Amanda said, 'You scared the living daylights out of me.'

'Just keeping you on your toes, cowboy. On your toes,' she said a second time, then they both burst out laughing.

Cindy removed her foot from the basin. The ice had long since melted.

'Amanda?'

'Yes, dear.' She was in the bedroom, putting on a pair of jeans and a check shirt. Coming out of the bedroom she asked, 'How's it feel now?'

'A lot better, thanks. What time is it?'

Amanda glanced at her watch. 'Ten-fifteen.' Cindy let out a sigh.

'What's the matter?'

'Oh, it's just that I dropped my watch into Steinberg's to be cleaned and I told him I'd collect it before eleven or so.'

'Shall I ring for one of the porters to go collect it for you?'

'Amanda, you'll think I'm an idiot, but is there any chance you'd collect it for me? Bob gave it to me – not that it's very expensive or anything, but it's, you know, sentimental value.'

Amanda sat down beside Cindy. Embracing her she said, 'I'm a fool. I've been so insensitive. Of course I'll collect it for you.'

'The ticket's in my bag.'

'It's only four blocks from here. I'll walk. The air will do me good.' Kissing Cindy on the cheek, 'See you in an hour or so.'

Cindy waited for Amanda to close the door behind her. Leaping from the couch like a deer, she grabbed the phone. 'Front desk.'

'Desk,' the voice said.

'She's on her way down. As soon as she's through the front doors you know what to do.' She hung up.

It was eleven-fifteen when Amanda opened the door to her apartment.

'Cindy,' she called from the hall. No reply. 'I'm back again.' No reply. Amanda shook off her mac. She laid the mac and her handbag on the marble-top table. 'Cindy, where have you got to?' She walked through the dining room and through the door to the lounge. She stood for a full minute, as if frozen. The profusion of flowers had completely flabbergasted her. Roses, tulips, carnations...

Amanda picked up the cards and read them as she went from sheaves to bunches. The cards all read the same:

To my wife and my best pal
To you, dear wife, I pledge
My eternal Love xxx
Brad
Happy Anniversary, Darling.

Amanda sat in a huge leather armchair and began to cry uncontrollably.

'Now, now. Let's be having none of that. Ruins your complexion, you know.' Cindy was standing in the doorway of the bedroom.

'When did they come?' Amanda asked.

'Early this morning.'

'This morning? But...'

Cindy danced around. 'I had to get you out of the apartment somehow.'

They embraced. 'He's so thoughtful and considerate. Busy and all as he is, I wish he were here.'

Cindy untangled herself from Amanda. She spun round. 'Your wish is my command.' From behind a cushion she produced a pair of binoculars. 'You'll need these.'

Amanda made a face at Cindy. 'I'm not with you.'

Grabbing her by the arm, Cindy walked her to the window. Handing her the binoculars, she said, 'See if you can spot anybody familiar.'

Amanda peered through the glasses. 'There's someone waving down there.' She adjusted the focus. 'It's Brad, it's Brad, it's Brad!' she screamed.

'Look beyond Brad,' Cindy told her.

'Where?'

'At the banner thing behind him.'

There were six of the hotel porters, holding a banner some seventy feet long and six feet high. The banner itself was gold, the words on it in large white letters. It read, '*Love You Forever, Brad*'.

At the opposite side, across from the hotel, Brad was standing on a hansom cab. The two horses which had drawn it were snow white, their master at the helm keeping them controlled. When Amanda first spotted him he was blowing her kisses, not caring about the many passers-by.

When Amanda finally calmed down and regained control of herself, Cindy said, 'He's waiting for you.'

'Yes, yes,' Amanda said, half out of breath. She got into a flurry again. 'What in God's name am I going to wear?'

Taking her by the hand, saying 'Come with me, my princess,' Cindy walked her to the bedroom. Lying on the bed was a large square box, wrapped in gold paper and with a huge gold ribbon tied round it. 'Well, are you going to open it or just stare at it?'

Amanda opened the box as if there was a bomb inside. When she pushed back the soft paper, holding her hands to her breast she moaned, 'Oh my God.'

'Betcha a million bucks it fits you perfectly.' She stood in the dress before the full length mirror. 'What did I tell you?'

'It's as if it were made for me.'

'Well, honey, with a few slight adjustments you could say it was.'

Amanda was wearing the gold strapless silk gown she had admired so much when she had accompanied Cindy to the catwalk rehearsal. 'But, but how did he know?' Amanda blurted, giving Cindy a you-dunnit look.

Cindy put her hands up. 'Hold on a minute, honey. Remember that call you got at my rehearsal?'

'Yes.'

'Well, Brad told me he had bought you something for your anniversary, but he felt it wasn't enough and had you hinted at anything in particular you'd fallen in love with the few days I'd been with you. Well, you never stopped talking about the rag.'

'I see, so all the nonsense with Morris was just a ruse so's he could get my exact measurements. I wondered why he seemed so nervous.'

'Yeah, Brad told him he'd buy the gown and that it had better fit you properly. But Morris wondered how to measure you without making you suspicious. That's your problem, Brad told him. So I knew your exact height, and the sheikh – oh, that was true. The model who was to originally wear that blue dress was an inch taller than you. Morris simply adjusted it to fit you. By the way, the sheikh really did have the hots for you.'

'Speaking of hots,' Amanda said, 'how do I look? Makeup all right?'

'Yes.'

'Hair?'

'Yes. There's just one more thing.'

Cindy pulled open the centre drawer of Amanda's vanity unit. Inside was a gold satin case.

'This is too much,' she said, leaning on her dresser. Inside was a gold diamond-studded necklace with matching earrings, together with matching bangle and a watch made by Gucci, also studded with diamonds. Looking at herself in the mirror again, 'What do you say, Cindy?'

'I say if those horses don't lose control over you, nobody can blame Brad if he does.'

'Come over here.' Cindy obeyed.

'You're a rogue, but I love you all the same.'

It was supposed to be a sightseeing tour by horse-drawn

carriage, but Brad hardly stopped kissing Amanda during the entire two hours.

'We're here, sir,' the driver said.

'Already?' Brad said.

'Yes, sir,' the driver replied.

Standing on the sidewalk, 'You never said how I looked in this monkey suit' Brad said, holding out the sides of his jacket. The lining inside was in gold, miniature castles in silver adorning it. 'You didn't.'

'Give me a chance to speak.'

'What?' he joked. 'I thought it was you who didn't give me a chance to speak.' Hand in hand they walked through the entrance of the Trump Towers Hotel, laughing.

As the maitre de walked them to their table, the 'oohs' and 'aahs' were coming from all directions. The maitre de snapped his fingers and a waiter appeared.

'Something to drink, sir, madam?'

Brad looked at Amanda. 'The usual,' she said. He nodded.

'Two tall glasses of iced mineral water, please.'

As they sipped their mineral water, Amanda ran her foot up the side of Brad's calf. Brad stood up and in his best Charles Boyer accent said out loud, 'Madam, what kind of a man do you take me for? I cannot be bribed.' Holding a finger in the air he said, 'No amount of money could entice me to go to bed with you.' He looked at his watch. 'Especially at three-ten in the afternoon. If you were a man, I would slap you with my glove. Never, never have I been so humiliated. Never.'

As he stood there fidgeting with an imaginary moustache, Amanda completely surprised him by replying, 'Sir, if I were a man I wouldn't be enticing you to bed.'

Brad sat down, laughing hysterically. Gentle clapping came from behind him.

The man stood over them. 'Very good, very good indeed Brad, and you too Amanda. Everything to your taste?'

Brad held up his glass and did his John Wayne bit. 'This hotel got anything stronger'n this ass's piss?'

'Brad,' Amanda rebuffed him, 'that's enough.'

'Sorry, darling, got carried away. Everything's fine, Boss.'

As the hotel owner walked away Brad shouted, 'Donald, where's your trousers?'

They had chosen the pheasant. As they ate, Amanda couldn't help but feel that she was being watched. She began to scan the huge dining room. In the farthest corner from them sat Linda Begg. The man whose back was to Amanda was obviously Chuck Brack. As soon as Amanda laid eyes on Linda, she immediately turned away. Amanda threw her eyes to the ceiling, saying to herself 'Poor woman.'

They had finished eating some twenty minutes earlier. Donald Trump himself pushed a silver trolley to their table. On the trolley was a beautiful white, gold-embossed cake. In the centre stood a lone candle. 'Happy First Anniversary' was written on it in pink. As Donald clapped his hands saying, 'Happy Anniversary to you both,' everyone in the room applauded, including Chuck Brack. Linda Begg kept her hands under the table.

Brad accepted the silver knife from Donald. He cut a slice and handed it on a plate to Amanda. The second one he cut for himself. They both thanked Donald. Donald snapped his fingers and three violin players came to their table.

'I'm sure everyone in the room would like to hear a song on this very special occasion from Mr Brad Conroy.'

He raised his voice at Brad's name. More applause. Brad stood up and bowed. He spoke to the musicians, who nodded and began to play. The dining room patrons gave Brad a standing ovation. If they thought that Brad was going to sing his usual deafening rock'n'roll numbers they were wrong, but pleasantly surprised. The song he choose was *The Black Hills of Dakota*. The only person in the room who knew why was Amanda. When he sat down she leaned across the table and squeezed his hands.

'You old romantic.' Her eyes filled with tears.

'Now, now, no more tears, OK,' he said, a finger raised. From the corner of her eye Amanda saw Linda Begg storm out of the room. Jealous, she thought. Chuck Brack was on Linda's tail.

Brad thanked the violin players, and after tipping them generously he sat down. Amanda cleared her throat.

'Everything all right, honey?' Brad asked in his most innocent of voices. Amanda glanced at the diners closest to their table. When she returned her gaze to Brad, her cheeks were showing the slightest signs of blushing.

'You're not coming down with anything, are you dear?' he asked again, innocently. 'I'm still not with you, dear.'

Amanda thumped the table, but not hard enough to attract attention from the other diners. 'Isn't it time we were going home?' she growled through clenched teeth.

'Oh yes, now I understand, darling.' From his pocket he took a key. 'We *are* home, darling. Well, for tonight anyway.' Amanda's face mellowed. 'I was only kidding, darling. Shall we?' he said, as he rose from his seat. They walked hand in hand through the lobby and into the elevator.

'Your floor, sir,' the elevator operator said. Brad stuck two twenty dollar bills in the pocket of the young boy's tunic. They had only walked a few paces.

'Here we are, sweetheart.' The brass plaque on the door read 'Bridal Suite'.

Amanda kissed Brad's cheek. 'And to think I almost begged you downstairs,' she whispered.

'You don't know the self-control I had to keep under wraps during that horse-drawn carriage ride,' he told her. After opening the door to the suite, Brad swept Amanda off her feet and up into his arms. At the same moment an elderly couple passed them.

'Just married,' Brad said smiling.

'Yes,' the man replied, 'just two days ago.' The elderly lady held her frail hand to her face, slightly embarrassed.

Inside the suite, 'That's the way I want us to be when we're that age' he told Amanda. Still holding her in his arms Brad asked, 'Bath, Jacuzzi, or shower?'

'Just drop me on that little ol' bed over there. I need a little time to make up my mind.'

Brad smiled down at her and started for the massive bed.

CHAPTER THIRTEEN

At eleven o'clock next morning, Amanda was going
through the all too familiar ritual of sitting in the VIP
Lounge at an airport waiting for Brad's flight to be
called. Amanda stared out of the window, not taking
any notice of the planes which taxied down the runway
every few minutes. She was thinking of the previous
night. Brad told her how he had warned Joe Quinn
when he was organising the tour dates that under no
circumstances was he to be booked for the fourth, fifth
or sixth of May; that he wanted to be with her, if only
for a few hours on their first anniversary. Brad had
flown from Minneapolis at midnight and now he was
returning there on the midday flight. He had also told
her that the gift he gave her in Acapulco was to throw
her off the scent that he would be returning to New
York for their anniversary. She smiled inwardly, thinking that apart from telling each other how much they
loved each other they had done very little talking until
the desk rang to tell Brad, as he had requested, that it
was seven-thirty. She felt the tears swell up inside her
as she caught a glimpse of Brad's approach, but she
regained control of herself knowing full well how he
felt about such silliness.

'How are you feeling, hon,' he asked.

'If you have to ask that after last night, then...' she
began to shake her head.

'You know something? You're dead right. A couple of

guys mentioned to me on the way from the men's room that I walked like John Wayne.'

They both burst out laughing. She kept waving and blowing kisses until he disappeared from sight. She watched his plane climb up into the clouds. Picking up her handbag, she slung it over her shoulder. The manager and staff bade her good afternoon as she walked from the lounge, smiling at each of them in turn. As she rode on the escalator, the tears were streaming down her cheeks.

Amanda collected her mail from the desk and took the elevator to her apartment. Once inside the apartment she felt very tired. Laying the bundle of mail on the magazine table, she flopped down into an armchair. It wasn't long before sleep overcame her.

Cindy let herself in. Seeing Amanda's head resting on her hand, she crept up behind her. She squeezed Amanda with both arms around the chest, shouting, 'How ya, cowboy?'

Amanda let out a loud yell as if in agony. Cindy walked round to face her.

Amanda, holding her breast, said 'You scared the living daylights out of me,' but she wasn't fooling Cindy, not by a long chalk.

'I'm going to make some coffee. Like some?' Cindy asked.

'Love some.'

As Cindy stood before Amanda, she started singing, 'It was a night, oh what a night it was, it really was'. Amanda picked up a magazine from the table and half-heartedly threw it after Cindy as she walked towards the kitchen.

'Common, that's what you are. Common,' Amanda called after her. As Amanda prepared to take a shower, she could still hear Cindy's laughter coming from the kitchen.

Amanda came out of the shower and sat down beside Cindy.

'Anything interesting on?'

Cindy had switched on the TV. 'Oprah will be on in a minute.' From the silver pot Cindy poured coffee and handed it to Amanda. Oprah came on the screen.

'Ladies and gentlemen, if you like movies then you will certainly like my guest for the entire show. After appearing in dozens of television series, it now seems she has at last broken into the big time. Ladies and gentlemen, the star of *The Virgin Wars*; would you please welcome Linda Begg.'

Amanda made a gesture of vomiting as soon as Linda walked on.

'I know you don't class her as a close friend but let's listen to the tripe that comes out of her mouth,' Cindy joked. Amanda began opening her mail.

The first half hour of the show Oprah chatted and showed clips of Linda's first venture onto the big screen. Linda lied about receiving several scripts but they were pure rubbish, she told Oprah.

'For a small budget film it has broken records, not only here in America but throughout Europe.'

'Stay with us,' Oprah said, as the show went into commercials.

'What do you think of this?' Amanda said, throwing an envelope at Cindy. The letter read:

Dear Mr and Mrs Conroy,
It would be a privilege and a pleasure if you would consider holding the coming benefit for veterans of all countries at my new home, which will be completed by the end of July. My home is at your disposal.
Sincerely yours
Walker Lewis.

'Wow, that's going to be the occasion of occasions! Only anybody who's somebody, like worth fifty mill plus, would be invited to that mansion's opening whether the benefit is held there or not. I hear tell he's got bowling alleys, Olympic size swimming pool and a ballroom that could easily fit two thousand people with no trouble. It's a seventy-five roomed private hotel. Of course it's not exactly like the guy's stuck.'

Walker Lewis was less than five feet six inches tall, bald and pot bellied. He was also one of the shrewdest businessmen in Bel Air. He had an eye for a good script and proved it by backing his hunches. He was worth in excess of eight hundred million dollars. Seldom were his hunches wrong, and everybody knew it was his money backing the new film *The Lost King.* Everybody in Hollywood would do anything to be in that film, and nobody more so than Linda Begg.

'What do you think of it all?' Amanda asked.

'Well, honey, I know Brad is very sincere about the benefit and if he wants it to be a huge success that's the place to have it. Those occasions are normally a couple of grand a place. Brad wants it to be voluntary. One thousand people jockeying to show that their hearts are in the right place could rake in a fortune.'

'I'll fax a letter to Brad. He should be the one to decide. I'm sure he'll make the right decision,' Amanda said.

On Saturday evening at precisely eight o'clock, Amanda knocked on the door to her apartment.

'Come in, cowboy.' Cindy closed the door behind them. As they crossed into the lounge, Bob Santos stood up.

'Bob Santos, meet Mrs Amanda Conroy.'

Taking her hand, he said, 'It is indeed a pleasure to meet you, Mrs Conroy.'

'Please, *Amanda.*'

'You're even more beautiful than Cindy's description.'

'And you are more handsome than Cindy described you,' Amanda answered, smiling.

'Well, Bob, this is one dame I sure don't have to worry about stealing my date. She is strictly a one-man woman.'

111

Amanda could sense that Bob felt uneasy. Deep in his eyes he had a little boy lost look about him, as if he wasn't sure of himself.

'Forgive my manners,' he said, 'I almost forgot to thank you for the use of your beautiful apartment.'

'Don't be silly,' Amanda told him.

'OK, let's hit a night club and enjoy ourselves,' Cindy ordered.

In the limousine they had decided on Toni's, on Forty-second Street. Bob's face shone like a child's in a toy store at all the TV and film stars who came and went at Toni's. Quite a few of the top movie stars had stopped and chatted with Amanda. All had asked her to dance, but gracefully she declined them all. Cindy, on the other hand, refused none.

Bob stuttered when asking Amanda to dance. He was equally shocked when she replied, 'Why of course, Bob.'

While dancing she said, 'Forgive me for prying, Bob, but I know what it's like really being in love. You seem to be in that category.'

'You, you, you are very perceptive, Amanda.'

'Well,' she said, 'what are you going to do about it?'

'I make around fifty thousand a year. How can I ask a girl who makes more than me to quit that kind of a job and marry me?'

'For God's sake, when Brad and I met we didn't even have an indoor toilet.'

'What?'

She pulled him closer. 'It's a long story. Remind me to tell it to you some time.'

Sitting back at their table, Bob said, 'Just look at her, Amanda. Movie stars, TV stars, people from the biggest shows in New York. Cindy's in her element around such people.'

Amanda touched his hand. 'Listen, that's on the outside, that's all for show. Take it from me, let your feelings be known and I promise you'll be very pleasantly surprised.'

112

'You really think so?'

'Trust me.'

At one o'clock on Monday morning, the phone beside Amanda's bed woke her.

'Hello?'

'Amanda, I'm engaged.'

'Oh Cindy, I'm so happy for you.'

'Bob proposed to me only an hour ago at the airport. It came as a total surprise. I suppose it comes as a shock to you, too.'

Amanda crossed her fingers. 'Yes, darling, it does. Have you set a date or anything?'

'My contract's up at the end of November, so prepare to be a matron of honour the first Saturday in December.'

'That will be my pleasure. Now stop crying and try to get some sleep. You have an early start this morning, or have you forgotten in your excitement? We'll celebrate tonight. I'll ring Brad tomorrow with the good news. See you tomorrow evening, darling.' She hung up. Throwing her fists in the air, Amanda shouted, 'Yes!' Then she began to cry.

CHAPTER FOURTEEN

Amanda was in the shower. She did not hear the door to her apartment open. Very silently, he closed and locked it. He was standing only ten feet from the shower, listening to her sing and hum. Before she stepped into the shower she had laid her robe over one of the armchairs in the lounge. When she emerged from the shower she was half way towards her robe when she noticed him. For a few seconds she froze. Finally she found the courage to say, 'What the hell are you doing here? Get out, you pervert, before I call the police.'

Before her stood what looked like an extra from a Russian ballet. Black fuzzy hair, black rimmed glasses, black knee-length boots and a below-the knees Red Army-type coat. A big black beard surrounded his face.

Forgive, please, please forgive, but my wife had dress exactly like that. Mind if I touch, see the material feel the same?'

For a moment she had forgotten her nakedness.

'How the hell did you get in here?' she roared. Grabbing the robe, she covered her nakedness. She grabbed the phone. 'This is Mrs Conroy. Send up security immediately.'

'If found here I get deported,' he blurted.

'If my husband finds you here, you'll be castrated.'

'I prefer castration than deportation,' he declared. He then dashed into the Jacuzzi room.

Amanda waited out in the hall. The two security guards came out of the elevator.

'What's the trouble, Mrs Conroy?'

'A Russian, it seems, somehow got into my room. He ran into the Jacuzzi room.'

'This won't take long, Mam,' one of them assured her. A couple of minutes later the two guards walked past her.

'Everything's OK now, Mam,' they said, touching their caps.

Amanda looked amazed. They had gone past her without the intruder. Slowly she made her way to the Jacuzzi room. She knocked.

'Open the door.'

Sitting in the middle of the tub, with a huge grin on his face, was Brad. 'Why don't you switch to the dress you were wearing when you came out of the shower?' he asked.

'You, you, you crazy Irishman! You took the heart out of me,' she began, splashing him wildly.

'It was a surprise, darling? I led you to believe the tour wouldn't end until tomorrow.' Pulling her to the tub, gently he removed her robe. 'Now,' he said, 'let's behave like uncivilised people.' Through the tears she began to laugh.

*   *   *

The next morning, Brad's gentle kissing of Amanda's cheeks awakened her from her slumber. She placed her hands at the back of his head, forcing his lips on hers. After making love they lay wrapped in each other's arms. Brushing her hair from her eyes Brad said, 'I didn't think it was humanly possible to love someone with the intensity my heart holds for you. That tour did all but break my heart.' Kissing him hard on the lips, 'My mind, as well as my heart, that tour almost destroyed, darling' she told him.

'I promise you, darling, we'll never be apart for so long ever again.'

'I know you mean it, darling,' she said, 'but I also know that you were born to sing, and only God can stop what flows through your veins.'

'A month into the tour I instructed Joe Quinn to cut my work load by sixty per cent.' She was about to protest when he put a finger to her lips. 'No arguments, OK?'

'OK,' she replied. 'Now let's have some breakfast.'

Over breakfast Amanda told Brad how Cindy had saved her sanity for the first month of Brad's tour. The second month had brought her closer to her mother than she had ever been. They did lots of shopping and sightseeing, and went for long walks together.

'And Ireland?' he enquired.

'Oh, Ireland! Your brothers each in turn took a week off from work to drive me, it seemed all over the country. I visited Kerry, Cork, Waterford, Wexford, Kilkenny; and Wicklow was particularly beautiful.'

'Yeah, no wonder you feel in love with that part of the country. They call it the garden of Ireland,' he told her.

'But I'm not finished,' she told him. 'I also visited Galway, Clare, Sligo, Donegal and Dublin. The pubs at night were great fun. It seems everybody in Ireland is a poet or singer. The people wherever we went were always kind and courteous.'

'That's us Irish for you, love, and you have a prime example right here having breakfast with you,' Brad quipped.

Squeezing his hand, 'Of that, you never have to remind me,' she whispered.

'Now, what would you like to do today?' he enquired.

'How about just strolling through Central Park?'

'You got it.'

During their walk through Central Park, Brad and Amanda discussed the invitation sent by Walker Lewis to hold the Veterans' benefit at his new home.

'Sure, anybody who's anybody will be there,' Brad told Amanda.

'But, but?' Amanda enquired.

116

'You must be the only person connected with show business who doesn't know that he's hopelessly into cocaine.'

'You're right, I didn't.'

Walker Lewis had one other secret, but Brad decided not to mention it to Amanda. When they got back to their hotel Brad went to the telegraph desk to send a telegram to Walker Lewis, thanking him for his generous offer and telling him he would be grateful to hold the benefit at his new home.

Amanda stood by the elevator. Taking her by the hand, 'I've sent the acceptance telegram', he told her, 'let's hope all goes well.'

On entering their apartment Brad immediately began undressing. With a wide grin on his face he said 'Let's shower together.' She nodded and began to get undressed. In no time Brad was in the shower. The zip of Amanda's frock got stuck. It didn't seem to want to budge. As she fumbled with it, the phone rang. She lifted the gold and ivory handle from its cradle.

A minute later Brad, soaking wet, came into the room. 'What's keeping you?' Instantly he sensed trouble. Amanda's face had gone ashen grey. Her left hand covered her mouth and, weeping, she handed him the phone. Through blurred eyes she watched as the blood drained from her husband's face.

*　　*　　*

Brad stood at his father's side along with his three brothers and watched as old friends and neighbours threw long red roses into the grave in which his beloved mother now lay. After shaking hands and thanking numerous people, he glanced around in search of Amanda. He spotted a lone figure some hundred and fifty feet away, standing beside a tree. As Brad and Amanda walked towards the waiting limousine, Brad instructed the driver to wait at the graveyard's entrance for them. Brad and Amanda walked towards the lone figure. The girl seemed very nervous, and was also crying. Throwing his arms around her he said, 'Susan, how very thoughtful of you. Amanda, you remember Susan Brown, my favourite DJ?'

'Of course, How are you, Susan?'

Susan climbed into the limousine beside Amanda, Brad got in after her, then they drove to the pub that Brad's father loved.

Three days later, high over the Atlantic on their way back to New York, tears still streamed from Brad's eyes. Amanda tried to comfort him the best she could, but seeing him in such pain she could only weep with him. Brad's mother had gone to bed that night in perfect health. When his father failed to wake her next morning, he sent for the doctor. Mrs Conroy had had a massive heart attack. At seven that morning, the doctor pronounced her dead.

'We'll be arriving at Los Angeles International in ten minutes, Mr Conroy,' the pilot said over the intercom system. Brad had hired a private ten-seater just to take them to Los Angeles. In three days' time the Veterans' benefit would be held at Walker Lewis's mansion.

Turning to Amanda, Brad said, 'I've been lousy company these last three weeks, darling.' She shook her head. 'You, you've been my rock,' he told her, 'you kept me sane.'

*   *   *

Chuck Brack was sitting up in bed, reading *Variety*. He was searching through it to see if there was any mention of the new mini series he had just completed. Disappointed that there wasn't, he returned to the front page. Nudging Linda, who lay asleep, he said, 'Read this, sweetheart.'

Linda growled. 'Read what?'

'That Brad Conroy's shindig is to be held at Walker Lewis's mansion.'

She was sitting upright in a flash, grabbing the journal from him. Throwing the paper on the floor, she said, 'I have to get an invitation to that.' Turning to Chuck she barked, 'What the hell are you laughing about?'

'That one, honey, is strictly for the upper crust. First of all, Walker Lewis doesn't know you exist. Secondly, Amanda Conroy does, and both of them are in charge of the invitations, five hundred apiece.' He was still laughing as Linda leapt from the bed naked and walked into the bathroom, slamming the door behind her.

At nine o'clock next evening Chuck and Linda were watching television when the phone rang. Linda picked it up. 'Hello, Linda Begg speaking. 'It's for you,' she said, shoving the phone into Chuck's hand and adding, 'Sounds like an old broad.'

When Chuck hung up, 'Great news, honey' he shouted.

'Tell me, tell me,' she said excitedly.

'That was Debbie DeRich. You know, the producer of that mini series I did a few weeks ago.'

'And?' Linda said.

'And she wants to know if I would be her escort to the shindig at Walker Lewis's mansion.'

'*That* old bag! Why'd she choose you?' Through clenched teeth she added, 'You banging her, or what?'

'No, honey. You know I love only you. God knows I've asked you to marry me often enough.'

'Don't give me that shit,' Linda screamed, 'that broad must be sixty-eight if she is a day. It must be fuck-an-old-lady week.' Then she began throwing dishes and anything she could lay her hands on against the walls. Chuck retired to the bedroom.

* * *

Three days later, Linda sat before her vanity unit applying her makeup. She was wearing a mauve two-piece suit, a white blouse under the jacket. Chuck placed his hands on her shoulders. 'You look beautiful, darling.' They hadn't had sex since he was asked to the party at

119

the mansion. He ran his hands down her waist and onto her knees, then they began to travel up.

Slapping both hands, 'Piss off' she growled, 'don't you know I'm a guest at one of those boring talk shows in two hours?'

'But I love you, honey,' he said.

Walking towards the apartment door she said, 'Kiss my ass.' She banged the door shut.

'I'd love to, honey, wouldn't I really love to,' he said to an empty room.

If Linda was in a foul mood when she arrived at the television studio she became furious when she learned that, instead of being the last guest on the show, she was the first. But she contained her fury within. After all, she could unleash it later on Chuck. The television presenter stood up, shook hands, and thanked Linda for sparing time from her obviously heavy schedule to appear on such a relatively new network. Linda smiled and waved for the audience and cameras.

An executive escorted her to the dining room back stage, but as he was about to walk through the doors he was called away. Linda, already through the doors, was fit to be tied. The dining area was packed with electricians, carpenters, painters, fixers. She was about to turn and walk out when a voice called, 'Miss Begg, Miss Begg.'

Turning in the direction of the voice, a boy of about eighteen stood beckoning her to his table. To avoid embarrassment she walked in his direction.

'There's plenty of room at this table, be a real pleasure if you'd dine with me, Miss Begg.'

Having no choice, 'Thank you' she said.

Sticking out his hand, 'Roy Baker's the name, loved you in *The Virgin Wars*, watch every show you do.'

'You're so kind.' The young man whistled and a waitress came to their table.

'Only way to get service in this place,' he told Linda. The young man ordered a large steak. Linda chose the smoked salmon. As they ate, the young man asked Linda if she was going to the benefit at the mansion.

'Haven't made up my mind yet,' she lied.

'It's young, talented people like you who should be invited to those parties, not pensioners like that old fart Hugh Dietrick.' Linda for the first time smiled genuinely.

'Don't blame you for smiling, Miss Begg. That old bastard never married, but because he's a lawyer and handles business for some of the biggest stars in tinseltown he gets an invitation to every party, different girl on his arm at each party. He's almost seventy and still loves 'em young, the younger the better.'

'Ideas were running through Linda's head as the young man chatted on and on. Dietrick. Yes, she'd heard Chuck mention that name several times before, but had taken no notice. Dietrick was Chuck's lawyer. Linda had never met Dietrick. It was time they did, and when they did the ball, so to speak, would most definitely be in Linda's hands.

CHAPTER FIFTEEN

Linda walked through the doors of the seventy-storey-high Tennison building at 1.45. The afternoon she had left the television station after her chat with the young man, she had immediately phoned Dietrick's office. She had been told Mr Dietrick would not be free until two p.m. four days later.

She took the elevator to his penthouse suite of offices. The elevator doors opened into his reception area. The receptionist, aged about twenty-seven, asked her to take a seat, telling her Mr Dietrick would be free presently. Forty-five minutes later she was still waiting. The receptionist apologised and asked her if she would like something to drink. 'Property developers. They always take forever,' she offered.

Linda thanked her and said she quite understood. Ten minutes later four well-dressed men, all middle aged, came out from an inner office. It was another ten minutes before the receptionist beckoned Linda to a door. Opening the door for her, 'Miss Begg to see Mr Dietrick, Miss Kelly.' The inner office was that of Frances Kelly, Private Secretary to Dietrick for the last sixteen years.

'Good afternoon, Miss Begg,' Frances said, as she stood up and knocked on the huge oak door to Dietrick's office. 'Miss Begg to see you, Mr Dietrick.'

'Thank you, Miss Kelly. Come in, my dear. I'm so sorry for the delay, but my meeting was fraught with complications.'

'That's quite all right,' she said in a matter-of-fact voice.

Frances Kelly closed the door, sat back at her desk and pressed down the answering button on her intercom. Taking a pocket tape recorder from a drawer, she placed it an inch from the intercom. As usual, she recorded everything of importance that went on in her boss's office – without his knowledge, of course.

Dietrick came from behind his twelve feet-long, French-polished, solid mahogany desk.

'My dearest Miss Begg, can you ever forgive me for keeping you so long?' Guiding her to a chair in front of his desk, his hand accidentally brushed against her right buttock. This could be easier than I thought, Linda said to herself.

*   *   *

Twenty years previously, Frances Kelly had arrived in Bel Air with a few dollars in her purse. She tried more than a dozen restaurants for work, any kind of work. On the thirteenth attempt she got lucky and was hired as a waitress at York's Restaurant. Frances stood five feet ten, slim build, brown eyes. Her long black hair reached the small of her back and her thirty-six inch bust was admired and envied by those she served. She rented a tiny room, all she could afford on her meagre wages, but at least she had her own washroom. As her popularity grew with the customers, so did her tips. Frances had graduated from Hobart High School in Seattle. The extra money she made she put to good use. She enrolled in a secretarial course, which she attended three nights a week. During her studies she struck up a friendship with Harry Savin.

Harry suited Frances, as he was quiet, shy and seemed not in the least bit ambitious. Harry lived only a block away from where Frances lived. After classes they would stroll home, chatting about books, music and movies. Harry's class was on the floor above Frances'. He was studying electronics. Knowing Harry had as little money as herself, she would insist that he visit the restaurant several times a week for a meal on the house. Most evenings the chef would allow her to take home the odd steak, chicken pieces or pizzas, and Frances would cook them for Harry after evening classes. Though their friendship lasted twelve months, Harry never made an advance towards her. Frances didn't mind, as she grew to treasure his company.

Twelve months after they met, Harry informed Frances that a large electronics firm in San Francisco had offered him a position and he had accepted. The night before he left, Harry treated Frances to an exquisite expensive meal at the Bel Air Hilton. Before he climbed into his taxi next morning Frances, who was sitting outside his apartment, kissed him on the cheek. He promised to keep in touch. He would write her. As she watched the taxi pull away, she knew he would.

Four weeks after Harry had left, Hugh Dietrick walked in to York's Restaurant alone. He sat at a table reading some papers.

'May I help you sir?'

'Yes,' he said, without taking his eyes from the official papers. 'I'll have the lobster.'

'Something to drink, sir?'

Again not taking his eyes from the papers, 'Scotch, plenty of ice.'

'Right away, sir.' She placed a napkin on the table, then placed the glass on the napkin. 'Lobster will be ready in five minutes, sir.' He nodded.

He laid the papers on the seat beside him as she placed the plate before him. As she walked away, he called after her, 'Miss.' As she stood before him, he took his glasses from the table and put them on. Looking up at her, his mouth dropped open.

'Something wrong, sir?' she asked.

'No, no, it's just that your beauty took me totally by surprise.'

'Thank you,' she said.

'Could, could I have a telephone, please?' he blurted out.

'Certainly, sir.'

Dietrick beckoned for his check. As she scribbled on her pad, 'Do you mind if I ask you a question, miss?' he said.

'No, sir.'

'Can't a beautiful young woman like you find any other rewarding employment?'

She explained she had just finished a secretarial course and was sure something would come her way eventually.

He produced a card from his wallet. 'Would you consider working for me? It would only be as a receptionist, but I guarantee you promotion within one year,' he told her. He also offered to double what she was making at the present, tips included.

She took less than a minute to make up her mind. Dietrick spoke with the restaurant manager. Dietrick being a valued customer and powerful attorney, the manager wished Frances all the luck in the world in her new job the following morning. Again the number thirteen had come up lucky for Frances Kelly.

Dietrick was true to his word. Six months after Frances started working for him, he made her a junior clerk. Three months later, Frances received the most devastating news of her young life. Both her parents had been killed in an automobile accident. Frances was an only child, with no known living relatives. Her father, who could find work only as a night watchman and had scraped just enough money together to pay for Frances' education, had died penniless. Dietrick not only paid for the entire funeral but also paid for and accompanied Frances on her trip back home. Sitting beside Dietrick on the flight, Frances looked up to him as if he were a saint.

*   *   *

Three months later, sitting before Dietrick in his office, 'You know my Private Secretary, Miss Hopkins, is leaving us at the end of the month?'

'Yes sir.'

'Well,' he said, getting out of his leather chair, 'come,' extending his hand. 'I want to show you something.'

'His chauffeur-driven Rolls-Royce pulled up outside the most fashionable apartment block in Bel Air. Frances walked from the lounge to the kitchen, to the dining room, to the completely fitted bathroom, then the bedroom with its six-foot bed. Holding out the keys he said, 'It's all yours, plus Miss Hopkin's job.' As his words sank in, she seemed welded to the floor. Moments later she leapt into his arms.

'You're so kind, Mr Dietrick. You're like a father to me. Wait till Harry Savin hears about this.' She didn't take any notice of the angry look on Dietrick's face at the mention of Harry's name.

In a soft voice he asked, 'Harry?'

'Oh, he's just a pen pal of mine, lives in San Francisco.' His face relaxed.

Six weeks after starting as his Private Secretary, Frances walked into Dietrick's office.

'Anything planned for next Saturday night?'

'No,' he smiled.

'Then you're invited to my apartment for dinner. I know you'll like what I cook. Eight o'clock all right?' she asked.

'Precisely,' he smiled.

Dietrick sat at one end of the immaculately laid out table, Frances at the other.

'Like it?' she asked.

'Best I ever tasted,' he told her. She had cooked his favourite, lobster.

After they had finished eating, 'Let's retire to the lounge,' Dietrick suggested. As he sat on the sofa, 'Kill the lights, let's watch a little TV,' he said.

'Not yet,' she said, anxiety in her voice. Handing

him a wrapped package, she said, 'Happy Birthday, Mr Dietrick.'

'Please, Frances, once we're out of the office, *Hugh*, please.' Tearing the wrapping paper from the box, inside was a gold hand bracelet. Dietrick's name was engraved on it.

Beside him, she asked, 'Like it?'

Taking her face in both his hands, he kissed her full on the mouth. 'Frances, I loved you from the moment I first set eyes on you.'

He had taken her totally by surprise with such an admission. To her he was her employer, a father figure. 'How do you feel about me?' he enquired.

'I'm, I'm, I don't know what to say, Mr...'

His finger touched her lips. 'Hugh.'

He kissed her full on the mouth again. 'How would you like to be Mrs Hugh Dietrick?'

The words made all the tension leave her body. Once again his lips pressed hers, his hands squeezing her breasts. His hand travelled to her knees, trying to prise them apart.

'You'll be the toast of Bel Air,' he whispered into her ear. His hand found no more resistance. Lifting her up in his arms, he walked to the bedroom. Laying her gently on the bed, as she watched this fifty-year-old undress she hardly heard him say, 'I've been waiting for this night for so long.'

*   *   *

Seven years later, Frances was still a single woman. Dietrick showered her with gifts, paid for her apartment, but came to collect any evening he felt in the mood.

All through the years Frances had kept in touch with Harry Savin. She had just finished writing him a letter, inviting him to Bel-Air for either a long weekend or a week's free holiday at her apartment, when Dietrick came on the intercom.

'Miss Kelly, could you come in please?'

127

A week later, Frances sat behind her desk reading Harry's letter of reply. He would be delighted to see his old friend again. She laughed as she read how upset his boyfriend was that he would be spending the weekend with a 'woman'. Harry would arrive on Friday and fly back on Sunday evening.

Frances and Harry had been chatting for hours about old times when they both had nothing, and how Frances had saved his life feeding him from the restaurant. They were both earning more than fifty thousand dollars a year.

'How things change,' Harry said in a concerned voice. 'What's the matter, my old friend? You're hurting. I can sense it, and I should know. I've been there, my love.'

Frances began to weep uncontrollably. He pulled tissues from the box and began wiping her tears.

She opened her heart to him, telling how Dietrick told her he loved her and promised marriage, but too late she had realised he only wanted her body.

'All those fat cats are the same out here, love,' he told her.

'I'm getting too old for him, now I'm almost twenty-eight. There are twenty-year-olds going into his office and I'm quite sure they are not spending long periods of time in there discussing their arrears. He used to come to my apartment five nights a week, now I'm lucky if it's once a fortnight.'

'Do you love him?' Harry asked.

After a pause she replied, 'I thought I did at first.'

The next morning, after breakfast, Frances asked Harry if he'd like to go anywhere special. After some thought Harry said, 'How about showing me your place of work?'

'Of all the places – but if that's what you want.'

'Dietrick won't be there?' Harry enquired.

'No, he's in San Diego on so-called business. Would you like her name?'

'No thanks,' replied Harry.

Using her master key, Frances showed Harry round the penthouse suite. Harry fidgeted around Frances' desk.

'Good grief,' he shouted, 'your boss must have been sent to the same school as Scrooge,'

'What do you mean?'

'Will you look at this intercom system? The first one ever invented.' Harry walked into Dietrick's office and studied the intercom.

Harry called to Frances, 'Would you like to know – well, hear – what goes on between your boss and his clients?'

'I don't understand,' she said.

'It would take me all of ten minutes to work on this antique equipment. I could fix it so that any time you wanted to listen to what goes on in here it would only mean that you put a little extra pressure on your answer button. Could be useful and,' he said, raising a finger, 'if it were ever discovered it would simply look like a faulty switch.'

'Get to work,' Frances said with a smile.

'Any tools in this building?'

She opened a cupboard. 'Help yourself.'

*   *   *

Three years later the most handsome young man Frances Kelly had ever laid eyes on was escorted into her office by the receptionist. Instantly she knew she was in real love for the first time in her life. Opening the door to Dietrick's office she announced, 'Mr Chuck Brack to see you, Mr Dietrick.'

Chuck Brack was twenty-five years old.

*   *   *

'Mr Dietrick, you're a busy man.'

'Please, Miss Begg, *Hugh*.'

'You're a busy man, right, Hugh?'

He nodded. Linda stood up slowly, undid the knot on

129

the belt of her mackintosh, and expertly let it crumble to the floor.

Dietrick's eyes almost popped out. Before him was a deeply tanned body wearing black stockings, black suspender belt and black nylon see-through bra, containing a perfect forty-inch bust. She wore no briefs. She removed the black fedora from her head and pulled a clip from the bun in her hair, which fell, almost covering her buttocks. She unclipped her bra and tossed it to the floor. She walked over and placed her hands wide apart on his desk.

Running her tongue slowly round her lips she said, 'I'd do anything, anything, if you would take me as your partner to the Veterans' benefit at Walker Lewis's mansion on August the thirteenth.'

Dietrick pressed his fingers to his lips.

'You find something funny, Hugh?'

Shaking his head and still laughing, he said, 'Before we begin, would you mind removing your tits from my inkwells?'

Seconds later he pressed his intercom switch. 'Miss Kelly.'

'Yes, sir.'

'Would you cancel all my calls and appointments for the next hour?' Linda stuck two fingers in the air. 'Sorry, Miss Kelly. For the next *two* hours. Something's come up.'

'Of course, sir.'

On the eleventh of August at nine p.m. Frances Kelly stood in the hall facing the door. She could not remember ever being so nervous. She pressed the door bell. When he opened the door, her heart skipped a beat.

'Miss Kelly? Please come in.'

'Thank you.'

'Something to drink?' She shook her head. 'Please make yourself comfortable.'

She had been asking herself all day long, 'Am I doing the right thing?'

130

'Miss Kelly – sorry, you said it was important.'

From her handbag she took a large brown envelope from which slid a dozen Dictaphone tapes. She placed the recording machine on the table.

'I can leave these for you to listen to on your own.'

'Miss Kelly, you have my curiosity. Please stay.'

They had listened to the tapes for over an hour. Chuck leaned on the mantelpiece, sobbing like a child. Frances was crying for his pain.

'I'm so sorry, Mr Brack. Nobody should have to go through such torture.'

He nodded. 'You were right to bring this to my attention.' He sat down next to her on the sofa. Without realising it, she held his hands.

'He promised to marry me many years ago,'

'You, you, poor soul, must be as hurt as me.'

'No,' she said, 'I only thought I was in love. There's a world of difference.'

'If I may ask, how did you obtain the tapes?'

'It's a long story. Perhaps...' She stopped.

'Perhaps?' he continued.

'I was going to say perhaps if we got together some time, maybe over dinner, I could tell you the whole story.'

'It would be my pleasure, Miss Kelly.'

After Frances left, 'That bitch!' Chuck roared. 'And to think we were going to announce our engagement at the premiere next week. Think, think, Chuck,' he told himself, 'it's payback time. She's been banging him two hours every day for the last three weeks, just to get to that benefit. Why?' Chuck smiled. 'Of course, you fool. But I too will be there.'

As he rang his fingers through his hair he thought to himself, 'Dietrick's inkwells must be quite a distance apart.'

CHAPTER SIXTEEN

As limousine after limousine pulled up outside the magnificent mansion, Walker Lewis greeted and welcomed each of the guests. He spent some minutes chatting with Brad and Amanda.

As Brad and Amanda walked into the dining room, 'Did you see his eyes?' Amanda asked. 'Is he drunk?'

'No, my love,' Brad whispered into her ear, 'they're cocaine eyes.'

During his speech, the Governor of California paid special praise to Brad.

'To say the least, it's very unusual for someone who wasn't even born during the Second World War to think of the men who were involved in it. I'm sure I speak for every veteran of all nations as I extend my heartfelt thanks to this unique human being.'

He directed his hands towards Brad. To thunderous applause, Brad stood up and bowed gracefully. Various actors and comedians gave speeches during the dinner. The last person to be called was Brad.

The MC announced, 'ladies and gentlemen, it is with the greatest of pleasure I present the man responsible for this evening's benefit. I give you Brad Conroy.'

The standing ovation lasted ten minutes.

'I can't tell you how grateful I am to you all for supporting this worthwhile benefit.' Taking an envelope from his inside pocket he took out a slip of paper. 'I have in my hand the total amount subscribed by your good selves.' Looking down at the thousand guests, he said, 'The world will be proud of you all. You have very generously donated five million dollars! You are a credit to the human race. I thank you.' Brad walked off the stage to thunderous applause.

After the meal the guests moved into the ballroom. Everyone, it seemed, wanted to shake hands with Brad. It was almost an hour before Brad and Amanda took to the floor to dance. It was during their dance that Amanda first laid eyes on Linda Begg. They came within a few feet of each other. Linda gave Amanda the victory sign, only she didn't include her index finger. Amanda simply ignored her.

During the course of the evening Walker Lewis paid several trips to his private bathroom, where he made small mountains of white powder disappear up his nose through a solid gold snifter. He was extremely high when Linda Begg asked him to dance. As Linda and Lewis danced, their every move was watched by Chuck Brack. After their first dance, Linda didn't return to Dietrick. She stayed chatting to Lewis, who seemed intrigued by her. Dietrick didn't mind. A redhead aged about nineteen kept him busy dancing.

After a dozen or so dances, Brad and Amanda sat at their table.

'Mel,' Brad said, 'the very man I'm looking for.' After introducing Amanda, he asked Mel if he wouldn't mind finding Hugh Grant.

'For you, my friend, anything,' Mel said, and went in search of Grant.

By midnight two-thirds of the guests had left. Dietrick had left with the redhead. Linda never left Walker Lewis's side, except when he went to his private bathroom. By one a.m. there were only some fifty people left in the ballroom. By this time Walker Lewis was completely stoned. Chuck Brack watched as Linda, her arm supporting Walker Lewis, staggered out of the ballroom. He asked his partner to excuse him and followed them

133

discreetly. They seemed to take forever to climb the marble stairway. He watched as they walked to the end of the corridor then entered a room. Five minutes later, Chuck turned the knob on the door. It opened, and he checked to see if he was being watched. There was nobody about, so he went inside. Linda and Walker were in the bathroom, both snorting cocaine. Chuck slipped by them and into the bedroom. To the right of the four poster bed was a walk-in wardrobe. Chuck slid open the door and stepped in.

Chuck watched as Linda had to literally carry Walker who by now was totally spaced out across the bedroom floor. A couple of feet from the bed, Walker's dead weight sent them both crashing backwards onto it. Expertly, Linda removed Walker's off-white jacket. She removed his shoes, then his trousers and underpants at the same time. She placed his feet on the bed and rolled him to the centre of it. In less than a minute she undressed and climbed naked onto the bed. Kneeling over Walker, she began showering his face with kisses. The only response coming from Walker was snoring. She tore open his white shirt, sending buttons in all directions. She began to massage his grey-haired chest. She pressed her lips to his, sending her tongue deep into his throat. Clearly he was not responding to her love-making. Her tongue travelled under his chin and down between his breasts.

Chuck was grinning like a Cheshire cat as he watched from a slit in the closet door. 'That's it, my love,' he whispered. 'Have tongue, will travel. You don't know it, but you're giving the performance of your life.'

Every move she made was being captured on film by the camera that Chuck had brought with him.

Brad had ordered and laid out the breakfast table as Amanda came out of the bedroom. Bending over him, she kissed him full on the mouth. She didn't remove her lips for a full minute.

'Wow,' Brad said, as he gazed up into her eyes, 'let's skip breakfast.'

Amanda laughed and sat across from him. 'Love you,' she purred.

'Then let's skip breakfast,' he teased.

Amanda held her glass of orange juice to her cheek and ran her tongue over her lips. 'Darling,' she said 'we have all week.'

'Darlin',' he said in a craggy voice, sounding like Victor McLaglen in *The Quiet Man*, 'I don't just love you, I adore you.' Handing her the morning paper 'Look how stunning you look.'

She glanced down at the photo on the front page. It was of both of them after emerging from the limousine on their way into the Walker Lewis mansion. 'Not bad,' she said with a smile, 'but how do I look this morning?'

Even more beautiful,' he replied. 'Now eat your breakfast. I've just had a brain-wave.'

Shaking her head, she burst out laughing.

'Could you send someone up to collect our suitcases?' Brad said into the phone.

'Immediately, sir.'

'Thank you.'

Amanda was on the other phone to her parents. 'See you both soon. Brad sends his love. Bye bye.' She hung up.

Just then there was a knock on the door. 'I'll get it, darling,' she said. She came back into the lounge. 'It's someone for you, darling.'

Brad, who was listening to some music, walked out into the hall.

'Mr Conroy,' his bodyguard said, 'this soldier wants to know if you will see him for five minutes.'

'What's this about?' Brad asked, a puzzled look on his face.

The soldier, who was about Brad's age, removed his

cap. 'My name is John Brady, sir.' Brad still looked puzzled. 'I'm sorry for the intrusion, sir. Louis Brady was my father,'

It was like a kick in the teeth to Brad. 'I'm so sorry. Please forgive me. That's all right,' he said to the bodyguard. 'Please come in.' Shyly the soldier stepped in. 'Please make yourself comfortable.'

'Thank you, sir.'

'Please – *Brad*.'

'I'm sorry, sir, I'd feel uncomfortable.'

'As you wish,' Brad said.

'I know you're busy, sir, it's just that I felt that I had to thank you personally for everything you've done for ex-servicemen of the Second World War worldwide.'

Amanda came into the room from the dining room. Instantly the soldier was on his feet.

'Amanda, my wife. This is John Brady, the son of Louis Brady.'

Extending her hand, 'It's a pleasure to meet you, John.'

'Likewise, I'm sure, ma'am.'

Brad couldn't help noticing how immaculately the soldier's uniform was, not the slightest crease in it. His black shoes shone like mirrors. 'What rank are you, John?' Brad asked.

'Major, sir.'

Pointing at the decorations on the left breast of his jacket, Brad said, 'Seems to me you are as brave as your late dad. My condolences to you, by the way,' Brad added.

'And mine to you, sir,' the soldier replied.

'Thank you. Would you like something to drink?'

'No, sir.'

'Something to eat?'

'No thank you, sir. I've got to be on a bus in thirty minutes. I've got to be back in barracks in San Diego this evening.'

The three chatted for another fifteen minutes. Standing up, 'I'd better be on my way, ma'am sir,' he said. They shook hands. Brad walked him to the door.

Reaching into his inside pocket John said, 'By the way, sir, I'm sure Dad would have been proud if you would accept this on his behalf.' Handing Brad a brown paper package, he saluted and left.

About the same time as Brad and Amanda sat chatting with John Brady, Susan Brown sat across from her mother having breakfast. The doorbell rang.

'Who can that be at this hour of the morning?' Mrs Brown said as she rose to answer it.

When she came back into the kitchen she carried a large package in her hands. 'It's for you, Susan,' she said, as she placed it in front of her. 'I had to sign for it. Look at the postmark, Los Angeles. We don't have any relations in Los Angeles.'

'I'm as curious as you, Mum,' Susan replied, as she began cutting it open with a pair of scissors.

Inside the packaging was a large white box. When Susan lifted the lid off the box she placed her right hand over her heart. Smiling back at her from the box was her heart-throb, Hugh Grant, in an eight by ten autographed photograph. The next photograph was of her other idol, Mel Gibson, also autographed. There were a dozen photographs altogether. Amanda with Hugh, Amanda with Mel, Brad with Hugh, Brad with Mel, Amanda, Brad and Mel, Amanda, Brad and Hugh. All had handwritten notes of affection on the back, written for Sue.

'Good God, girl, I have never seen you blush so much in your life,' Sue's mother said, smiling.

'Can you imagine, Mum? As busy as Brad and Amanda are, they still found the time to do all this for me.'

Tapping the back of her daughter's hand, 'Decent people never forget kind deeds, no matter who they are, rich or poor,' she told her.

CHAPTER SEVENTEEN

By mid-November Brad had completed his new album. He had written ten new songs. They were in complete contrast to his usual throaty rock numbers.

Joe Quinn sat with Brad and Amanda in their New York suite. A copy of the album had just been delivered to Brad, who put the CD in his stereo unit. When the last song finished, 'I'm flabbergasted' Joe Quinn said.

'Disappointed?' Brad asked, apprehensively.

'No, no, not at all. They're beautiful, beautiful ballads, each one a gem, each one a love song. Where did the inspiration for them come from?'

Brad placed his arm around Amanda's shoulders.

'Aren't I the stupid one?' Joe said, smiling. 'Your love for Amanda shines through in each song,' he added. 'Thought of a name for the album yet?'

Black and Red, Amanda's – my world's – favourite colours,' he told Joe.

Black and Red went straight to the number one spot on both sides of the Atlantic. Amanda was in the bedroom preparing herself. She and Brad were having dinner at the New York Hilton. Joe Quinn was in the lounge chatting with Brad. As she added the final touches of makeup to her face she could hear Joe say to Brad, 'The Las Vegas Hilton are offering you three million dollars for just two concerts, on New Year's Eve and New Year's Night.'

'I know what you're trying to say, Joe, but I'm just not

interested. I want to be with Amanda all over Christmas and the New Year. You know we are spending Christmas at Amanda's parents and the New Year with my father and my brothers.'

'I know,' Joe sighed. 'Mecca Executives will be hopping mad.'

Send them a photograph of Amanda, then they'll understand,' Brad joked. At that moment Amanda had never been more proud of her husband.

Joe Quinn whistled as Amanda entered the lounge.

'What do you think?' she asked, spinning around.

Kissing her on the cheek, 'Positively beautiful. We should have put you on the cover of the new album,' Quinn said.

Amanda was wearing a new dress Brad had had specially made for her. The top half was black silk, from the waist down was a stand-out red chiffon, barely touching the knees. Her stilettos were two-toned, also black and red. The back of the dress was bare from the shoulders to the hips.

'You'll have trouble keeping the wolves at bay tonight,' Joe told Brad. 'You have to admit, Amanda, he's got great taste.'

'I know, Joe. You should see what I'm wearing underneath.' Quinn blushed. 'Should I show him, Brad?' Amanda said, grabbing the hem of her dress.

'Only if you want the poor man to have a coronary right here in the suite, dear.'

Letting go of the hem, 'We couldn't have that, could we, Joe?' she said, smiling.

'I wasn't thinking of him, sweetheart,' Brad said. 'I was thinking of poor auld me.' Brad placed a black stole around Amanda's shoulders. 'Let's be going then.'

Joe kissed Amanda and shook hands with Brad, wishing them both a Happy Christmas. Brad and Amanda climbed into the waiting limousine.

'I'll see you both back home in Limerick, New Year's Day.' The limousine pulled away.

*   *   *

Amanda's parents waved after Brad and Amanda as they walked down the terminal to the flight which would take them to Ireland. Mrs Gordon squeezed her husband's hand.

'We're the luckiest parents in the world.'

'I know, my love,' her husband told her.

'Brad's love for our daughter radiates from her. He dotes on her hand and foot.'

'That he does,' her husband said. 'If he buys her any more jewellery she'll have to keep it in a bank.'

Brad had woken Amanda at seven o'clock on Christmas morning. He blindfolded her and walked her to her parents' garage. Standing her in place, he removed the blindfold. Amanda was totally flabbergasted. Before her, wrapped in a huge black and red ribbon, was a brand new two-toned Rolls-Royce, its colours black and wine.

Amanda's parents were also waiting in the garage, to see the shock on their daughter's face. Amanda almost kissed the face off Brad. It was her father's clearing of his throat which brought her back to earth.

'I'm sorry, daddy,' she said shyly.

'So am I,' said her father. 'I've only got a beat-up old jeep.'

They all burst out laughing and walked back into the kitchen.

That night, as Amanda lay in Brad's arms, he was kissing her eyelids, forehead and cheeks as their bodies slowly began to get in motion.

'We have to be very quiet,' Amanda whispered. 'Remember, this shack is made mostly of wood.'

'Quiet? Quiet, woman? Why should we be quiet? After all, we be married now, it be allowed.'

Tears were streaming down Amanda's cheeks. Her laughter couldn't be heard, for she had half the bed sheet stuffed into her mouth so as to prevent it.

Amanda's father turned to his wife. 'Youth takes beating, all the same,' he told her. They too fell asleep laughing.

Brad and Amanda arrived at his father's home with three trunkloads of clothes and shoes for his three brothers and their wives. As they tried to thank him, all he said was, 'Who else am I going to spend a few quid on?'

Holding up a cowboy belt, his older brother asked, 'Just this one item, how much did it cost?'

'A few quid,' Brad replied.

'Please?' his brother persisted.

'Three thousand dollars. Now can I have a little peace?'

Brad gave his father a solid gold pocket watch, wrapped in five one thousand pound notes.

Brad spent every afternoon walking the countryside with his father. His father kept bringing back bitter sweet memories of when they were all young when most families were lucky to have a meal placed before them.

'But, my God, they were happy times, son,' he would say. 'I remember when you and Joe Quinn would be down in the shed. "Listen to that racket," I would say to your mother. All she would say was, "They're happy. Let them be happy while they're young. The years will fly by soon enough".'

'She was right on that count, Dad.'

'Too true, son, too true. Amanda's looking better every time I lay eyes on her. You're a lucky man, son.'

'I know, Dad, I know.'

'Do you remember to thank God for all your blessings?' Brad was silent. 'When everything's doing fine, it's easy to forget God. But the minute there's trouble, who do we turn to?' his father asked.

During those walks Brad turned from his father several times, saying there was something in his eye. But he wasn't fooling the old man, not for a minute. The memories his father brought back made Brad cry many times.

141

It also made Brad realise how much his father loved and missed his mother.

Brad shook hands with his brothers and kissed his father before he and Amanda turned the corner to walk down the terminal. He looked back, waving to his father and shouting, 'See you in the summer, dad.' Amanda felt Brad's loneliness as they held hands while the aircraft taxied down the runway. Brad wasn't to know that it was the last time he would see his father alive.

On arriving back in New York, Brad set about writing new songs. After two weeks he realised that when Amanda left the apartment to buy clothes, or just to browse around taking in the city, the inspiration for his songs went with her. From then on, any time she mentioned that she might go for a walk Brad accompanied her. During those walks he also realised he was falling deeper and deeper in love with her. If that were possible, he told himself. Everywhere they went, Brad's bodyguard would be only a few paces behind. Brad didn't need a bodyguard in Ireland or England. But since John Lennon had been so savagely gunned down, when Brad was in the States he would phone an agency and both he and Amanda had protection twenty-four hours a day.

CHAPTER EIGHTEEN

Tony Lorenz sat behind his desk. He reached down and pulled out the bottom drawer. From it he took out a half full bottle of bourbon. Into a plastic cup he poured himself a generous amount. He downed it in one go. He was the sole owner of *Sleeze* magazine. *Sleeze* concentrated totally on tinseltown's scandals, and its owner spared none. Things at the magazine had been relatively quiet for the last few months. Lorenz would go around his printing works like a raging bull, shouting and threatening his staff with unemployment at times such as these. As he squeezed the plastic cup and threw it in the waste paper bin on this Monday morning there was a bonus already in the post for him, which went beyond his wildest dreams.

'The mail, sir,' the young apprentice said, laying a bundle on his desk.

He browsed through a couple of dozen packages and letters before he ran his six-inch stiletto through the Scotch tape which encircled a foot-square cardboard box. Spreading out the coloured eight by tens on his desk, he couldn't believe his eyes. His high-pitched laughter echoed round his printing works. Every head turned and looked his way.

Lorenz studied each of the forty-eight photographs through a magnifying glass. Picking up the last one, it had a sheet of paper taped to the back. It read, 'Before you go to print, pay a visit to the Los Angeles Court

House. Seek out a clerk by the name of Philip Yates; for a fee of between five hundred and one thousand dollars he will let you browse through any file. The file of most interest to you is File Number 93568/074.'

The note had been typewritten and was, of course, unsigned. Opening his office door, he yelled 'Farson!'

'Yes, Boss.'

'Farson, I have a particularly sensitive assignment for you. I want you to go down to the Court House and find a clerk by the name of Philip Yates.' Handing Farson a piece of paper, 'Tell him you would like to glance through the file I have written on that piece of paper.'

'That's it, Boss?'

'That's it.'

Farson was almost through the door. 'Hold up there.' Farson returned to the desk. Lorenz took a key from his pocket and opened the top drawer of his desk. He spread ten one-hundred dollar bills across his desk. 'You'll need this to bribe Yates.'

Farson whistled. 'Must be hot stuff, Boss.'

Lorenz thought for a moment. 'You know, you might just be right.' Lorenz took another thousand dollars from his drawer, handing it to Farson. The guy just might be greedy.' Before Farson left, Lorenz said, 'I don't know what's in that file, but whatever's in it make sure you photograph it.'

'Gotcha, Boss.' Farson closed the door behind him.

Two weeks later, *Sleeze* magazine went on sale throughout California. Tim Deski kicked in the door to Walker Lewis's bedroom. Jumping onto the bed, he screamed 'Bitch, bitch, bitch!' At the same time, he punched and slapped Lewis on the face.

'What the hell has gotten into you?' Lewis yelled.

Deski sobbed like a child and threw the magazine at him. 'Read for yourself you bitch! Our secret, that's what you said it would be. Our secret. Now the whole bloody world knows!'

144

As Walker Lewis glanced through the pages his eyes seemed to grow bigger, and his mouth dropped open. Each photograph showed Linda Begg in various positions, making love to him.

'How could you do it with a tramp like her? If it were with another man, I might understand. But a woman! How, how could you?' Deski sobbed.

'Tim, I swear on my mother's grave I never made love to Linda Begg, or any other woman for that matter.'

'Those pictures don't lie. This is the thanks I get, travelling all round the country looking after your business interests while you carry on with that – *that*!'

'Tim, I swear to you I never made love to a woman in my life. I don't even remember that bitch being in my bedroom.'

'She's been around the place often enough these last few months.'

'I know that, darling. She's hoping to get a part in that new film I'm financing. But I'll tell you something, she'll never work in this town again. That I promise you.'

'This must have happened when I was away on business, if you can't even remember the night it happened.'

Lewis shook his head. 'Haven't a clue, darling.'

'That's your trouble, you bastard, you're so spaced out on coke you don't know who the hell you're screwing,' Deski roared. 'But I'll tell you something, this is going to cost you half of what you're worth. I'm packing my things. You'll hear from my lawyer real soon.'

Lewis got out of bed and tried pleading with Deski. Deski just pushed him aside and started throwing clothes into suitcases. Lewis almost tore the phone from its connection in temper. He rang all the major studios which he had shares in, instructing them not to allow Linda Begg inside their gates. He did the same with some dozen television networks he controlled.

When Deski opened the front door to leave, a plain clothes detective was about to knock on it. There were a half dozen uniformed policemen behind the detective.

'I have a warrant here to search this house for narcotics,' the detective said.

'Be my guest,' Deski roared, 'most of the stuff's in that bitch's bedroom.'

Within two days, *Sleeze* magazine was sought after in every state across the country. Tony Lorenz was in seventh heaven. He was sure Walker Lewis would hit him with one hell of a lawsuit. But after a month hearing nothing from Lewis's lawyer, who was none other than Hugh Dietrick, Lorenz came to the conclusion that a trial would only rake up more muck on Walker Lewis and that's exactly what Walker Lewis knew would happen, so he had decided against suing.

Amanda was walking home after buying some new shoes when she spotted the magazine hanging from a vendor's stand. As she came into the apartment she dropped the packages she carried.

'Brad, Brad, have you seen this?' They both sat down on the settee. Amanda went through it page by page, reading every word to Brad. When she finished reading 'My God,' she sighed.

Brad was laughing. 'Why do you seem so surprised?' he asked.

'Walker Lewis gay?'

'Yes, my love, is and always has been.'

'I didn't know that,' she told Brad.

'Everybody in tinseltown knew that Lewis was gay. That is, everybody except Linda Beg. Somebody obviously forgot to tell her. Poor Linda.'

'Poor Linda my ass. She was the queen of gold diggers if ever there was one,' was Amanda's reply.

As Deski threw his suitcases into the back seat of his convertible Porsche, Chuck Brack was sitting up in bed. He hadn't felt so good in years. Linda had gone shopping. Chuck knew she never missed an issue of *Sleeze*, and could hardly wait for her to return.

He heard the door almost come off the hinges as she slammed it. She was screaming obscenities as she stormed into the bedroom. In his best acting voice, sounding very concerned, he asked. 'What seems to be the matter, darling?' More obscenities as she threw him the magazine.

'I'd love to know what bastard's responsible for this!' she screamed.

Chuck read out the various headlines accompanying each photo. The photograph with Linda spreadeagled across Walker's genitals read, 'Virgin on the ridiculous'. He read on, 'She huffed and puffed but she couldn't blow the guy up.' He continued, 'Linda gives Walker a hand'. 'Linda Begg's Walker tries to stand up, but no matter how hard she tried all her efforts were in vein'.

'Shut up, shut up!' Linda screamed.

'I'm sorry, darling,' he said, placing an arm around her shoulders. 'Things will work out,' he told her.

'You stupid bastard, you, you idiot! You don't seem to understand. I'm finished in this business! That fag Lewis has got more clout in this town than anyone.'

'You don't know that for sure, darling.'

'Don't I?' she said, slamming down the phone. 'The show's been cancelled. Cancelled an hour ago by Walker Lewis!' Six days later, Linda Begg arrived back in Buffalo, N.Y., and began scanning the papers looking for a job.

Chuck had driven Linda to the station. He placed her suitcases in her compartment. 'Sure you won't change your mind and stay?' he enquired. Linda lit a cigarette and ignored him. He stood on the platform and watched as her train pulled out. He was thinking it didn't even occur to her, as he read and looked at those pictures in *Sleeze*, that he was in love with her and had hoped to marry her before Christmas passed. The thoughtless self centred heartless whore. Good riddance to bad rubbish. He walked out into the sunshine and got into his car.

That evening Chuck pressed a finger to the doorbell.

'Mr Brack, what a pleasant surprise, please come in.'

'Scotch on the rocks all right?' she asked.

'Perfect,' he replied. She poured two and handed him one. She sat on the armchair across from him.

'How was your day?'

Smiling, she replied, 'Absolutely fabulous. The phone's been ringing all day, same as yesterday. Clients are leaving Dietrick by the dozen. Talk about a bear with a sore head. Walker Lewis may be gay, but his influence is enormous and far reaching. Apart from the pastor who married Lewis to Deski, the only other person on earth who knew their secret was Hugh Dietrick. When Lewis came to the office, I listened in. He was screaming so loudly at Dietrick I didn't need the intercom. Lewis maintained that Dietrick must have drunk too much one night and let it slip about their marriage. All Dietrick's pleading did him no good whatsoever. Lewis told Dietrick in no uncertain words that the only business he'd be handling from now on were parking fines, and that was if he was lucky. Cancelling all his business with Dietrick, he stormed out of his office. Refill?' she asked.

'Yes thank you.'

'Now, how was your day?' she asked.

'Oh,' he said, hanging his head, 'I've had an awful day. The girl of my nightmares left me and went back to Buffalo.' Looking up at her, he began to laugh. Standing up he said, 'As for you, Miss Kelly, you have saved me an awful lot of pain and aggravation.' He placed his glass on the mantelpiece, offering her his hand.

Taking it she said, 'You know, taking those photos to ruin Linda's career was satisfying enough, but when you wanted a slice of Dietrick and told me Lewis's secret, our plan couldn't have gone any better.'

'The only loser is poor old Lewis.'

'Poor my eye. When Deski is finished with him, he'll still be worth a considerable amount of money. Anyway, how much does a seventy-year-old need?'

Chuck pulled the clip from the bun at the back of her

hair. Her silky black hair fell beyond the small of her back. He began to undo the buttons of her blouse. She let it fall to the floor. He unclipped her bra. Looking at her thirty-eight inch bust, he said, 'My, oh my, Miss Kelly, but there's more to you than meets the eye.'

He kissed her hard on the lips, she pushed her tongue deep into his mouth. In all her dreams she had never thought it possible that here in her own apartment the man she had adored for so long was about to make love to her. He eased her slowly to the white rug in front of the fireplace, the artificial embers emanating from it making the scene perfect.

Fifteen minutes later, as they both lay on the rug breathing heavily, 'That was fantastic, Frances.'

'You're pretty good yourself.'

'Mind if I make a suggestion?' he said. She crossed her fingers.

'Not at all.'

'Would you mind terribly if I moved in with you?'

'Only on one condition,' she replied.

'And that is?'

'That you never move out.'

CHAPTER NINETEEN

As the aircraft flew over the Atlantic, Amanda had Brad's head pressed on her breast. He cried like the rain. On February the tenth his father had had a stroke. Three days later he had a heart attack and died. Brad had held up well at the funeral, shaking hands, smiling and thanking everyone who attended. But when they were an hour out of Shannon Airport he fell to pieces. Words of consolation at times like this are useless. Amanda didn't try. She simply cried with her husband.

Two months later, Joe Quinn sat across from Amanda having lunch in a Chinese restaurant. He had phoned her the previous day, asking her to meet him.

'Tell me if I'm out of line, Amanda, but I'm worried about Brad.'

'That makes two of us, Joe.'

'He doesn't seem interested in anything any more. He's not writing, doesn't want to know about concerts, TV interviews, nothing.'

'What do you suggest, Joe?'

Joe rubbed his hands and swallowed hard. 'With your help, I can organise a tour. I know he's hurting, losing both parents in such a short time, but we've got to get him back to work.'

'You seem very nervous, Joe.'

'I'll be straight with you, Amanda. Australia, Japan, New Zealand, Brazil, Egypt, I could go on and on. They're all crying out for him to tour. He's more popular now than he ever was.'

'I understand why you're nervous, Joe. I'm the problem, right? He won't tour with me and he won't tour without me, right?' He nodded his head. 'I'll do my best, Joe. I want to see Brad out of his grief as soon as possible.'

Two weeks later, in spite of all her hints about touring, Brad would simply say, 'There's no rush.' Every afternoon they would walk through Central Park, always accompanied by their bodyguard. One evening after returning from their walk, as they entered their apartment the phone was ringing.

'Hello? Amanda Conroy.'

'How ya, cowboy?'

'Cindy! Brad, it's Cindy.'

Amanda chatted with Cindy for half an hour. Sitting next to Brad on the settee, she said, 'Cindy and Bob are coming to New York for a week's vacation next week. I've invited them to stay with us. Is that OK, honey?'

He smiled at her. 'Of course it is, my love.'

Bob and Cindy Santos were like a breath of fresh air to Brad. Their lifestyle was so different from Brad's and Amanda's. Brad and Amanda got great pleasure taking them shopping and to the fanciest restaurants and hotels in town. Brad and Bob both loved football, baseball and basketball. The women didn't object when they wanted to go to games. When Brad and Bob mentioned in the nicest of ways that such a game was on, the girls would say, 'OK guys, we'll take in a show.'

At ten o'clock on Friday morning, Brad and Bob set off for the bowling alley. Half an hour later, Amanda shook Cindy awake.

'I'm going out for an hour.'

'Hold on, cowboy. I'll go with you.'

'No way, pet. Stay where you are. After all, you are on vacation. Bye.' She closed the bedroom door.

                    *   *   *

Cindy helped Amanda lay out the dining room table.
When they had finished, they both stood back. 'Perfect,'
they said together.

The table was laid out for six people. Amanda had
phoned Joe Quinn, whose wife rarely left London but had
accompanied him on this trip to New York, and invited
them both to dinner. At five minutes to eight, Brad lit the
half dozen candles on the table then turned the lights
down. At exactly eight-fifteen the waiters brought in the
food. When everybody had been served, Brad handed one
of the waiters a wad of dollar bills. The waiters thanked
him and left.

When they had finished the meal, Brad raised his
crystal glass of mineral water. 'A toast,' he announced.

'To what?' Joe Quinn said with a smile.

Brad thought for a second. 'To love and friendship.'

'Hear, hear,' Quinn shouted.

They were about to rise from the table when Amanda
spoke. 'Hold on, everybody. Sit, please. I have an announcement to make.'

She walked to the opposite end of the table, where Brad
sat. Standing behind him, she put her arms around him
and kissed the top of his head. She cleared her throat.

'Ladies and gentlemen, I am delighted to inform you
that my husband and I are going to have a baby.'

Everyone's eyes immediately were fixed on Brad. He
was on his feet in seconds, squeezing and kissing Amanda's
face all over. Their guests applauded them and in turn
shook both their hands and congratulated them.

'When did you find out?' Brad asked through misty
eyes.

'Yesterday morning, darling.'

'So,' Cindy said, 'that's where you sneaked off to yesterday morning.'

Embracing her, Amanda said, 'Yes.'

As they lay in bed that night, Brad said, 'I forgot, in all
the excitement, to ask when the baby is due.'

152

'December, darling, around the twentieth.'

Brad lay back on his pillow.

'Hmmm,' Amanda blurted.

'Something the matter, dear?' he enquired.

'Don't I get a bonus?'

'Should we?' he said, sounding concerned.

'I'm barely two months. Of course we can.'

In his best W. C. Fields accent, Brad shouted, 'If my wife wants a bonus, a bonus she shall have. Come to think of it, my dear, you are going to get two bonuses.' Bob and Cindy heard him and were laughing uncontrollably. Amanda, also laughing, began beating Brad with her pillow.

The next morning, Amanda phoned Joe Quinn.

'Joe, organise a tour. My husband's returning to work.'

'Fantastic,' Joe shouted down the phone. 'Amanda, you told me you'd try your best. What in fact you did was create a miracle.'

'I'm afraid God will have to take all the credit for that, Joe.'

She handed the phone to Brad.

'I don't care where you send me. Just make sure I'm back sometime in the second week in December.'

'Done,' Joe said, 'that I promise.'

Brad rehearsed every day until two days before the tour began. Joe Quinn stuck his head in the door.

'Whenever you're ready, Brad.' He waved at Amanda.

'Well, honey, your old man's got to go to work.' She forced a smile. 'Now, now, that's no way to send your old man away. After all, I do have a family to take care of. We need the money,' he joked. They kissed and embraced. As he walked to the door he turned round. 'Ah, ha.' He waved a finger at her. He could see she was filling up.

'I know, I know,' she said, 'see you in five months.'

'I'll phone every day,' he said, then he was gone. She watched from the VIP lounge as the chartered jet taxied down the runway. Before she reached the escalators she had used several tissues.

A week later Amanda was sitting alone, watching the late movie on television. Her phone rang.

'Hello, Amanda Conroy.'

'Howya, cowboy?'

'Cindy! Your voice, oh, it's so good to hear your voice. How's Bob?'

'He's fine. He sends you his love.'

'How are things in Chicago?'

'The rain, you have to see the rain here to believe it. When it starts, the cars come to a standstill.' After ten minutes Cindy said, 'I had something delivered to your apartment. I told them to leave it outside your door, so it should be there now. Will you go and check?'

'Hold on a minute.'

Amanda opened the door. Standing outside with a mobile phone in her hand was Cindy.

'Oh, you and Brad with your jokes!'

After embracing, Amanda asked the bodyguard to bring in Cindy's suitcases.

'This was Bob's idea. Brad and you were so kind to us, he said I should come and stay with you for a few weeks.'

'I'll never forget him for this,' Amanda told her.

CHAPTER TWENTY

Brad's tour began in Australia. His first concert was in Melbourne, then on to Sydney, Brisbane, Gladstone, Darwin, Kimberley, Larmonth and finally Perth. Then it was on to New Zealand, visiting Dunedin, Timaru, Christchurch, Nelson, New Plymouth and finishing in Napier. Next was the Philippines: Davao, Mindanao, Manila, then Luzon. The next stop was Egypt. Brad was booked at Cairo and Alexandria for a week each. He was apprehensive about Egypt, but the response from the crowds amazed him. So far, it was the biggest sellout tour on record. Tickets to his concerts everywhere were fetching up to fifty times their face value on the black market. As November came to a close, Brad was in great spirits. As the plane left Egyptian air space, Brad clapped his hands. Canada would be like giving a concert in New York. Canada was the last port of call on Brad's tour.

Edmonton was no different from the other venues Brad sang at, and was completely sold out. Calgary, Vancouver, Winnipeg, Quebec, Ottawa, Toronto were no different. Brad's final week in Canada was in Montreal. Before his first concert in Montreal, Brad accepted an invitation to appear on the Sam Goodman Show. As Brad chatted on the live show, the switchboard was jammed by callers begging him to extend his concerts for another week. When Sam Goodman put this to Brad, he said, 'Normally it would be no problem, but my wife is expecting our first child and I promised I'd be with her when the baby comes.'

More than three dozen callers spoke live on the phone to Brad, mostly girls crying and begging him to reconsider. They told him that they had queued for hours in the freezing weather only to be told as soon as they reached the pay box that the concerts were booked out.

'Tell you what I'll do,' he told the live audience and viewers. 'I'll phone my wife in the morning and if she gives me the green light, I'll stay another week.'

He promised Goodman to phone him after talking with Amanda, so that he could let the viewers know the verdict.

Amanda wasn't in the least bit annoyed. 'It's cutting it rather fine, playing up to the nineteenth. Get your butt here after that last concert.'

He enquired about her health. She reassured him that everything was just fine, no problems whatsoever.

'Mother won't let me out of her sight for a moment.'

'They were my orders to her,' he joked into the phone. 'See you soon, darling. Love you so much.'

'Likewise,' she told him.

Brad's last performance ended at ten o'clock. Twenty minutes later he was being driven to the airport. The airport's manager came into the VIP Lounge.

'I'm very sorry, Mr Conroy, but you can see for yourself. In that fog, nothing's going to fly tonight.'

Brad thanked him. As soon as he left, he pounded his fist into the palm of his hand. 'Of all the luck!' he shouted. Joe Quinn cast his eyes to the floor.

By four next morning, the worst snow storm to hit Montreal for twenty years was born. By midday the airport was completely snowed under. Brad enquired about travelling home by limousine. That too was hopeless. He was told traffic throughout Montreal had come to a standstill. The weather people predicted the storm to last for five days. Joe Quinn had never experienced the anger shown by Brad.

At six p.m. on Christmas Eve the storm began to subside. The airport's snowploughs went to work. The airport manager told Brad that, with luck, he could be in the air by nine that night. At eight forty-five Brad's jet taxied down the runway.

'At last,' he said to Joe.

'That's the first smile I've seen on that face in four days,' Joe told Brad.

Tapping him on the knee, 'I know, I've been a rat's arse these last few days. I'll make it up to you, old pal.'

'Just be a good father,' Joe smiled back.

Amanda's waters didn't break until eight o'clock on Christmas Eve. She was driven immediately to St Andrew's Maternity Hospital. Amanda's father told Brad to follow the blue line. He ran all the way as he pushed the doors open. At two minutes to midnight, he gazed with amazement as his son came into the world.

*   *   *

Four days later Brad and Amanda agreed to allow several press photographers to take photographs of the new arrival.

'Have you decided on a name for the little guy yet?' one of them asked.

Brad was sitting on the bed, his arm around Amanda, the baby in her arms, looking down at her.

'You tell 'em, darling,' he said.

'Brad and I chose the name Chris.'

For the next ten minutes they both answered all the questions put to them: the child's weight, colour of his eyes, his hair.

'He actually arrived four days late,' Amanda told them.

The staff nurse came in and cleared the room in less than a minute. 'I should take her on my next tour,' Brad joked.

When they were alone, Amanda breast-fed the infant.

157

When the baby had taken his fill, Brad placed him in his cot. From under his overcoat, which lay on a chair, Brad brought out a package. It was gift wrapped and tied with a silk black and red ribbon. When Amanda opened the velvet box, 'This is too much, Brad,' she gasped.

Staring back at her was a necklace. It had four layers of emeralds, and they hung from twenty-four carat gold chains. Also in the box was a bracelet and ring to match.

Kissing her on the forehead, he said, 'You gave me a beautiful son, so in gratitude I spent a few bucks on you.'

'How do I look, darling?' she asked in a serious voice.

'Same old way. Astonishingly beautiful,' he told her, and kissed her full on the mouth.

Six weeks later, in the presence of Amanda's parents and brothers, their wives and girlfriends, Brad's brothers and their wives, Joe Quinn and Cindy Santos became God-parents to Chris Conroy. Bob Santos and Rose Quinn were also present. Chris Conroy was christened in the same Catholic Church where his parents had been married. Brad booked a private room at Frazier's Hotel in Montgomery for the reception afterwards. During the reception he pulled Joe to one side.

'I have a favour to ask of you.' Brad whispered instructions into Joe's ear.

Brad and Amanda stayed at her parents' house for a week after the christening, then returned to New York.

Chris lay asleep in his crib, Brad was soaking himself in the bath and Amanda was browsing through a newspaper when the phone rang.

'Amanda Conroy.'

'How you, cowboy?'

'Cindy! How are you?'

'How am I? Bob and I are over the moon, that's how we both are.'

158

Amanda was waiting for Cindy to tell her that she was pregnant. When Cindy got her breath back she said, 'Do you know what your husband did?'

'Cindy, for God's sake, what *are* you talking about?'

'Typical Brad. He didn't even tell you.'

'Tell me what?' Amanda said anxiously.

Just then Brad came into the room. Amanda indicated to him that it was Cindy on the phone. Amanda continued chatting on the phone for half an hour. Before she hung up, 'Cindy and Bob want to say thanks,' she said. Brad chatted with Bob and Cindy for ten minutes. At the end of the conversation he said, 'It was my pleasure. See you both soon.' He hung up.

Amanda sat on the settee, a cushion pressed to her stomach. Brad spread his arms.

'It was my way to thank Cindy for spending eight weeks with you while I was on tour.'

'You might have mentioned it at least.'

'Well, you were so busy, what with the baby, the christening, etc., I didn't want to bother you with such trivialities.' He sat down beside her.

'At the reception after the christening you asked Joe Quinn to fly to Chicago and meet Bob's partner, to ask him if Bob showed a special interest in any of the properties they had on their books.' Bob had mentioned to his partner a week earlier that he would love to be able to afford a six bedroomed mansion standing on ten acres in the swankiest part of Chicago. Amanda burst out laughing.

'Like to tell me what's so funny?' he asked.

Wiping tears from the corners of her eyes, 'The property cost half a million bucks.'

'So?'

'And you said you didn't want to bother me with such trivialities.'

He fondled her hair. 'I wonder, if it were the other way round, would I have been as noble as Bob was?' As they kissed passionately, baby Chris cried out to be fed.

159

In between changing nappies and feeding Chris, Brad tried to write songs. It was now mid-June. Only once had Amanda left the suite since she and Brad brought Chris home from Montgomery, and that was to celebrate their third anniversary. They went to see the show *Cats*. Afterwards they had a quiet meal, then straight home to their son on whom they both doted.

At two p.m. next day Brad watched Amanda as she laid Chris into his crib. They tiptoed out of the bedroom, leaving the door open. They sat on the settee.

'I was thinking, Brad. It's time we thought about buying a home, I mean a real home.'

'My thoughts exactly. I'll be back in a few minutes,' he said.

He was back in five minutes. He spread out a map of America which he had purchased in the hotel's newsagents. 'There,' he said, 'just place a finger on the spot where you'd like to live. Take your time.'

'I don't have to even think about it,' she told him. She placed a finger on the map.

Brad checked it, smiling at her. 'You auld romantic.' She had chosen Colorado, the state where they had first met.

Picking up the phone, 'This is Brad Conroy.'

'Hello Brad, Bob Santos.'

'How are you, Bob?'

'Fine, Brad.'

'And Cindy?'

'Just fine, thanks. And Amanda and Chris?'

'They're both having teething problems. Every day he looks more like Amanda. All he's got from me, it seems, is his blond hair.'

'Brad, I think I might have just the home you're looking for.'

'That's great, Bob. Where exactly is it?'

'It's outside Pueblo, about seventy five miles west of it.'

160

'How many rooms?' Brad asked.

'That's one thing you don't have to worry about. I think I counted twenty at least. It's got a reception room you could lose three hundred people in. It's got a kitchen about the size of your entire suite there in New York, and it's got a den where you can write and conduct your business from. Look, Brad, get yourself and Amanda out here, then judge for yourself.'

They made arrangements to fly to Pueblo the following Thursday.

Brad knew before Amanda had completed her tour of the house that she had fallen in love with it.

'It's perfect,' she smiled, clapping her hands, 'just perfect. Of course it needs a lot of converting.'

'Of course, darling, and that's your department,' Brad told her.

The front of the house had a twelve-foot-high solid stone wall surrounding it. Inside the wall there were oak, beech and elm trees. To get to the house you had to turn off the main highway some ten miles back. Brad and Amanda agreed the house had perfect seclusion. The drive from the main wrought iron gates was three hundred yards long. The back of the house had a huge veranda. There were various buildings to the left and right hand sides of the main house.

When Brad asked about one building in particular, Bob told him it was the bunk house. The last owners had had six hands working the ranch for them, and that was their living quarters.

'How much of this land would we own?' Amanda asked Bob.

'As far as the eye can see in any direction,' he replied. 'There's ten thousand acres goes with the house,' he added.

'We'll have to buy a couple of horses,' Brad said. He pinched Amanda's bottom.

'What's the asking price, Bob?' Amanda asked.

'Six million.'

'What do you think?'

'Well, Amanda, they'll accept five, I'm sure.'

Amanda looked at Brad.

'You like it, darling?' he asked.

'Love it,' she replied.

'Make the offer, Bob. Nothing's too good for my old lady.'

She jumped onto his back.

The house, apart from its foundations, was completely built with oak. The inside of the house had the most beautiful hand crafted panelling Brad had ever laid eyes on. The staircase was a work of art, carved by a man who obviously loved his work. Amanda began to make notes, not only of changes she wanted made but a list of all mod cons, a mile long. When she finally finished her list, Brad glanced over it.

'There's something missing,' he told her. He teased her for ten minutes before he told her. Amanda wrote at the bottom of her list, 'One swimming pool'. That was the one thing the ranch didn't have.

By early September the house, including the swimming pool with its underwater floodlights, had been completed to Amanda's satisfaction. Brad moved into it one week before Amanda and Chris were due to fly to Pueblo. He bought two palomino horses. When the truck with their feed arrived, he asked the driver where he could purchase a couple of saddles. Taking a map from his dashboard, the driver showed Brad the location of a small town about twenty miles south of the ranch.

'The place is mostly for tourists,' he told Brad. 'The town looks like a western movie set, all the shops look like they looked back in 1888. The tourists love that sort of thing. The revenue helps the folks through the winter months. Jackson Saddlers is the name to look for. Just give him your height and weight, he does the rest.'

Brad thanked him, handing the driver a hundred dollar tip. He watched as the truck pulled out of the yard. The two palominos were trotting around the corral. Brad climbed into his newly purchased jeep and headed for the small town to order the saddles.

When Brad went to meet Amanda and Chris, he was delighted to see Cindy appear from the terminal with them. After kissing and hugging all three, he loaded their suitcases in the back of the jeep and drove in the direction of their new family home.

As Amanda gave Cindy the grand tour, Cindy declared, 'This isn't a house, this is a hotel,' throwing her arms round Amanda.

'It's magnificent! May you all have a long and happy life here together.'

'It won't be for the sake of trying, I'll guarantee you that,' Amanda told Cindy.

'You've just got to see this little town,' Brad told Amanda as they lay in bed that night. 'It may have a shop with something that catches your eye.'

'Enough talk,' she interrupted him.

'Like I said, anything my old lady wants she gets.' He began kissing her passionately.

Brad climbed into the jeep, Amanda got in beside him. Cindy stood on the veranda with Chris in her arms.

'Shan't be more than an hour,' Brad said to her.

'No hurry, take all the time you want. Chris and I need to get better acquainted anyway.'

As they drove, Amanda removed the cravat from round her neck. She wiped the perspiration from her face. 'Sure is a hot one.'

'That it is, honey,' Brad replied.

Brad pulled up outside Jackson Saddlers. 'Look, honey, why don't you pop into James's Bar there and have a long cool drink? I'll join you as soon as I've finished with Jackson.'

Amanda agreed, and went down the dirt street and into James's Bar.

Brad came out of Jackson's, a saddle draped over each shoulder. He put them into the back of the jeep.

'My,' the man said, 'but you're a pretty thing. Like to buy you a drink.'

'Take a hike,' Amanda said, not taking her eyes from her drink.

'Don't be unsociable. I can show you a good time.' The man had a half bottle of whisky in his hand. He swallowed what was in his glass, then filled it again and pushed it towards Amanda. 'Drink, pretty lady.'

'You deaf, dumb, stupid or all three?'

The man stood up, kicking the chair backwards. Brad caught it and threw it to his right. The man swallowed two more glasses of whisky before he turned round.

'The lady told you to hit the road, mister.' The man turned round and swallowed another whisky. Brad walked to within inches of the man's face. He was at least six inches taller than Brad and thirty pounds heavier. The hair on his head looked like matted barbed wire. His full grown beard had bits of straw clinging to it. He looked like he'd walked straight off the set of *Deliverance.*

'You wearin' a mask, fella?' Brad asked. Before the man answered, Brad said, 'You must be nobody, but nobody could look that ugly.' He pulled at the man's beard.

'You're not,' Brad declared. 'I'll bet ten bucks that when you were born the doctor slapped your mother.'

Brad never saw the punch that sent him back out through the western-style swinging doors, head over heels. The man came through the doors like an express train. He dived at Brad, who somehow managed to roll out of his way. The man hit the ground with a thud that sent a cloud of dust into the air. As the man clambered to his feet, Brad sent a right fist crashing into his jaw. It only made the man madder. The man caught Brad by the lapels of his Levi's jacket, lifting him off the ground, and threw him hard against the steps of the bar. As Brad struggled to his feet, he was saying to himself, 'What have I walked into here?'

The man grabbed Brad round the throat. The man was as strong as a horse. Brad brought his right clenched fist down hard on the man's crotch. This made him release his grip on Brad. Brad sent a flurry of punches to the man's face and body. The man caught Brad on the right jaw, sending him flying backwards some ten feet. The fight continued, and by now blood was spurting from both men's faces.

The man stood in front of a shop, laughing as once again Brad picked himself up from the ground. He took a minute to catch his breath. Lunging at the man, hitting him in the solar plexus, the man's knees seemed to buckle. Hiking himself up, Brad drew on all his strength. He sent his best punch once again into the man's face. The man staggered back, arms outstretched. He went crashing through the shop doors.

Once again, Brad took time to draw his breath. He staggered into the shop. The man had caused a domino effect, knocking down the glass shelving which contained porcelain and bone china sold by the Robinson sisters, who were behind their counter. Their mouths were agape. The man was out cold amongst the debris. Brad walked over to the counter and took a cheque book from his pocket. He signed a check, handing it to one of the sisters.

'Please assess the damage, then add a thousand for the inconvenience. That all right?'

They both nodded. As Brad went through the door, an old timer was peeping in.

'Who's that guy anyway?' Brad asked him.

'That there is Willard Bull.'

'Now,' Brad said to the old timer, 'that's what I call a bull in a china shop.'

Amanda came running towards Brad. He fell to his hands and knees. She wiped the blood from his face with her handkerchief. He began to laugh.

'You're in bits! What's there to laugh about?' she enquired.

'I was just thinking, from the first day I met you I fell for you, and I'm still falling for you.'

'Come on,' she said, 'that gorilla could have killed you.'

As he climbed into the jeep he said, 'You'd better drive, darlin'. I can hardly see.'

*　　*　　*

Brad and Amanda had their official house warming party on the last Saturday in November. He was waiting at the airport.

'I'll take those,' he said, as the young girl was about to pick up her luggage.

Embracing her, he kissed her on both cheeks. 'Welcome to Colorado, Sue.'

'Thank you for sending the ticket and for inviting me,' Susan Brown said.

'How was your flight?'

'A little tiresome.'

'Well, you have plenty of time to freshen up before the party tonight, and its my pleasure to have you here.'

Brad and Amanda watched as Sue played with Chris. She had brought an assortment of toys for him all the way from Ireland.

'How's Limerick?' Brad asked.

'Oh, the same, Brad. Cold and damp.'

Brad was already dressed. 'You two ladies best be getting ready for the party,' he advised.

Amanda's parents and brothers and their partners arrived at six. Brad's brothers and their wives arrived thirty minutes later, Joe Quinn and his wife ten minutes after. Brad entertained them until Amanda came down. Amanda had deliberately kept Susan upstairs, as Brad had hoped a couple of special guests would be able to make it to the party.

Amanda and Susan came downstairs together. Amanda showed her to the mini-ballroom. The guests assembled

166

there applauded as she walked in. Brad took Susan by the hand. Standing before her was Hugh Grant.

'I believe you're a fan of this man.'

Susan felt her face burning. Going down the line, 'Mel, this is Susan Brown. Tom Cruise, Susan Brown. Charlie Sheen, Susan Brown.'

As Susan was introduced down the line, 'They're never going to believe it back home,' she said to herself.

'If you're going on tour in January, you'd better start getting into shape. You've put on weight since we've moved into this house,' Amanda told Brad.

Stepping off the bathroom scales, 'I'm twenty pounds overweight' he declared.

'Drive into Pueblo tomorrow, there's a fabulous gym called *Slim with Jim* there. I watched them work out a couple of times when I went to Pueblo shopping a few weeks ago.'

Brad joined the callisthenics class at *Slim with Jim* studio. He also went on a diet. His tour was due to begin in the last week of January and end in the second week of April. Brad and his group would tour the major cities of Europe. The tour would end in Ireland. He had three dates there, first Belfast, then the Point in Dublin and finally in his native city at the University. After that concert he would fly out of Shannon Airport and home.

CHAPTER TWENTY-ONE

The tour was over, and Brad told Joe Quinn he wanted at least a year off to concentrate on his ranch. He wanted to start stocking it with cattle, horses, sheep, chickens and ducks. He wanted Chris to become familiar with as many animals as possible.

Brad had to put his plans on hold after the tour. Amanda wanted the three of them to spend some time with her parents as, after all, Chris was their only grandchild. Brad told her he understood. They stayed with her parents until June. Then Brad, Amanda and Chris toured at their leisure round Europe, visiting France, Spain, Germany, Austria, Greece and London. Their last visit was to Ireland. September was coming to a close as they boarded their flight to return home.

'We'll be back in a couple of hours,' Brad told Amanda as he strapped Chris into the back of the jeep. He was going into Pueblo to meet a cattle agent. It was the end of November and Chris was one month from his second birthday. He was full of talk from the educational videos for children which Amanda purchased. She spent a couple of hours each day singing the songs and spelling and counting. Due to her efforts he spoke his words clearly. None of that baby talk was ever entertained by Amanda. When Brad had finished his business with the agent, he and Chris browsed through the stores. Chris got his hands on a racing car and neither for God nor man would he let it out of his hands. Brad paid for the toy.

Chris had a couple of hundred at home. Every time Amanda took him with her shopping, his collection increased.

As they walked through the mall, a Winchester caught Brad's eye. Grabbing Chris by the hand he went into the shop and asked the assistant if he could examine it. He had been less than a minute examining the weapon when he realised Chris was not by his side.

'Chris, Chris!' he called frantically. He searched the shop but there was no sign of Chris. He ran up the mall, shouting Chris's name. By now there was absolute panic in his voice.

'Chris, Chris, Chris!' As he got closer to the automatic doors, his heart almost stopped. Out in the middle of the road, Chris was lying belly down playing with his toy racing car.

As Brad went through the doors to his right, he saw an articulated truck thundering straight at Chris. He screamed at the child. He was too far away to be of any use himself. The truck was only feet away now. The driver wouldn't see the tiny body until it was too late. He began to run. The truck was less than twenty feet from Chris.

A man came from nowhere, picked up the child then, diving on his back, held the child against his stomach.

Brad was on his knees, holding Chris tightly against his chest.

'Are you all right, son?'

'Lost my car, daddy.'

The child seemed oblivious to the impending disaster. Thank God for that. If he realised the situation it could make him a nervous wreck. A crowd had gathered round them.

'The man, the man who saved you.'

'There he goes,' one man in the crowd said, pointing. With Chris in his arms, Brad began to run after the man.

As Brad got nearer to the man he called, but the man kept walking. Brad had called after the man several times, but his calls were ignored. The man turned up a side street. Brad increased speed. Finally he stood blocking the man's way.

'Didn't you hear me calling you?' The man remained silent.

'That truck would have...' His voice trailed off. He regained his composure.

'That truck missed your feet by inches.' The man remained silent. 'I just want to thank you and would like to make...'

'No,' the man said. 'You wouldn't be suggesting some kind of payment for saving another human being?' He made it sound so pathetic. The man walked away. Brad dropped to his knees sobbing.

The man stopped and turned back. Putting a hand on Brad's shoulder he said, 'Look, the boy's fine. Don't torture yourself. Kids run away from their parents all the time.'

Brad wiped his eyes and blew his nose. 'I'm sorry,' he said. 'I know you're, you're ... You're Bull, um, what is it, William ... no, Willard Bull.'

'That's right, but I've never seen you in my life,' the man said.

'We had a fight at Jake's Bar, do you remember?'

'Was that you who laid me out in that china shop?'

'Afraid so.'

'Don't give it a second thought. I more'n likely started it for nothin' anyway. Well, I'll be off then,' he said, patting Chris on the head.

'How about a job? I need a good man real bad.'

The man stopped in his tracks.

'Doin' what?'

'I have a ranch and I know nothin' about ranchin', doin' whatever people who work on ranches do.'

'Answering to who?'

'To no one. You'd be your own man.'

Brad brought the jeep to a stop at the back of the house.

'Hold the kid will you, Willard?' he said, handing Chris

to him. 'Now comes the worst part, telling my wife what happened.'

Willard cringed his face a dozen times as he listened to Amanda shred Brad to pieces with her tongue. She kicked open the mosquito prevention door. Standing before Willard she said, 'I can never thank you enough for what you did. Our home is your home for as long as you like.'

She hugged the giant. God, he stank to high heaven. She thanked him again and went into the house.

'Would you like to pick a bedroom?'

He shook his head. 'That a bunkhouse over there?'

'Yeah.'

'OK if I sleep there?'

'It's all yours. Like the lady said, as long as you like.'

Willard strolled towards the bunkhouse as the sun began to set. Looking back, he said, 'By the way, call me Will, just Will. OK?'

'You got it,' Brad answered.

The next morning, Amanda woke Brad. She was standing at the side of the bed with his breakfast on a tray. Tears rolled down her cheeks.

'I'm sorry for acting the way I did yesterday evening. I'm so ashamed.'

He put the tray on the bedside locker. They cried in each other's arms for some minutes, not speaking. He kissed her wet face.

'He's run away from me like that a dozen times, but I always caught him before he could get out of sight. I didn't give a second thought to how you must have felt. Your insides must have been coming apart. My darling, I love you so much.'

'I know that, my love,' he said, holding her head against his shoulder. 'Thank God for Willard Bull. He risked his life to save Chris. He could have all my wealth. All he'd have to do is ask me,' Brad told her.

'He's part of this family now,' Amanda declared.

Willard wasn't much for talking over the next few months. From bits of conversations they had, Brad pieced together that he was an only child. His father was from Ohio, his mother was Mexican. He joined the army at eighteen. While he did his stint in 'Nam, his parents separated. When he came home from 'Nam, his parents had remarried and moved away. He tried to locate them without success.

He then spent months drifting from one town to the next. The work he got on his travels was mostly from small farmers: picking potatoes, cabbages, carrots, cauliflowers, parsnips, turnips and tending their stock. It was long hours and backbreaking work, but it kept him in shape and, more importantly, he had three squares a day and a few dollars in his pocket for booze on Saturday and Sunday nights. His travels finally brought him to Colorado, where he ended up in tourist city. One Sunday night, and quite drunk with only a couple of dollars left in his pocket, a local who had befriended him in the bar and had been chatting with him for some hours realised that this man was a loner. He asked the bartender for some paper and a pen. He sketched out a map to the best of his ability.

'That's the old Baldwin place, 'bout ten miles north of here. The Baldwins are long since dead, but their shack's still there. If nothin' else, it'll give you shelter. That is, if you'd like to settle down round here for a while.'

'Thanks,' Willard said, swallowed his drink, took his rucksack from the counter, walked out through the doors and headed north.

He found the shack with ease. If there was one thing that Willard specialised in, it was map reading. Within three weeks he had built a still. There were plenty of farmers in the surrounding area. Will paid a visit to all of them. All of them told him they'd be mighty pleased to try his 'shine. So from then on, after selling his 'shine once a month, he would come down from the woods with a couple of hundred dollars in his pocket to tourist city to play cards, call on the local hooker and get slouched. The money never lasted more than three days. He was down

172

to his last half bottle of whisky when he and Brad had had their fight. Willard Bull was forty-five years old.

One night in bed Brad said to Amanda, 'I'm sure thankful to God that I didn't have to fight Willard on his first night in town.'

'What would you like to do for our anniversary, darling?' Brad asked Amanda. Amanda was busy cooking the dinner. Brad sat at the kitchen table, Chris was checking out the contents of the kitchen presses.

'I was thinking about that, honey. What do you say I cook us a simple home-cooked dinner?'

Brad looked surprised. 'I thought you might like to spend it in New York, L.A., or Paris.'

'No way. We came out here to get away from the hustle and bustle of New York. Anyway, I've seen all those other places and had my lover along to boot.'

Brad bit down on a pretzel. 'Anyone I know?'

She came and sat on his lap, and whispered intimacies into his ear. 'They remind you of anything?' She returned to the oven.

'Oh yeah, now I remember. I ran into a guy in a bar in Vegas some time ago and he described in exactly the same detail just what you've told me.'

She threw a tea towel at him. They both laughed. 'By the way, Brad, I'm going to cook for Willard as well.'

'What for? I've asked him dozens of times to eat with us. He's always refused politely, of course.'

Amanda removed the apron from round her waist. 'He shan't refuse me,' she said, storming out into the yard.

'Will?' She checked herself just in time. He never liked anyone to call him anything except Will. Willard seemed too girlish to him.

'Will,' she shouted at the top of her lungs, 'where the hell are you?'

'Over here, mam,' he called to her from the corral, where he was filing the hoof of an Arabian stallion which Brad had bought for him.

She stormed over in his direction. As she approached, he removed his white Stetson. He fidgeted with his hat like a child waiting to be scolded for something he'd done wrong.

'You like working round this ranch, Will?'

'Why, sure, Mam.'

'You got any complaints?'

'Why, no, Mam.'

'Brad and I treat you OK?'

'Course, Mam.'

'Everything satisfactory to you then.'

'Ye, ye, yes Mam.' He sensed there was a sting in her words, and thought there was a whippin' comin' his way.

'Well, damn it, everything isn't to my satisfaction round here.'

'I do somethin' wrong, Mizz?'

'Shut up and listen.'

He bowed his head.

'Every day since you got here, my husband asked you to dine with us at the house.'

'Well, Mam, it's just.'

'I told you to shut it. Four days from now is our fifth anniversary. We'll be dining at home. I'll be cooking for four. One of the names on a plate is yours.'

She continued to talk with him for some minutes. When she came back into the kitchen, 'Well, is he going to dine with us or not?' Brad asked.

'Dunno,' she replied.

There was a knock on the door.

'I'll get it,' Amanda said as she put the final touches to the dining room table. She opened the door. 'Yes?' The man was silent. 'Can I help you?'

The man hung his head. Frightened, she banged the door shut in his face.

She ran to the bottom of the stairs.

'Brad, Brad!' she shouted. He was dressing in their

bedroom. Sensing the urgency in her voice, he came running down the stairs.

'What's the matter, hon, Chris all right?'

'Yes, yes, it's, it's,' she was pointing, 'there's a stranger at the back door. Asked him what he wanted, he just stood there.'

Brad ran through the dining room, through the lounge, out into the kitchen. He kicked open the back door.

Amanda lifted Chris out of his playpen and ran into the dining room. She was in there for five minutes and there wasn't a sound. She was about to investigate when Brad walked into the room, the stranger behind him.

'Darling,' he said, grinning from ear to ear, 'that was an awful way to greet our honoured guest.'

'Honoured?' She was studying the man in better light now. 'Can't be,' she said.

'Afraid so, honey. It's none other than Will Bull.'

Amanda couldn't apologise enough to Will. He just shrugged his massive shoulders. 'Nothin' to apologise for, Mam.'

Will had asked Brad that afternoon if he could borrow the jeep. He drove until he found a barber shop. He asked for the full treatment and got it. Gone was the massive beard and moustache, his hair stood only an inch high on his head, combed back 'fifties style. Even his locks reached only half an inch below the top of his ears. He had also purchased a grey pair of trousers, white shirt and cowboy-style black tie. He also bought a black pair of shoes, which Brad knew very well were killing him to wear.

'For what we are about to receive let us be truly grateful, Amen.'

'Amen.'

CHAPTER TWENTY-TWO

Will helped the chauffeur load Brad's suitcases into the boot of the limousine. Amanda came out onto the veranda, Chris in her arms. After spending some minutes talking to Amanda and Chris, Brad kissed them both. He stood before Will.

'Well, Will, look's like I gotta go to work again,' offering his hand to Will, 'I'll see you in three months' time.'

As Will shook his hand, he said, 'Don't you go worryin' 'bout nothin'. I'll make sure no harm comes to Mizz Conroy or the little one.'

Brad embraced him. 'If there's one person on God's earth I can count on, it's you, Will Bull.'

As the limousine rounded the house, Amanda reached into the pocket of her apron and took out a bunch of tissues. Will walked up the steps, placing his huge arm around them both. 'Three months is nothin', Mizz Conroy, back in no time.'

*   *   *

Over the next couple of months the ranch began to look like a ranch. The hundred head of steers and the two hundred sheep Brad had bought were grazing on separate pastures. After Brad had left, Will got busy building a chicken coop and a separate one for the geese.

Will would call at the house every morning saying, 'Come on, little one.' Lifting Chris onto his shoulders,

176

they would go in search of fresh eggs. Those early morning trips became the highlight of Chris's day.

Will was in the barn, storing hay, when Amanda came in.

'Will?'

'Yes, Mam?'

'You're killing yourself with all the work you do around here. I don't think that's what Brad had in mind when he invited you here'

'Don't bother me none, Mam. Like I told you afore, I sure like it here.'

'We love having you here too, Will. But just the same, you go to town tomorrow and find a couple of men to help you round here, even it's only to ride the range keeping an eye on the herd and sheep.'

As she walked out of the barn, she turned around. 'That's an order, Will. You hearing me?'

'Loud and clear, Mam.'

As she walked back to the house, her thoughts went back to the night of her anniversary. In bed that night Brad asked, 'What did you say to that poor man that made him come and eat with us?'

'Simple women's intuition. I told him if he didn't come and eat with us, from then or any time I hollered for him I'd call him Willard.'

Will was right about the three months. They flew. Between Chris, keeping her house spick and span, and helping round the ranch which she loved most – Will having more patience with her than God – Amanda was learning more and more about running the ranch every day. Chris wouldn't allow anyone else to fed the chickens and geese, that part of the ranch being his personal domain. Will would load the pick-up with bales of hay and take Amanda and Chris to help him feed it to the steers.

On one such occasion, he tried with some difficulty to apologise for coming on to her in Jake's Bar back in

Tourist Town all those months ago. Amanda put him at ease by saying, 'Why, Will Bull, I'd have been terribly disappointed if you hadn't. After all, they tell me I'm quite pretty.

Will simply said, 'Thank you, Mam.' She knew he had unloaded a huge burden that had been with him from the first day since his arrival at the ranch.

It was ten o'clock in the evening, and Amanda looked in on Chris. He lay fast asleep. Down in the kitchen she made a pot of coffee. She poured herself a mug, placing it on the table. She went about closing the curtains.

'Will and his fire,' she said, shaking her head. Since his first night at the ranch, Will always lit a fire about six feet from the bunk house every night. Then he'd sit with his back to the bunk house, sometimes until two a.m.

Hearing her before he saw her, he was on his feet as she came into view.

'Use some company?'

'Don't mind, Mam,'

She handed him a mug of black coffee, no sugar, the way he liked it. Will brought a stool from the bunk house.

Sitting on it she said, 'Thank you, Will. Kinda chilly tonight, Will.'

'Sure is, Mam. They'll be snow in them mountains by the end of the month. The little one asleep?' he added.

She nodded. She decided to take the Bull literally by the horns.

'You're a strange man, Will Bull.'

'How's 'at, Mam?'

'You're up and at work by six a.m., you hardly ever finish until well after dark. You know Brad and I don't want you working so hard.'

'I like work, Mam, helps keep the mind occupied.'

So, she said to herself, Will Bull is trying to forget someone. She pressed further.

'Tell me, Will Bull, you ever fall in love?'

178

She could see the question took him completely by surprise. He shifted restlessly. Realising she must have hurt him she stood up, pulling her three-quarter length sheepskin coat around her.

She said 'If you never forgive me, Will Bull, for asking such a personal question, I won't hold it against you. Goodnight.'

She had taken a few paces. 'Mizz Conroy.'

Turning to him, 'Yes, Will.'

He indicated the stool, and finished his coffee.

'Jo was her name, Jo Peters ... Little Jo,' he whispered, as she stared at the flames of the burning wood. 'She was no more'n five-two. I met her in Oklahoma City, leaving a shopping mall. We crashed into each other in the car park. I had a beat-up old pick-up, she had a beat-up Volkswagen. If we sold both of them there and then, we'd have been lucky to get forty dollars. We had a heck of a row, lasted an hour. After an hour, both out of breath, I said, "You like a drink?" She said "Yes." It went on from there. She sold her Volkswagen, I had a tent in my pick-up and we drifted all over the place – Little Rock, Arkansas, Fort Worth, Austin, San Angelo. We tied the knot in El Paso. After we got hitched I got a job in Phoenix. We rented a small house 'bout five miles from the city. For more'n a year we were blissfully happy.'

There he paused for almost five minutes.

'It was a Friday. I drove home at lunch time as usual with my wages. We kinda fooled around – you know.'

She nodded.

'For half an hour. She drove me back to work, said she'd collect me after work.'

A blind man could have read the pain in his face now.

'She drove to the mall to buy groceries. As she left the mall there was an armoured truck being held up. She was caught in the crossfire. Her tiny body stopped three blasts from two twelve-bore pump action shotguns.'

The piece of wood he toyed with snapped. Amanda knelt beside him and placed his head on her shoulder.

179

'I'm so sorry, Will.'

'She was three months pregnant,' he whispered.

It was fifteen minutes before he said, 'I'm all right now Mizz Conroy.'

They sat in silence, staring at the fire for another ten minutes. Then he said with a smile, 'Now it's your turn.'

'My turn?'

'Yeah,' he said, 'tell me how you and the boss got together.'

When she finished telling him, 'A fairy tale,' he told her. As she walked back to the house she said to herself, 'Now I understand why he's so fond of Chris.'

*   *   *

'Is there anyone in the house, anyone at all, at all?' came over the intercom system in Amanda's kitchen. It was the voice of Brad, fooling in his Irish brogue. With Chris in her arms she ran out back, down the steps of the veranda.

'Will, Will! Brad's back!'

Brad drove around the back of the house. He jumped out and began kissing Amanda and Chris all over their faces. Chris kept wiping his cheeks, 'Yuk, Daddy.'

Handing Chris to Will, Brad began to kiss Amanda passionately. After some minutes Will cleared his throat.

'My stallion's watchin', Boss. Might just give him ideas.'

They all laughed.

'Give me a couple of minutes, hon, I want to show Will something.' Brad opened the door into the brand new camper he had arrived in.

'It's magnificent, Boss. Colour TV, bar, fridge, cooker, phone – and look at the wood panelling, entirely double glazed, too.'

'And as you can see, sleeps two comfortably. Plenty of luggage space,' Brad said. 'You like it, Will?'

'Like I said, Boss. Magnificent.'

'Glad you do, Will, 'cos it's yours,' Brad said, throwing him the keys. 'Paperwork's in the glove compartment; see you later.' He closed the door, leaving Will alone.

Twenty minutes passed. Brad was telling Amanda about the tour, with Chris sitting on his lap. There was a knock on the door.

'Come,' Amanda called.

Will walked in, hat in hand. ''Scuse, folks.'

'Will Bull, how many times have I asked – no, *pleaded* with you – not to knock on the door, to just come right in?'

'Will you leave the poor man alone,' Brad intervened.

Will bent down. 'Little one, would you prefer to listen to Mammy and Daddy talking or would you like to come look at the chickens?'

Leaping from his father's arms, 'Chickens, chickens, chickens!' Chris shouted.

Will reached the chicken coop. 'Up on your shoulders,' Chris demanded. As he swung Chris up, Will caught a glimpse of Brad drawing their bedroom curtains.

'I've another idea. Why don't we take a ride on my horse, King, and go check on those other two fellas? Make sure they're mindin' the sheep and steers.'

'Yes, Will. Yes, Will.'

When Brad's luggage arrived next day, Chris's eyes lit up as Brad showed him an exact replica, three feet long, of *HMS Bounty*. The model was a labour of love, the attention to detail the work of a master craftsman. Its sails were of canvas, tiny figures beside its cannons.

'That guy there, that's Captain Bligh.'

'Who's Captain Bligh?' Chris enquired.

Brad told the story as best he could remember. Finishing the story, he said, 'He was an all round bad guy.'

'Can I sail it please, Daddy?'

'Maybe in a couple of years' time, son,' Brad said. 'But right now I'm going to ask Will to make a couple of brackets and hang it in my den. But I have another surprise for you.' Reaching into the trunk, he pulled out a pair of the latest craze in slippers.

'They look massive, son, but they're quite comfortable. Take off your shoes.' Brad fitted the *Kermit the Frog* slippers on Chris' feet.

'How do they feel?'

'I love 'em, Daddy.'

Chris wouldn't take off the slippers for the rest of the day.

Will didn't return with Chris until it began to grow dark. Chris ran into the kitchen, Will trailing behind him.

'Mammy, Daddy, I've been minding the sheep and cattle. Will was showing me how to rope a calf, it was great.'

Brad looked at Will and mimed 'thank you'. Will nodded.

'Sit yourself, Will. We're about to have dinner,' Amanda said.

'I ain't cleaned or nothin', Mam.'

'You're fine just as you are,' she said, indicating a chair.

After dinner, Brad asked Will into the den. Will, too, had admired *HMS Bounty*.

'It sure is a work of art, that's for sure, Boss.' The phone rang.

'Excuse me, Will.'

When Brad finished his conversation on the phone, ''Bout here all right, Boss?' Will asked. Brad swivelled on his huge black leather chair, and used his feet to pull himself on the chair's wheels along the varnished oak floor. Will was holding the ship about five feet high against the wall.

'Perfect, Will.'

'I'll carve the brackets in the morning, have it in place before lunch tomorrow.' He was about to thank Brad for his gift.

'Time you got your head down.'

Over dinner the following evening, Brad announced

182

the next tour 'will be my last'. Amanda looked at him in amazement, then she looked at Will. Chris was only interested in his ice cream.

'My husband comes home yesterday afternoon and waits till now to tell me this.'

Brad put his hand on hers. 'You didn't give me a chance till now, remember?' he said, winking at her. She began to blush.

Brad turned to Will. 'Will, you collected Chris at nine this morning, right?'

'Right, Boss.'

'Didn't bring him back home till near six, that right?'

'That's right, Boss.'

Brad opened his arms. 'I rest my case.'

By now Amanda's face was bright red, almost as bright as the red dress she wore, which Brad had bought her while on tour. Smiling, Amanda said, 'Will you excuse me, Will?'

He stood up. 'Sure thing, Mam.'

When she was clear of the room, Brad and Will burst out laughing. Amanda was also fighting back her laughter as she heard them all the way back in the lounge.

CHAPTER TWENTY-THREE

Brad was on the phone to Joe Quinn in London. October was drawing to a close. When he finished his conversation, he walked out on to the veranda. One of the hands brought his galloping horse to a halt outside the barn, where Will was busy storing hay. Brad leaned against one of the veranda's uprights, humming one of his own songs. Will came storming out of the barn, his saddle draped across his shoulder. He walked to the corral. Brad didn't pay much attention until Will came out of the bunkhouse carrying his Winchester. Brad walked quickly to the corral.

'Hey, Will, what's with the rifle?'

Will removed his Stetson. ''Fraid we lost some sheep last night, Boss.'

'Oh? How many?'

'Twenty-five dead.'

'How?'

'Has all the signs of a cougar, Boss.'

'Were you thinking 'bout going after that cat alone?'

'Yes, sir.'

'Wrong. They are my sheep, my responsibility.'

'But, Boss...'

'There's no buts, Will. You hold up for me now, ya hear?'

Will cursed under his breath. He climbed down from his mount and went back into the bunk house. When he came back out he was carrying his saddle bag and a blanket.

Amanda tried to dissuade Brad from going after the cat. She made sure he wore a pair of long johns, a thick cotton shirt and a heavy woollen sweater. He held his three-quarter length sheepskin fur-lined coat.

'Honey, I'll pass out before I reach my horse,' he laughed. He picked up Chris, kissing him on both cheeks. 'You take care of Momma while Daddy's away, OK son?

'Yes, Daddy, I'll mind Mommy.'

As Brad kissed Amanda, he squeezed her buttocks.

'Keep it warm for me, hon,' he whispered.

'It's been on fire since we first met, you know that,' she whispered back.

'Love you both.'

As Brad walked to the corral, Will was putting the finishing touches to saddling Brad's horse.

'We ready then?'

'Yes, Boss.'

'What's this?' Brad asked.

'Just a precaution, Boss.'

Brad removed the knife from its scabbard. 'Jeez, it's almost as long as a sword.'

'It's called an Arkansas toothpick, Boss.' Will handed Brad a chunk of chopped firewood. 'Try it, Boss.'

'Brad held the wood with his left hand and brought the knife down hard on it. The wood split into two pieces.

'God, that's what I call sharp!'

'Put it on and let's be on our way,' Will suggested.

Brad began to unbutton his coat.

'Outside, Boss. It's not goin' to be much use if you need it in a hurry.'

'Of course. You're the boss,' Brad replied, placing the belt round his waist and buckling it.

Three hours later they were about a thousand feet from the mountains.

'Will you look at that?' Will said.

'What?' Brad asked. A strong wind was blowing in their faces.

'There.' Will pointed atop the boulders, quarter way up the mountain.

'I see him,' Brad said. The cat was sitting in an upright position. 'He's sitting there as if he owns the world.'

'Out here, Boss, he does,' Will said as he dismounted. 'I need your shoulder, Boss.'

Brad dismounted. 'You'll never hit him at this range.'

'Worth a try anyway, Boss.' Will adjusted his sight. Licking his thumb, he ran it over the sight at the end of the barrel. Pressing the butt tightly to his shoulder, 'Stay right where you are for another thirty seconds, baby,' he whispered. With the sight pointed at the cat's throat he gently squeezed the trigger. The explosion shattered the tranquil peace of the prairie.

'You hit it?' Brad asked anxiously.

'Negative. The bastard moved as I squeezed the trigger.' Both men remounted.

'Best find a place to bunk down for the night. It'll be dark less 'n an hour.'

'You're the boss,' Brad replied, 'lead the way.'

As the last embers of light began to fade Will pointed to two huge boulders. 'Won't find a better place 'n this.'

The two boulders were about fifteen feet high. They supported a huge flat granite slab.

'You take care of the horses, Boss, I'll get a fire started.' Brad returned with both saddles one on top of the other. He let them fall to the ground.

'Horses secured?'

'Yes.'

'You leave 'em where they can get at grass?'

'I did. Done this sort of thing before,' Brad replied. There was ice in his voice.

Remembering Amanda's story of how they met, Will said, 'Sorry, Boss. I'll go get the blankets and saddle bags.' When Will returned, he asked Brad for the 'toothpick'

186

then went and cut some tree branches. He made several such trips. 'That should do for the night.' He reached into his saddle bag and took out a sharpening stone. Lovingly he began to sharpen the knife.

Half an hour later he said to Brad, 'Salmon or stew?'

'Stew.'

Reaching into his boot, he took out a double edged serrated knife. Expertly he opened two cans of stew. 'Get that into you,' he said, handing one to Brad. Will took two forks from his saddle bag. He tossed one to Brad.

'You think of everything, don't you?'

'Habit,' Will replied.

Some hours later, Brad sat bolt upright from his uneven slumber. Will was smiling.

'You look like you seen a ghost, Boss.'

'What the hell was that?' Brad asked.

'That roar came from our quarry. He's letting us know that he knows we're on his path.'

Will indicated the fire. Brad removed the knife from its scabbard and sunk it into the earth a few inches from his head. Will smiled and replaced his Stetson over his eyes.

At daybreak, Will opened two tins of salmon. After they ate, they began to ascend the mountain. After four hours Brad said, 'It's useless. It's like looking for a refund from the tax people. Plain useless.' Will remained silent. They rode on for another hour. Will dismounted.

'What you looking at?' Brad asked.

'The bark of this tree's damp.'

'So?'

'It's urine, his urine. That's how they mark their territory. Other cats get the message and vamoose.'

'Or piss off,' Brad said.

As he remounted, Will said, 'Better keep our eyes peeled from here on. That bastard could appear at any time.'

Will carried his rifle across his saddle. He advised Brad

to do likewise. They approached a canyon. Will's horse became restless. He patted the horse's neck. 'Easy boy, easy.' Will, who was leading the way, hardly had the words out of his mouth when from behind some rocks the cat dived at him. The powerful cat knocked Will clear out of his saddle and, as he fell to the ground, his rifle went flying into some bushes. As the cat pounced Brad's horse reared, sending Brad flying backwards hard on to the ground. Brad was on his feet in seconds, rifle in hand. As Will struggled with the cat, Brad realised that in this situation the rifle was useless. He could quite as easily hit Will as the cat. Will's powerful arms kept the cat's fangs at bay. But the cat's front paws played havoc with Wills shoulders and chest.

Brad removed the toothpick. He waited until Will rolled over so that the cat was on top of him. Placing his left arm round the cat's neck, he plunged the knife deep into its throat and pressed down hard. Brad felt the fight go out of the cat. He let the animal's body fall to the ground, then he sat down on the ground, shaking like a leaf. A few minutes passed.

'You all right?' Will asked, forcing his head from the ground. Brad sat shaking, the animal's blood still dripping from the knife. 'I ask you all right?'

'So, so sorry,' Brad said.

'That was a brave cat.'

'Wha, what do you mean?' Brad asked.

Forcing a smile, Will said, 'Look at all the guts he had.'

'You're amazing,' Brad told him. 'That bastard almost had you for lunch and you make wisecracks.'

'Wait till you see my underpants,' Will said, laughing. 'Now, go get the horses, will ya, Boss? Afore I bleed to death.'

Brad returned with the horses.

'There's a roll of cotton wool in my saddle bag,' Will said. Brad tore the wrapping from it and placed some inside the shirt on Will's injuries, then inside his trousers on his thighs.

He helped Will into the saddle, then had one last look at the cat.

'What's this?' he said in a high pitched voice. 'This is a bullet hole. It seems you hit the bastard after all.'

'The size of him,' Will said, 'he would have been hard to miss.'

The cat was ten feet long. It's weight, Will guessed, was around thirteen stone.

As soon as they got off the mountain, Will advised they ride as fast as possible. He was growing weaker from loss of blood. They rode hard for an hour. After that they had to canter both horses, and Will looked done in.

'You still with me, Will?'

He nodded with difficulty. Half an hour later, Will slid off his horse on to the ground. Brad leapt from his.

'Will, Will!'

He opened his eyes! 'Still with you, Boss.'

Brad grabbed his Winchester and let off half a dozen rounds. If the hands were tending the cattle and sheep, they would surely hear the shots. Brad removed his coat and placed it over Will. Slowly Will pulled it off his body.

'Cold helps stop the bleeding,' he told Brad.

It took the two hands fifteen minutes to respond to the shots. They lifted Will back into the saddle of one of their horses. Brad climbed up behind him and they began to ride.

'I let off half a dozen shots as soon as I heard yours,' one of the hands told Brad.

'Good,' Brad said.

If Amanda was at home, she would have heard them. She'd know what to do.

Amanda had heard the shots. Six was the signal for trouble. She immediately phoned the paramedics, giving them precise directions to the ranch. She strapped Chris in the back seat of the jeep and drove out into the prairie. In her panic she didn't realise she was doing ninety miles an hour. Ten minutes later, Brad and the hands placed Will's now unconscious body on the floor of the jeep.

Leaving Chris with the hands, Amanda drove like the devil.

The paramedics came round the house just as the jeep came out of the prairie. They placed Will into the ambulance.

'Plasma,' one said to the other, as he gave Will an injection.

Brad and Amanda travelled with Will. The driver radioed ahead.

'Prepare surgery, lacerations to the shoulders, chest and thighs. Blood transfusion required, patient extremely weak. Be with you ten minutes, over.'

Will was rushed straight to surgery. Brad and Amanda sat on a settee in the hall. Brad removed his gloves.

'Look at your hands,' Amanda gasped. 'Doctor, doctor would you look at my husband, please?'

Brad had to have three fingers of his left hand stitched. During the struggle, the cat had bitten through Brad's gloved hand. He had not even noticed or felt the pain until he removed his glove.

It was two days before Will opened his eyes. When he did, the first people he saw were Brad and Amanda smiling back at him. Amanda laid a gentle kiss on his cheek.

'Welcome back,' she said.

'How you feeling, my friend? Brad said with a smile.

'A little sore, Boss. How long have I been out?'

'Two days.'

'Any food in this place?'

'I'll see to it immediately,' Amanda said, leaving the room.

'Getting to be a habit.'

'What are you talking about?' Brad asked.

'Saving people's lives.'

'Oh. Amanda been bragging again?'

'I forced it out of her one night while you were on tour.'

'It's my fault you were up that mountain in the first place,' Brad told him.

'Comes with the territory, Boss. All part of the job. What happened to your hand?'

'Few scratches, courtesy of the cat.'

'How long do I have to stay here?'

'Doctor says at least two weeks.'

Amanda came into the room and held the door open for a nurse with a tray. The nurse was about thirty-five years old, with flaming red hair. She placed the tray on the locker.

'I'll feed him,' Amanda said.

'You attached?' Will asked. The nurse shook her head. 'You guys have other things to do. Let the pretty nurse feed me,' Will winked at Brad.

'You're the boss,' Brad said.

'You're getting better by the minute,' Amanda added. 'See you later.'

Looking at the nurse, Will said, 'Knock before you come in.'

Amanda and Brad drove Will home from the hospital two weeks later, with strict instructions that Will was not to do any sort of work for at least four weeks.

'I'll see to that,' Amanda assured the doctor. She had also prepared a room at the house for him. They spent Thanksgiving together. Amanda cooked a goose served with roast potatoes, creamed carrots (Brad's favourite), broccoli and peas. For dessert they had apple tart with custard.

'I think I'm putting on weight,' Will announced.

'Me too,' Brad said. Four weeks later the four of them sat around the same table, about to sample Amanda's turkey. It was Christmas Day.

By February Brad had gained twenty pounds and was ordered by Amanda to return to *Slim with Jim* to lose it again.

'I don't want the fans to see that pot belly, especially since it's your last tour.'

The tour was due to begin in July: three months touring Europe, then back to the States for another two and a half months.

After two weeks at the gym, Brad had lost eight pounds. He was walking through the hall.

'Hi.' He turned round. 'You're Brad Conroy, aren't you?'

'Guilty,' he replied.

Extending her hand, 'I'm Tanya Evans.'

'My pleasure I'm sure,' Brad said.

'I've got your CDs.'

'Thank you,' Brad said.

'Getting in shape before your tour?'

'Yes,' he said, patting his stomach, 'too much easy living I'm afraid. What's your reason for being here?' he enquired. 'You look in excellent shape.'

'Thank you. I'm a body perfect freak, I'm afraid.'

'What line of work are you in?' he added.

'Oh, I'm out of work at the moment. Last year I came fourth in the Miss Colorado contest,' she told him.

'Ah, the judges must have been blind,' he told her. 'It's been lovely meeting you,' he said, extending his hand.

'Likewise,' she said.

As he drove out of the car park, he spotted her waiting at a bus stop. 'Which way you headed?' he enquired.

Pointing, she said, ' 'Bout ten miles.'

'Don't you have wheels of your own?'

' 'Fraid not; have to use the bus both ways.'

'I'm going that way. Hop in.' As they drove, she told Brad that she was an only child. Her father had passed away two years ago, and she lived with her mother. Brad waved to her as he pulled away.

'See you next Tuesday,' she shouted. Brad went to the club Tuesdays and Thursdays.

For the next three weeks Brad picked up and dropped off the beautiful Tanya. More than once she made suggestive remarks which he pretended not to understand. The following Tuesday Brad picked Tanya up as usual. As he drove to the gym, 'She means business today,' he told himself. Tanya wore very short yellow ski pants, and the matching sweater had the lowest neckline he had ever laid eyes on. As they drove, she brushed her thigh against his half a dozen times.

When Brad came out of the gym, Tanya was waiting for him, leaning against the car. She turned a as he approached, placing her sports bag on the back seat of his car. Taking her time placing her bag in the back, her aspirations were quite obvious. For the whole ten-mile journey her conversation revolved round sex.

'Hold old are you?' Brad asked.

'Twenty.'

'Twenty. Then you must have a world of experience of men.'

'I've had my share, Brad.'

'Here we are,' he said pulling up outside her house. She leaned at his side of the car. He was staring at her bare breasts, as she wasn't wearing a bra today. He could see all the way to her belly button.

In her sexiest voice she said 'I know a more pleasurable way we can lose weight. My old lady ain't home.'

Smiling, he said, 'Thanks very much, but no thanks. Trouble is mine *is* home, and that's where I'm headed right this minute.' He drove a few yards, then called to her. A smile flashed across her face.

'From now on, Tanya, take the bus. There's a good girl.'

She kicked the car. She could hear his laughter as he sped away.

'You're too bloody old anyway,' she screamed after him.

Will convinced Amanda that she and Brad should spend the night in Denver. It was their fifth anniversary and Brad had booked a table for them at the Denver Springs Hotel. They would fly from Pueblo to Denver. There was a return flight at midnight which Amanda wanted to come back on. But after Will, who was doing the baby-sitting, finished chatting with her she agreed to stay overnight. Brad packed his tuxedo, shirt and shoes into his suitcase. He threw socks and underwear into a holdall. Amanda sat before her dressing table. All she was wearing was her pantyhose. Brad came up behind her and ran his tongue along the nape of her neck.

You taste so delicious, my darling.' He cupped her breasts in each hand.

'I love the ground you walk on,' she told him. 'I adore...' She noticed his expression change in the mirror. 'What's the matter, darling?' He let go of her breasts as if they were diseased.

She examined them. 'Oh God! Oh my Lord!' she gasped. There was a lump under her left breast.

CHAPTER TWENTY-FOUR

Amanda insisted on going ahead with their planned anniversary celebration. From the moment the plane touched down at Denver International until it took off again the following afternoon, no matter what she did to ease Brad's fears, nothing – not as much as a smile – did she get from him, such was his concern for her.

As soon as they arrived at the ranch, Brad went immediately to his den. Flicking through his phone number index, he dialled Dr Troy's secretary.

'How may I help you?'

'This is Brad Conroy here. Could I speak with the doctor immediately, please?' She put him through straight away. Brad explained the situation to him.

'My advice to you, Brad, is to take Amanda to see Doctor Sands as soon as possible. He's got a clinic out on Long Island, New York. I'll phone ahead from my office, put him in the picture. He'll have a room prepared for her.'

'Thank you, doctor. We'll be on the first available flight out of Pueblo.'

Brad phoned the airport at Pueblo. The desk girl told him that there was a flight to Georgia in three hours. An hour later there was a flight to Kennedy International. Brad booked Will and Chris on the Georgia flight and Amanda and himself on the New York flight.

Brad conveyed the flight information to Amanda.

'I'll start packing his things.' Brad held her in his arms.

'Sweetheart, just a few toys for the flight. Your parents can buy him anything he needs in Montgomery.' He looked down at her. 'OK?' She nodded.

She went into Chris's playroom, where he was on the floor with an assortment of aeroplanes surrounding him. She bent down, arms outstretched. 'Darling, how would you like to visit Grandma and Grandpa?' Running into her arms, 'Yes, Mammy, yes please.' She sat on the floor and sat him in front of her.

'Darling, would you be brave enough to make this trip with Will?'

'Why,Mammy? Why not with you and Daddy?'

'Daddy and I have to fly to New York. You know how Daddy's got to fly away every so often with his band?' He nodded. 'Well, this time they need me along.'

'Why, Mammy?'

She was trying to think hard. 'Because ... because ... well, because Daddy says he won't make this trip without me. He wants me along for luck. Did you ever hear of anything so silly? Now give Mammy a hug.'

He held onto her as if for life itself. She lost the battle to fight back the tears.

'You're crying, Mammy. Why are you crying?'

Wiping away the tears with her fingers, 'You know I don't like being parted from you for any length of time, darling. Anyway,' she said, getting to her feet, lifting him up in her arms, 'as soon as Daddy's finished his business, we'll be flying straight down Grandma's and Grandpa's to pick you up.'

Brad came in with a small holdall.

'Put some of your toys in this, son. You can play with them on the plane and show them to Grandpa when he and Grandma pick you up at the airport. Will's ready,' he said to Amanda.

She buttoned Chris' tiny furlined overcoat and placed a ski cap on his head. Brad held him in his arms.

'You do me a big favour, son?'

'Yes, Daddy.'

'I want you to take care of Will on the plane. He's scared of flying.'

'Big Will?' Chris said, wide eyed.

Brad put a finger to his lips. 'Don't tell anyone I said so, OK?'

Chris copied his father's actions and shook his head. He kissed him on the cheeks and forehead. Amanda held him for another five minutes. They both stood on the veranda and watched as Will criss-crossed the safety belts around Chris. Touching his Stetson, 'Don't you worry none, Mam. I'll take good care of him. Good luck in New York, Mam.'

He climbed into the jeep. Once again Amanda's tears began to flow.

It was eight p.m. when the limousine cruised through the gates of the secluded clinic. Brad climbed out and took Amanda's hand as she got out. A porter opened the door as they approached. As they reached the reception area, a nurse came towards them.

'Mr and Mrs Conroy?'

'Yes,' Brad said.

She showed them into an office.

'Doctor Sands will join you presently,' she said. She closed the door behind her. Amanda locked her fingers with Brad's.

'No need to be nervous, honey. This could be a false alarm, congealed blood or something.'

'You're not nervous, darling?' she asked.

'Of course not,' he lied. 'We'll be out of here in no time.'

'My darling husband, since the day we met you never lied to me,' she said to herself, 'but you are lying now. She couldn't help noticing the collar of Brad's blue shirt; it was soaking with sweat.

The door behind them opened and in came a man of about Brad's age and height, his one-time black hair now almost grey.

197

'Robert Sands,' he said, with an outstretched hand. Brad stood up, accepting it.

'Brad Conroy and my wife, Amanda.'

After a five minute relaxing chat, the doctor suggested a preliminary check. He opened the door to an inner office.

'If you'll come through, Mrs Conroy. This'll take no more than fifteen minutes,' he said to Brad.

Amanda handed Brad her scarf and coat. It was the longest fifteen minutes of Brad's life. He spent the time pacing up and down the room, wiping perspiration from his face several times. At last the door opened. Amanda sat beside Brad, the doctor sat before them.

'From my experience, I'm afraid it is cancer.'

Amanda gave no indication of fear. Brad wiped his face with his hands.

'Now,' said the doctor, 'let's not be thinking the worst here. It could be in the very early stages, and if so can be operated on immediately.'

He tried to assure them by telling them that he carried out such operations every day, and ninety-nine per cent of such operations were successful. 'But I would like to suggest that Mrs Conroy return in the morning, say ten o'clock, and we'll put her through every test for cancer known to man. Those tests take about three days to complete and, I'm sorry to say, no visitors during those three days.' Brad was about to speak. 'No, Mr Conroy, not even the husbands. I'll look forward to seeing Mrs Conroy in the morning.'

Brad stood up. 'How about phoning, doctor? May I have permission at least to phone my wife?'

The aggression in Brad's voice didn't go unnoticed. 'Absolutely not, Mr Conroy. For three days your wife will be going through the most stringent of tests, after which she will need rest; total rest. Now, if you will excuse me, I have patients to attend to. Good evening.' He walked out of the office.

'He's a bit of a pri...'

Amanda put a finger to his lips. 'He's probably got more on his plate than we can ever imagine.'

Brad helped her into her coat. 'Let's be off to our suite, enjoy a nice Chinese meal and watch TV together,' she suggested.

After driving to the clinic next morning, Brad stayed with Amanda in her private room until he was asked to leave an hour later. When he returned to his suite he phoned Amanda's parents and filled them in on the situation. He spent the next half hour chatting with Chris. Then he rang Cindy. Cindy began to sob.

'Now there's no need to cry, Cindy. She's only having tests, it could all be a storm in a teacup.'

He then rang his oldest brother and asked him to let his other brothers know. If he didn't know better he was sure his brother, who to Brad was as tough as nails, sniffed several times during their half hour conversation. Next on his list was Joe Quinn. He was in London. He sounded as shocked as Brad's brother and wanted to fly to New York immediately. Brad persuaded him otherwise.

'I'll ring you as soon as we know the results of the tests,' he told Joe.

For the next three days Brad never left his suite. He killed time phoning friends in Hollywood. Many were on location in San Francisco, Houston, San Antonio, Rome, Athens, Paris. He spent hours chatting with each one, never mentioning that Amanda was in the clinic. When they asked after her, he would tell them that she had gone shopping. Finally he phoned Will. When eventually Brad got an answer, 'Where in God's name were you?'

'Workin', Boss.'

'I've been tryin to get you for hours.'

Brad put Will in the picture. As soon as he did, Will seemed to run out of conversation. Finally Brad said, 'See you soon, friend,' and hung up.

At last the third day dawned. Brad shaved and showered. He unwrapped a brand new white shirt, and chose a grey pin-striped double breasted suit after trying to match a necktie from some three dozen. He decided on a wine-coloured bow tie. After brushing his hair, he splashed Old Spice on to the palms of his hands then rubbed them hard against his cheeks.

'She'll be crazy about you,' he said, looking into the mirror. He picked up the phone.

'Brad Conroy. Would you please have my limo brought round to the front right away?'

Brad was shown to Doctor Sands' office. They shook hands, greeting each other at the same time. The doctor toyed with some paperwork for some five minutes before he spoke. When he did, Brad Conroy was devastated. Amanda not only had breast cancer, which was spreading at an alarming rate, but she also had cancer of the pancreas. Cancer of the pancreas, he told Brad, was inoperable. Half a dozen times Brad asked the doctor if there was any chance there could be a mistake.

'I carried out three individual tests. There's no mistake. I'm terribly, terribly sorry, Mr Conroy.'

It took Brad almost half an hour to regain control of himself.

'She's only twenty-seven years old, doctor.'

'I know,' the doctor replied.

'But why, doctor? Why do such things happen?'

The doctor didn't have an answer. Brad stood up and began to pace the floor.

'This can't be happening to me. I must be having a nightmare, please let it be a nightmare.'

Finally Brad asked the question the doctor dreaded.

'How long does she have, doctor?'

The long pause made Brad return to his chair. 'How long, doctor?' he asked a second time.

'One week.'

Brad collapsed to the floor. The doctor injected Brad with a sedative. Two hours later he woke up in bed. When the doctor came into the room Brad said, 'Tell me I had a nightmare, doctor.' The doctor remained silent.

200

Brad staggered to the sink and washed his face. Turning to the doctor he asked, 'Would you take me to my wife, please?'

Amanda welcomed Brad with open arms.

'I love you, darling, more than life itself. I adore the ground you walk on.'

'Is it that bad, darling?' She tried to push his head from her shoulders, but he resisted. For a long time she brushed his hair with her hand. She pushed his shoulders back.

'Doctors and nurses are in and out of here all morning, all with faces as long as a wet weekend. Therefore, my husband, I can only come to the conclusion that they have come up with the worst kind of diagnosis – I do have cancer.' He began to cry.

She held him. 'Now, now, now, you know as well as I that everything born on earth was born to die. Everyone's called sooner or later. I'll tell you a secret, my husband. I prayed for years that when my time came, God would give me the strength to face it with dignity. Now I know he has.'

'I hear you, but I can't believe what you are saying,' he told her.

She tried to dry the continuous flow of tears. 'I want you here and now to make me two promises.'

'Of course, darling, anything. Name it.'

'Number one, I want you to live, live for our son, love him and care for him as you did me.'

He nodded. 'I promise, darling.'

'Number two is much easier. From this moment, no more tears.'

'I'll try.'

'No, you'll succeed.' He nodded.

Doctor Sands came in. 'Mr Conroy, could you wait outside please? We could be some time. We've got to take Mrs Conroy to theatre.'

Brad asked for, and was shown to, a tiny office where he could phone the awful news to all concerned. Like

Brad, Amanda's mother collapsed on hearing the news. It was nine p.m. before Doctor Sands allowed Brad back in to see Amanda. When he walked through the door, in a matter of hours the cancer had begun to show its ugly head. She lay asleep. Her beautiful tanned complexion had turned a stone grey. Her hair looked thinner. Her stunning face seemed to have shrunk. He was about to burst into tears, but remembered his promise. An hour later she came round, and spoke in a whisper. They chatted until she fell asleep. Before he left he watched as a nurse administered an injection into her already thinning arm.

As Brad walked up the corridor he heard, 'Mr Conroy.' He turned. It was Doctor Sands.

'Take one of these at night. They'll help you to sleep, especially tonight.' Brad thanked him as he walked away. He stopped.

'Doc?'

'Yes, Mr Conroy?'

'She knows she's got cancer.'

'Yes, she does.'

'But she never asked me how long she had left.'

'I know, Mr Conroy. She spared you that. She asked me instead ... by law I'm duty bound to tell her.'

Brad leaned against the wall, but he kept his promise.

It was one in the afternoon the next day when Brad walked into the clinic. As he approached the private waiting room outside Amanda's room, he was totally surprised to see the room full: Amanda's parents, brothers, Brad's brothers, Joe Quinn, Cindy and Bob Santos. Each in turn cried on his shoulder. Cindy was almost out of control.

'How could anyone change in such a short time?' she cried in Brad's arms.

He apologised to all, telling them he had taken a sleeping pill late into the night. They understood.

'You've all seen her?'

They all nodded. Brad threw his arms around Amanda's parents.

When Brad went in to see Amanda, he hardly recognised her. The change overnight was shattering. Her eyes were sunk deep in her face, half her hair had fallen out, her arms looked like twigs. He gently placed his head on her chest.

'I've been luckier than most. God gave me a marvellous man and a beautiful healthy son, and the few years we had together were better than most who've been together a lifetime and have not loved as much as we have each other.' She began coughing blood.

'Doctor'. He pressed the bell. A nurse came in instantly. 'Leave us, please,' she said. He obeyed.

'I'd like to be alone,' he said, as his brothers made towards him. As he walked down the corridor, he asked a nurse, 'Do you have a chapel?' She pointed the way.

Brad walked into the tiny chapel. He doused his finger into the holy water font and made the sign of the cross. He walked up the aisle. He pushed open the brass gates. He knelt on the bottom of the three steps up to the altar.

'Almighty God in heaven, I know I'm the last person on earth to be asking you for favours. For years I've lived outside the Commandments. You know I've used drugs, drink, women. I abused them all. All the time I was making buckets of money, I never once thought of going to Mass and thanking you for my good fortune. I know I'm the bottom of the barrel, the lowest creature on this earth. But I beg of you with all my heart, please. My wife Amanda never harmed a fly, not to mention a human being. Please give her life back. I'm asking you to perform a miracle, please. If you need someone to do your work, I would go gladly in her place. I beg of you, Lord, take this miserable specimen which you see here before you. Please give my wife back her life.'

He began to pray. 'Our Father, Which Art In Heaven . . .'

*   *   *

A pair of eyes and ears watched and listened to Brad's pleas.

An hour later, Brad walked out of the chapel. As he walked back to Amanda's room he was met halfway by Will Bull. Will almost crushed Brad with his embrace. Without saying a word, he shook Brad's hand as they walked to the room together.

The doctor came out of Amanda's room. He placed an arm around Brad. Opening the door he whispered, 'She's fading fast.'

Brad sat on the chair beside the bed. As he picked up her frail hands, her wedding, engagement and eternity rings slid off her finger. She opened her eyes. As she tried to speak, he had to place his ear to her lips.

'I ... love ... you ... more ... than ... life ... itself ... love ... our ... son ... as ... you ... did ... me ...'

He saw the slightest glimmer of a smile on her frail lips. It disappeared as fast, her head tilted, resting on his right palm.

His wailing told the people outside that Amanda Conroy's life had come to an end.

CHAPTER TWENTY-FIVE

'I christened Amanda Gordon Conroy, I gave her her first Holy Communion, I officiated at her confirmation, I married her, and now I am officiating at her burial. As I look around at the congregation gathered here, my heart goes out to Amanda's parents and brothers. You will be always in my prayers. But I would ask each and every one of you to remember Amanda's husband, Brad. Many times, when she came to visit her mother, she often called on me for a chat. And I hope you will forgive me, Brad, for saying this, but she said to me once that God must have bestowed a special blessing on her. In her own words, 'It doesn't seem fair for a woman to be as happily married and in love as much as I am.' Now let us say a decade of the rosary.'

The crowd shook hands one by one as they began to disperse. Eventually he was alone. In his hand were two roses, one red, one black. He placed them on the coffin in the shape of a cross. As he placed them he said, 'I will always love you, be it from a distance.'

As Brad approached the limousine, Cindy caught him by the elbow.

'I heard you that day in the clinic chapel, asking God to perform a miracle. Well', she said, sniffling, 'he didn't, or maybe he wasn't listening.'

Brad placed his arms on her shoulders. 'He's always listening and he always answers. His answer to me was no.'

The limousine was almost out of the graveyard when Brad caught a glimpse of someone he thought he recognised.

'Stop the car.'

He climbed out and started walking. She was kneeling at the graveside, praying alone, white rose in her hands. When she stood up and turned around to leave, Brad's smiling face stared back at her. With his thumbs he wiped away her tears.

'Susan Brown,' he announced, placing his arms around her, 'my mother's saviour. You've travelled all the way from Limerick to pray and place a rose on my wife's coffin, and you tried to do it without anybody noticing you. What a true friend you are.' Slowly he walked her to the car. 'After you,' he said.

The limousine came to a stop outside the entrance to the Frances Hotel. Extending his hand, Brad helped Cindy and Susan out. Cindy and Susan walked into the hotel, followed by Brad and Bob Santos. The hotel manager was waiting in the lobby.

'Mr Conroy, on behalf of my staff and myself I wish to express our deepest sympathy?'

Shaking hands with him, 'You are all very kind. Please tell the staff it's much appreciated.'

The manager showed Brad and his party to the Atlanta Suite, booked by Brad for the one hundred invited guests to the funeral.

'We'll need an extra place,' Brad told him.

'No problem, sir,' the manager said.

As soon as Brad walked through the French doors and into the suite Chris, who was sitting on his grand-mother's knee, came running towards him.

'Daddy, Daddy, Daddy.' Brad picked him up in his arms. 'Where's Mammy, Daddy?'

Brad looked at Mrs Gordon. With tears in her eyes, she shook her head. Since Amanda's demise, Mrs Gordon had told Brad that she would try to explain as best she could to the child.

Brad sat in a corner and took Chris on his lap. 'Remember all those nights when Mammy brought you to bed?'

'Yes, Daddy.'

'Remember the stories she used to tell you?'

'Yes, Daddy.'

'I'll give you a little test then. Who made the world?'

'Holy God, Daddy.'

'And who made all the people?'

'Holy God, Daddy.'

'Now, Mammy told you that Holy God made the world and the people, right?' He nodded. 'Now, did Mammy tell you that sometimes Holy God needs some of the people back in Heaven to help him with his work?'

'Yes, Daddy.'

'Well, son, three days ago Holy God paid Mammy a visit and he told her that he needed her back in Heaven with the other angels to help him with his work.'

'But why didn't he pick someone else's Mammy, Daddy?'

Brad held him tightly to his chest. 'Because son, Holy God just doesn't pick anyone, you know. He only picks very special people to help him with his work and your Mammy was indeed a very special person. Now do you understand?'

Chris nodded, but he didn't understand at all. Susan Brown came to Brad's rescue.

'Hello, Chris.' It took him a time to take to her. She bent down.

'This is a very special person, too,' Brad said. 'Say hello to Susan.'

'What do you say we find some ice cream?' Taking her hand, 'Yes, please, Susan.'

Brad watched Sue and Chris walk through the French doors in search of ice cream. He ran his index finger along the inside of his shirt collar.

'Phew, thank God that's over,' he said in a low voice.

Brad spoke and shook hands with all his guests, thanking them for making the effort to attend; most of his movie star friends had tight schedules and had to travel almost immediately to various locations throughout America. As Brad scanned the room, he smiled as his eyes fixed on Will Bull. He nudged Will in the ribs.

'Hi, Boss.'

Smiling at him, Brad said, 'Do you know what you look like?' Will shrugged his shoulders. Laughing, Brad said, 'You look like a deer at a lions' convention, but,' Brad added, 'you know I appreciate it very much, the trouble you took to pay your last respects to Amanda. I know you'd rather be back on the ranch and how much you hate these gatherings.'

It was the first time Brad had seen Will Bull in a tuxedo. Brad handed Will a piece of paper on which was the address of a bed and breakfast.

'In your own time, Will, go to that address, pay whatever is due and bring the suitcase to the Gordons' house.'

On the way from the graveyard Brad had asked Susan where she was staying, and she told him. She had only booked in that morning and hadn't had time to unpack.

Brad stood before Joe Quinn and his wife. After a brief conversation Brad asked, 'Would you mind very much if I borrowed your husband for a little while?' Brad put his arm around Joe and walked him out into the hall.

As they walked, Brad said, 'Let's sit here.' There was a two-seater settee at the end of the hall. Brad began, 'Joe, my old friend, I'm getting out of the game.' Joe made a gesture of protest. Brad raised a hand.

'No, Joe, it's over. My last tour was my last tour. Cancel the one that is due to begin in July; I'm sure the fans will understand. My heart isn't in it any more. When I buried my wife an hour and a half ago, I also buried part of myself. I don't think I'll ever sing again. When does my contract with Mecca run out?'

'Next March some time, I think.'

'How many albums are due between now and then?' Brad asked.

'Two,' Joe replied.

'I wrote quite a few songs during my last tour; I think I wrote enough for two seven-song albums. I'll be on the phone to Mecca first thing in the morning, then I'll come out to the Gordons' house and put you in the picture. You've been watching me like a hawk, old friend, since Amanda passed away, right?'

Joe hung his head.

Brad placed an arm on Joe's shoulder. 'You have nothing to worry about, old friend, I'm not going back on drugs or booze. I made a promise to Amanda to take good care of Chris, and that's exactly what I'm going to do.'

At eight o'clock the following evening Brad, Will, Susan, and Mr Gordon sat at the dining table of the Gordon's home. Mrs Gordon served dinner. Chris lay fast asleep in his bed. After they had eaten, Brad said, 'Mr Gordon, remember the Christmas Amanda and I spent here with you?'

'Sure, Brad.'

'Remember how much you admired my Christmas gift to Amanda?'

'Of course, Brad.'

'Well now it's yours, and I won't entertain protests of any kind. Anyway, it looks out of place on a ranch.'

With the sincerest of humility Mr Gordon thanked Brad.

Looking at Will, Brad said, 'would you mind flying home in the morning, Will, and fly or drive the machine down here?'

Smiling, Will said, 'I'll drive, Boss.'

'Thought so,' Brad said.

Later, when Brad was alone with Mrs Gordon, he said, 'Apart from Amanda's wedding, engagement and eternity rings, which I placed back on her fingers, I'll send the rest of Amanda's jewellery by courier down to you.' They held each other for a long time.

Susan Brown had arrived in Montgomery with one suitcase, now she was returning with ten. Mrs Gordon had taken her shopping every morning for eight days, fitting her out from head to toe many times over. The watch, earrings, three gold neck-chains, bangle, bracelet and half a dozen rings were all made by Gucci. After checking her luggage through, Brad sat with her at the bar.

'Did you even enjoy yourself?' Brad asked with a smile.

'Yes, Brad, but under the most awful circumstances.' He held her hands.

'She's with God now. If I didn't convince myself of that, I'd go crazy.' Her flight was called, and they kissed and embraced.

'Oh, I almost forgot.' He took a large envelope from his inside pocket. 'Just a letter thanking you for making the effort.'

They waved at each other until she disappeared from view. As Brad drove back to the Gordons' home, he was thinking, 'Poor Sue, she above all made the greatest effort to attend Amanda's funeral.' He was quite sure that she had had to borrow some, if not all, of the money to make the trip to Montgomery. Brad Conroy was very proud to have a friend such as Susan Brown.

Half an hour into her flight, Sue took the letter from her purse. It read, 'My dearest Sue, it is hard for me to put into words how much I appreciate the trouble you went through to attend Amanda's funeral. Mr and Mrs Gordon asked me to send their thanks also. We all love you. You are a rare human being. Tell your parents that they reared a wonderful daughter. Give all my love to all your family.' It was signed 'Brad Conroy'.

As Sue replaced the letter, she realised there was a smaller envelope in the larger one. Opening it, she read, 'P.S. Please accept this gift in the same manner in which it is given.'

Brad had put twenty-five thousand dollars into the smaller envelope. He didn't want his friend returning to Ireland owing anybody money due to her thoughtfulness towards the Conroy family.

210

The next day Brad flew home to the ranch. The Gordons had begged him to leave Chris with them for another month. Remembering how much he needed Amanda after the deaths of his mother and father, he couldn't refuse them. He had been home a week. It was late into the afternoon. He sat on the bed. Standing up, he walked to Amanda's closet. He had tried, but couldn't, for the last week. He slid the doors open in opposite directions. Slowly he walked in. To the left and right hand side of him hung her clothes. Most of her dresses were in black and red. He clasped his hands around a dozen or so. He pressed his face against them. Her fragrance was all over them. He could smell her, he could taste her, but he couldn't touch her. He let out a scream, falling to the floor, pulling half a dozen dresses with him. He lay there weeping for more than an hour.

Will Bull, who was watering the horses, looked towards the open bedroom windows when he heard Brad's screams. Mounting up, he said, 'C'mon, King, let's go check on somethin'.'

Will Bull knew love pains when he heard them. He too had been down the same pain alley which Brad Conroy was now treading.

Since Brad returned to the ranch house he hadn't taken one step outside it. Two days after he walked into Amanda's closet he was out in the yard calling for Will. Will came out of the bunk house.

'Yes, Boss?'

'Got any work round here for me?'

'Plenty, Boss.' Will pointed to a huge pile of wood. 'That needs choppin' and when you get through that lot, give me a shout. There's plenty more for you to do 'round here.'

As Will walked away, he said to himself, 'Welcome back, Boss.'

Three weeks later Brad was feeling fit and healthy. Will had made sure he didn't have too much time to think. He worked Brad from dawn till dusk. Brad sat in the kitchen sipping a cup of coffee, tapping his fingers to the tune on the radio. Will had flown to Montgomery the previous evening to collect Chris. They were due home any time now. The radio announcer averted his thoughts.

'This is Larry Brown at K.L.C. Radio. I have a very special request for Amy Emmers, who is celebrating her Golden Anniversary today. Congratulations Amy, Fifty Years today, and the request comes with love from your husband, Henry. Here now is the song he requested, it's from *My Fair Lady*, Rex Harrison sings *I've Grown Accustomed To Her Face.*'

Brad had heard the song a thousand times, but this time the words pierced his heart. It was as if Lerner and Loewe had written the song especially for Brad and how he felt about Amanda. He felt the flood gates about to burst, when he heard, 'Daddy, Daddy, Daddy.' Chris Conroy was home.

By mid-July Maria Gonzales was part of the Conroy household. Brad hired her as a cook. Her expertise with food knew no bounds. She was of Mexican extraction, and this rather large, plump lady loved children. She would sing all day long as she went about preparing the meals for Brad, Chris and Will, who now ate at the house every day. She was fifty-five years old. She drove her own car. The only condition she asked was to have Tuesdays and Sundays off. No problem, Brad told her, and any time you want time off, you only have to ask.

Brad hired a studio in Pueblo. His band flew over from London. They began working on the two new albums. Brad told Joe Quinn that he wanted them out of the way by Christmas. Brad sat with Joe in the kitchen at the ranch.

'Mecca are asking for you to fly to London on the first of March. They ask, Brad, no *insist*, that you sign off the end of a long and fruitful partnership where it all began, as they say, all those years ago.'

'How long will the trip last?'

'No more than three days. They hope that you'll give a couple of one-hour interviews on TV. If you agree, you fly out on first March, you're home in bed by midnight the third.

'I'll think about it, Joe.'

'That's all I ask,' Joe replied.

'Have you anything lined up after I quit?' Brad enquired.

'Not that I'll ever spend the money I've got already, but you know me, Brad, I love the business, thanks to you. There's a dozen groups just dying to make me their manager,' he laughed.

'How are your family?' Brad asked.

'Thanks to you, old friend, they'll never want for anything.'

They chatted late into the night. At midday next day Joe flew back to London.

Maria insisted on putting up the Christmas decorations herself. When she finished, Brad and Will were amazed at her expertise. She had a real motherly touch, Even the crib which she built herself from the bark of trees must have come close to an exact double of the stable in which Jesus was born.

On December twenty-fourth, Maria baked the cake for Chris's fourth birthday. Will, Maria, and Brad sat around as Chris opened his presents. Maria had bought him a huge truck, together with a trailer and its cargo of real logs. Chris kissed her and thanked her. Will bought him a Superman set of pyjamas; the cloak could be detached before going to bed. Chris kissed and thanked Will.

'My pleasure, little one.'

'Now it's Daddy's turn,' Chris cried out.

'Oh dear,' Brad said, putting his hands over his mouth, 'I forgot all about your birthday.'

'Come on, Daddy, come on. You never forget.' Chris cried, pulling his father's hand.

213

Lifting him up in his arms, 'My present's outside.'

Will went through the door first. As Brad went through he looked back. 'Well, Maria, aren't you curious?'

'Si, senor.'

Will came out of the stable. At the end of the reins he held was the smallest horse that not only Chris had seen, but also the smallest Maria had seen. Placing Chris on its saddle Brad said, 'It's called a Connemara pony, all the way from the Emerald Isle.' Chris was beside himself with happiness.

'Thank you, Daddy, thank you very much.'

Later, when Will and Maria had left, 'Aren't you the luckiest boy in the world?'

'Why, Daddy?'

'Well, today is your birthday, and tomorrow Santa's coming.'

In mid-January, Brad phoned Joe to tell him that he would fly to London to sign the end of his contract with Mecca.

'I owe them that much,' he added.

Joe thanked him, telling him he would meet him on his arrival at Heathrow Airport.

The second week in February, Maria complained of severe stomach pains. Brad drove her to the hospital, where she was diagnosed as having appendicitis. A couple of days after her operation, Brad brought flowers and chocolates to Maria. All that she was worried about was that she wouldn't be at the ranch when Brad travelled to London. Brad put her mind at ease, telling her he would think of something. The school in Pueblo had accepted Chris in September. He loved school and Brad didn't want to disrupt his school routine. He would think of something told himself as he left the hospital.

Brad had climbed into the jeep. Will approached.

'Goin' to town, Boss?'

'Yes, Will, got a list of groceries here a mile long.'

214

'I was thinkin', Boss, I could look after the little one while you're away in London.'

'Thanks, Will, but you've got more than enough to do around here, the stock has almost doubled. Anyway if the worst comes to the worst, I'll take Chris along with me.'

'That'd be a shame, Boss. He's settled in so well at school, most kids don't. Brad closed the jeep's door.

'We'll just have to play it by ear for the time being.'

'See you later, Boss.' Brad drove away.

Brad was walking through the mall.

'Hi, Brad.'

'He turned to his right. Standing against the wall was Tanya Evans. He walked over.

'How are you, Tanya?'

'Fine thank you, Brad. Very sorry to read about your wife's untimely death. I realise how much you must have loved her.' Brad wanted to divert her from talking about Amanda.

'How are things with you, anyway?' he asked.

'Oh, I got engaged since we last spoke.' She showed him her ring.

Taking her hand, he whistled. 'That's a real beauty,' he told her.

'Thank you; been going steady with Frank, that's his name by the way, Frank Lewis.'

'What's he do?' Brad enquired.

'He's a trainee manager.' She pointed in the supermarket.

'He must love you a lot to buy you a chunk of ice that size.'

'Yes, Brad, we're pretty much in love.'

Brad chatted to Tanya for another few minutes. He was about to say goodbye, when an elderly lady pushing a wheelchair came over to them.

'Brad, I'd like you to meet my mother, who's been a fan of yours, dare I say, since before I was born.'

'That statement's going to do my ego the world of

good,' he replied, smiling. Brad bent down. Taking the lady's hand, he kissed it. 'The pleasure's all mine, Mrs Evans.'

Six weeks previously, Tanya told Brad, her mother had had a mild stroke, she couldn't walk for more than five minutes every two hours.

'And this is my aunt, my mother's sister, Alice Farmer.' Brad shook hands with the lady behind the wheelchair. 'Aunt Alice is a widower; after Mum had her stroke she came to live with us. Two welfare cheques are better than one, wouldn't you agree?' Brad nodded. He had bade them goodbye, was walking away, when he stopped and turned round. They had gone through the doors out into the car park. He walked towards the doors. He caught sight of Tanya and her aunt helping Tanya's mother into a beat-up twelve-year-old Volkswagen. His heart went out to them. He called to Tanya, standing before him.

'Can I help you, Brad?'

'Tell me, have you got a job yet?'

She shook her head. 'Afraid not, nothing round here suits me.'

'Look, I'm not promising anything, but how are you with children?'

'I think they're adorable. I mind my cousin's three boys every other weekend.'

'What ages are they?' Brad asked.

'Two, six and nine.'

Brad took a notebook from his pocket, 'Would you mind giving me your phone number?' I've got to fly to London on the first of March, should be home by eleven on the third. My son, Chris, just started school and I need someone to look after him and drive him to and from school. If I decide on you, Tanya, would you be able to stay over those three days?'

'I'd be delighted, Brad. Folk round here say I cook the best pizza in town.'

Brad smiled inwardly. I'll phone you in a week or so, one way or the other, OK?'

216

'Bye, bye,' she said, flicking her fingers.

Walking back into the mall, he noticed a small crowd outside one of the shop windows. His curiosity got the better of him. Standing on his toes, he peered over their shoulders. They were watching the most beautifully laid out model railway that Brad had ever seen. The layout must, Brad thought, have been at least twenty feet square. It had platforms, shops, signals, countryside, trees, miniature trucks and cars, level crossings, tunnels, and half a dozen diesel engines which pulled six carriages each. Miniature rail staff, as well as passengers, stood at various locations.

Brad walked in.

'May I help you, sir?'

'Could you deliver that,' pointing at the rail set, 'as it is?' he asked.

'Oh no, sir.' The salesman went on to explain that this was an exhibition layout. It would be at his shop for two weeks, then delivered to one of their other shops for another two weeks.

'I understand,' Brad interrupted him. 'What you are saying is that everything's for sale but I've got to build it myself.'

'Yes sir.'

Brad rubbed his chin. It would be a challenge all right. He'd have to try building it unbeknown to Chris. 'What kind of tools would I need to build this lot?'

The salesman began, 'You'd need a jigsaw, wood chisel, screwdriver...'

'Tell you what, you put what I need into a box or something, together with trains and stuff, and don't forget the dimensions for the base.'

'No sir.'

'I've got a list of shopping to do. When I've finished, I'll call and collect the packages.'

'I'll have everything ready, sir, and thank you, sir.'

The cost of the train, everything included, was two thousand dollars.

*   *   *

Will helped Brad carry the groceries and the other packages into the house. They brought the packages containing the train set to a room at the end of the left wing of the house which was rarely used. Brad emptied the box containing the tools onto the floor. Picking up the jigsaw Will said, 'This is one handy gadget.'

'Yeah, and it comes with an extension lead I swear could reach Denver.'

As Brad locked the door, 'Not a word to Chris.'

'My lips are sealed, Boss,' Will told Brad.

That night Brad began working on the layout of the model railway. One week before he was due to fly to London, a tornado hit the entire south-east region of Colorado. It took two days to blow itself out. Smack in the middle of its path was Brad's ranch. As Brad and Will assessed the damage, the main house had withstood the powerful tornado, but not so the bunkhouse, stables, barns, tack room and various outhouses. They had all taken a terrible beating.

That evening, when Will rode back after inspecting the stock, 'Couple of steers, half dozen sheep dead.'

'Not too bad,' Brad said.

'No, Boss, but the fencing was almost all blown from here to kingdom come.'

'In time,' Brad said, 'everything will be fixed in time.'

'I'll get to work on the barns, stables, bunkhouse first thing in the morning, Boss.'

'Goodnight, Will.' Brad went back into the house.

Brad did his share of the work, helping Will to repair the bunkhouse, barns, and stables. The day before Brad was due to fly to London Will told him, 'You're sure getting the hang of this ranchin' lark.'

Brad kept reminding Chris that he would have a nanny minding him for the three days he'd be away. Slowly Chris got used to the idea. Brad dialled Tanya's number. They chatted for a minute, then Brad told her he'd come and collect her so she and Chris could get acquainted before he left the next day.

Brad was elated. Chris had taken her to his heart straight away. Next morning Will picked Tanya up at her house. Brad held Chris tight to his chest.

'This is the last time we will be parted,' he told Chris. 'When I get back it's you and me all the way, OK?'

'Yes Daddy, but what about Will?'

'Will was within hearing distance.

'Oh, that big ol' bear Will be looking after us both.' He kissed his son. 'Now, off to school with Tanya.'

Chris raised his arms for a hug from Will. Picking him up, 'You learn plenty at school. You hear, little one?'

'Yes, Will.' Tanya strapped him in.

'You use this jeep whenever you want,' Brad told Tanya. 'Will can use the other one if he needs to go to town or whatever.' Brad's eyes misted as he watched the jeep drive off.

'You mind if I borrow that fancy jigsaw of yours, Boss?'

'Sure thing, Will. I won't need it for a few days anyway.'

Will waited until Brad's plane was in the sky. He returned to the ranch and, with one of the hands, began to repair the corral. The jigsaw was a Godsend, he told the hand. After collecting Chris from school, Tanya set about cooking the evening meal. She was by no means a Maria Gonzales when it came to cooking, but Chris, who never was fussy about his food, ate what she put before him. When she put him to bed she would read as many stories as he wished until he fell asleep. He was into the routine of going to bed at seven every evening, and because his father was away he didn't give Tanya a hard time about staying up later.

As soon as he was asleep, Tanya began a tour of the house. When she opened Amanda's closet she was staggered at the amount of clothes she had had. She walked in, admiring one dress or frock after another. The hats, scarves, jackets and shoes, as well as an assortment of handbags and purses, she couldn't resist. She began to try them on one after the other, admiring herself in the bedroom's full length mirror. She matched shoes with dresses and put scarves around her shoulders, with purse to match.

★   ★   ★

Brad was kept busy in London. Photographers took photos of him ending his association with Mecca. 'No bitterness on either side', the papers would print. 'Brad Conroy to take up full-time ranching on his ranch in Colorado. Says he'll miss the business, but naturally wants to spend time with his son.'

Brad obliged three TV stations, spending an hour chatting on each show.

It was Wednesday the third of March at four p.m. when Will walked up the steps onto the veranda. He knocked on the door.

'Come in, Will,' Tanya said.

'I've got to go out to the east ranch. I'm takin' the two hands with me. There's a whole lot of fencin' down out there. I just come to see if you need anythin' before I head off. I reckon I won't be back until well after dark.'

'We've got everything we need, Will, thank you.'

'I'll be seein' you later then.'

'Bye, Will,' Chris called. Will pointed a finger at him and made a cracking sound from the side of his mouth.

At six-thirty, two pick-up trucks pulled around the side of the ranch house. Amongst the twenty or so people aboard them was Tanya's boyfriend. When they had called to her through the intercom, she pressed the button which opened the automatic gates. As they climbed down, they were already in a boisterous mood. The men carried cartons of canned beer into the house. By the time Tanya got round to introducing them to Chris, he asked if he could go to bed. He was tired, he told her. As Tanya left the kitchen, Chris in her arms, she put a finger to her lips and winked at the crowd.

220

The third of March was Tanya Evans' twenty-first birthday. The party she had planned was put back until the fourth, but the crowd had come out to the ranch just to have one or two drinks on her actual birthday. They would be out of there in an hour or two.

Chris was asleep in fifteen minutes. The crowd downstairs began tearing open cans of beer. An hour later, one of them drifting around the house discovered the main reception room.

'Look, look, look what I found,' he shouted. 'Our own dance floor, together with stereo and disco lights. Let's have the party in here.'

Tanya, who had had several drinks, each of them spiked, was in no condition to protest.

As the partygoers began lighting up joints and passing them around, someone raised the volume on the stereo to its maximum. The immediate change of volume brought Chris out of his slumber. He climbed out of bed and began descending the stairs to investigate. Slowly he made his way to where the music was coming from. The door into the reception room was slightly ajar. He peeped in, and started to laugh as he watched boys and girls dancing in a very funny way. He had never seen that kind of dancing before. He watched others sitting on chairs with girls on their laps. They were all kissing. He watched for a little while then he decided to return to bed.

On his way back, he noticed the his father's den had been opened. He peeped inside. No sign of anyone. Running to his father's leather chair, he began to push it towards the back wall. With the chair pushed firmly against the wall, he climbed up onto it. His tiny fingers barely lifted the ship above its brackets. Holding the ship under one arm, he climbed back down onto the floor. Chris made his way out of his father's den, through the lounge and out into the kitchen unnoticed. Pushing the back door open, he ran smiling towards the swimming pool.

Holding the ship by its mast, he gently laid it onto the water at the shallow end. The ship seemed anchored. Chris ran back towards the house. He smiled as he picked up a two-foot twig. As he ran back to the pool, someone in the house must have hit the switch turning on the pool's underwater lights. Chris was thrilled. He began moving the ship, using the twig. It was halfway up the pool when a slight breeze sent the ship towards the middle. Chris's face grew sad.

After a couple of minutes, his face broke into a smile. The ship had changed direction again and was heading towards the foot-high diving board. Chris walked out onto the end of it.

'Come on, come on,' he called. Now it was only inches from his twig, then once again it lay dead in the water. Kneeling down, he began to splash at the water, hoping the ship might edge towards him. He could almost touch the top mast, and reached out to it. A slight wind sent the ship a bit further away. Not noticing this, he tried to stretch a little further.

Nobody heard the splash as his tiny body made contact with the water. Brad, Amanda and Will had played many times with Chris in the pool. He had been quick to learn a few strokes and under normal circumstances would have made it to the ladder, only four feet from where he now struggled for his life. But tonight, unfortunately, circumstances were different. Several times Chris called for his Daddy. Ironically, the last voice he heard before his head disappeared under the water was his father's. The name of the song was *Make My Day*.

HMS Bounty had claimed yet another casualty.

Thirty minutes later, Will and the hands rode out of the darkened prairie.

'What the hell is goin' on?' he said out loud. Climbing down from his horse, he began making his way across the yard. The two hands went into the bunkhouse.

Some sixty feet from the house, he spotted that the

pool's lights were on. He changed direction and headed towards it, half expecting to find the party people naked in the pool. At first glance it seemed empty, but a dash of red caught his eye.

'CHRIS!' he roared, as he dived in the direction of the tiny body at the bottom of the deep end.

As Will's body touched the water, the wheels of the plane bringing Brad home touched the tarmac at Pueblo Airport.

*   *   *

Four days later Brad was once again back in Montgomery, staring at an open grave. Will Bull lifted the tiny white coffin from the hearse. He laid it on the straps which ran horizontally across the grave. This time Brad never heard a word the priest said. He was still in shock. Many people shook his hand. Will guided him to where Joe Quinn stood by a limousine.

'You go ahead,' Will told Joe, 'I'll walk back.'

Will walked back to the white coffin. Taking a white rose from an inside pocket, he laid it on the coffin, adding the words, 'Vaya con Dios, little one.'

An hour later, a yellow cab pulled up outside the graveyard.

'Please wait.'

The two ladies spent fifteen minutes in prayer by the graveside. Mrs Brown touched her daughter's arm. Susan looked at her and nodded as they walked back to their waiting cab.

One week later, Brad was still moping around the house. Inadvertently he opened the door where he had begun to build his railway.

'I'd better start doing something. It's what Amanda would have wanted,' he said.

Out in the yard, he began to call to Will. Several times he called, but there was no reply. He searched the tack room, barns, stables – no sign. He headed for the bunkhouse, and checked on top of the bunks, under them, in the cupboard. He was about to walk out when he spotted a black refuse sack at the back of Will's bunk. Lifting it out, he reached inside. What he brought out turned his blood to ice.

Will's massive frame, standing blocking the sun from entering through the door, almost turned the bunkhouse into darkness.

'I, I, I was looking for the jigsaw and I found these.'

Will placed his hand over his face.

'Tha, tha, thank you, my friend, for trying to spare me.' Brad sat on a bunk. In his hand were Chris's *Kermit the Frog* slippers. They were still soaking wet from being in the plastic bag.

'The, the, these are really what killed my son. I, I mean, even I couldn't swim in these. Did you feel the weight of them, Will?'

Will nodded his head. He had meant to bury them. Why on God's earth hadn't he? He would ask himself that question for many years to come.

'Of course you did. Sure, it was you who brought Chris up from the bottom.' Right now Brad was in another world. 'Did you ever watch *Sesame Street* Will?'

'No Boss.'

'Kermit sings a song, how does it go?' Brad tried hard to think. 'Oh yes. *It's Not Easy Being Green,*' he began to sing.

The next morning, Brad called Will.

'Yeah, Boss?'

'Will, I want you to sell everything that moves on this ranch.'

'Sorry, Boss?'

'You heard me. Sell everything and keep whatever you get for them.' Brad raised a finger. 'By the end of the week, Will.'

Brad remembered on his way back from Pueblo that there was a demolition team at work, knocking down a factory.

224

After meeting with the foreman, 'Saturday at ten.'

'Ten it is, sir.' The foreman stuck a bundle of notes into his top pocket.

At nine forty-five on Saturday morning, Brad handed Will a grocery list. 'Would you get these for me please, Will?'

'Sure, Boss,'

Brad watched as the jeep sped out of the yard. Fifteen minutes later a crane with a huge ball hanging from it, accompanied by a Caterpillar digger, turned in to the Conroy ranch.

Will Bull returned an hour later. His mouth dropped open as he drove through the gates. The house had simply vanished. The swimming pool was covered in. All the outside buildings had also been demolished.

Will jumped as Brad laid a hand on his shoulder. 'Too many memories, too much pain.' Brad handed Will an envelope.

'Have a good life, my friend.' He climbed into the jeep. 'All our personal belongings, Amanda's clothes, Chris's, everything packed into trunks and sent to the Gordons.' Brad put the jeep into gear. 'So long, my friend.'

Will called after him. 'Brad, where you goin'?'

Brad smiled. 'To hell, I think.'

It took Will five minutes to soak up the situation. He opened the envelope. 'Pay the bearer one million dollars.'

Will tore the cheque into tiny pieces. Opening his fist, the wind did the rest.

Will stopped his trailer outside Jake's Bar in Tourist City.

'Whisky.' The barman poured a glass. Will grabbed his wrist. 'Leave the bottle.'

The barman stared in awe at Will's trailer. 'You come into money, Will?'

Will caught him by the shirt. 'I came into drink, OK?'

An hour later Will loaded six cases of whisky into his trailer and drove in the direction of his shack.

'To hell with civilisation,' he shouted, 'it hurts too much.'

Back in his suite in New York Brad rang his drummer in London.

'Pete, I ask only two favours of you.'

'How can I help you, Brad?'

'I want the names and numbers of your dealer; here in New York and in L.A. Thank you.'

CHAPTER TWENTY-SIX

For the next two years Brad Conroy sunk lower and lower into oblivion. He would not see anyone, not even his brothers or Joe Quinn. He became a total recluse. Finally, after travelling between L.A. and New York, he settled in New York. For weeks Joe Quinn had tried to talk Brad into letting him in to talk to him, but no way would Brad agree. Finally Joe gave in. He asked the cleaning lady at Joe's hotel to phone the number on his card if Brad became so bad that he couldn't take care of himself. He pressed five hundred dollars into the woman's hand.

Six months later Joe got a call from the house cleaner, telling him that his friend was in a very bad way.

By the time Joe flew to New York Brad was practically dead. Dr Sands kept Brad at his clinic for two days, then recommended that he be transferred to the Fr O'Brien clinic for abusive substances, located in County Wicklow. It was six months since Joe Quinn had had Brad admitted to the clinic. Joe was also paying the bills. He hadn't seen Brad for the last four weeks, as he was touring England with the new group he now managed.

*   *   *

'Mr Conroy is ready for you now, Mr Quinn.'

He turned around. A sweet eighteen-year-old nurse was smiling at him.

'Thank you, nurse.' He chatted with her as they walked towards the building.

227

'I'm Dr Paul.'

'Joe Quinn.'

The dark haired doctor walked with Joe. 'I know she can be frightening.'

'Who?' Joe asked.

'Matron,' he smiled, 'but deep down she's an angel. Nobody cares for the patients like she does.' The doctor got serious. 'Your friend doesn't seem to have the will to live. He hardly ever eats and his body doesn't respond to our drugs.'

'What can be done, Doctor?'

'Hope and prayer.'

There were twenty beds in the ward. Brad's was the last on the left-hand side. As Joe got nearer, he was shocked at the sight of Brad. His eyes were like huge duck eggs, his hairline had receded at an alarming rate, there was a bald patch on the top of his head, and he couldn't have weighed more than eight stone. His once beautiful golden blond hair was now pure grey and streaky. For hours Joe tried to coax words from Brad, but to no avail. Joe noticed that the robe he wore had been given to him by Amanda many years ago. Its collar was frayed and full of dandruff. As hard as Joe tried to get Brad to talk, it was useless.

'Mr Quinn.' Joe looked up at the other end of the ward. Standing holding the door open stood the Matron. 'Do you know what time it is?'

He shook his head like a child.

'It's eight o'clock, two hours after visiting time.'

Joe kissed Brad on the forehead. 'See you next week, my old friend,' he said. Brad grabbed Joe's wrist. Very slowly he took a velvet case from the pocket of his robe. He handed it to Joe. Joe saw Brad give the slightest nod of his head.

'Mr Quinn.'

'Coming.'

As he passed the Matron he said, 'I'd like to thank you for being such a caring person.'

228

As the Matron walked slowly to Brad, she swallowed hard. 'Let's be getting you to bed, Mr Conroy, and out of that wheelchair.'

'Matron,' a young nurse called, 'phone.'

'I'll be back in a minute, Mr Conroy.' She thought she heard him say something. 'Did you want something, Mr Conroy?' She got no response.

Joe sat in his BMW. He switched the inside light on and opened the velvet box. There were three two-inch square colour photos inside. One was of Brad and Amanda, broad smiles on their faces, taken the day they got married. He picked up the next. Brad was sitting on the bed, his arm around Amanda. Held firmly in her arms between them was four-day-old Chris. The third photo was of a three-year-old, blue-eyed, blond boy, who looked exactly like his mother except he had one of his front teeth missing.

Joe smiled, wiping tears from his eyes. At the same time, from under the photos he lifted a pale blue ribbon. Dangling from it was a badge in the shape of a five-pointed bronze and enamel star. Resting on a wreath, suspended from a bar bearing the word VALOR, sat an eagle with outspread wings. The centre of the medal showed the head of Minerva. Just above the eagle was a pattern of thirteen white stars. There was a piece of paper under the medal. It read:

For courage above and beyond the call of duty.
Presented to Louis Brady by General Dwight D. Eisenhower

How did Brad come by this, Joe asked himself, as he turned the key in the ignition.

'Now Mr Conroy,' the Matron said as she came back down the ward.

When she had got within six feet of him, she knew he was dead.

EPILOGUE

One hour later a mother lay beside her daughter, trying to console her.

'Why, Mam, why?'

'I don't know, love. Only God can answer such questions.'

'But why did so much tragedy befall one family? It doesn't seem right, it's not right at all.'

Her mother climbed off the bed, and closed the bedroom door quietly. Susan Brown would continue to cry into the wee hours of the morning, until eventually surrendering to sleep.